# Baller Dreams

# Baller
# Dreams

## TASHA MACKLIN

Kensington Publishing Corp.
http://www.kensingtonbooks.com

DAFINA BOOKS are published by

Kensington Publishing Corp.
119 West 40th Street
New York, NY 10018

Published by arrangement with Wahida Clark Presents Publishing,
60 Evergreen Place, Suite 904, East Orange, New Jersey 07018

www.wclarkpublishing.com

Copyright © 2012 by Tasha Macklin and Wahida Clark

Library of Congress Cataloging-In-Publication Data:
Macklin, Tasha
Baller Dreams / by Tasha Macklin
ISBN 13-digit 978-19366493-2-7 (paper)
ISBN 10-digit 1-9366493-2-2 (paper)
LCCN 2012913558
1. Urban   2. Detroit   3. Drug Trafficking   4. African American—Fiction
6. African American criminals

This is a work of fiction. Names, characters. places, and incidents either are
the product of the author's imagination or are used fictitiously, and any re-
semblance to actual persons, living or dead, business establishments,
events, or locales are entirely coincidental.

All rights reserved. No part of this book may be reproduced in any form or
by any means without the prior written consent of the Publisher, excepting
brief quotes used in reviews.

If you purchased this book without a cover, you should be aware that this
book is stolen property. It was reported as "unsold and destroyed" to the
Publisher and neither the Author nor the Publisher has received any pay-
ment for this "stripped book."

All Kensington Titles, Imprints, and Distributed Lines are available at special quantity discounts for bulk purchases for sales promotions, premiums,
fund-raising, and educational or institutional use. Special book excerpts or
customized printings can also be created to fit specific needs. For details,
write or phone the office of the Kensington special sales manager: Kensington Publishing Corp., 119 West 40th Street, New York, NY 10018, attn:
Special Sales Department, Phone: 1-800-221-2647.

Dafina and the Dafina logo Reg. U.S. Pat. & TM Off.

ISBN-13: 978-0-7582-9405-0
ISBN-10: 0-7582-9405-0

First Kensington Mass Market Edition: January 2014

10  9  8  7  6  5  4  3  2  1

Printed in the United States of America

# DEDICATION

To my cousin, Stephon Macklin. There are so many words left unsaid. To my mom and dad who are scheduled to hit the bricks in 2013. May God keep you both safe and in good health.

# ACKNOWLEDGEMENTS

All praise is forever due to the Creator. I have many blessings to count all because of Him.

To my husband and best friend, Trae Macklin. Thank you for challenging me to write this book. It was therapy for me and I enjoyed penning it. I think that a few people will get at least one lesson out of it. I am looking forward to your book: *Flippin' The Hustle*. What's taking you so long to finish it? Are you trying to outdo me? ☺ Well, good luck!

I gotta give a special shout out to my editors and proofreaders: Intelligent Allah (welcome home. 18 years is a long, long time!) Erick S. Gray, you are such an underrated author. Linda Wilson, girl, you are such a professional! You are awesome at what you do. Rosalind Elaine Nobel Hamilton. Wahida loves you to death. Y'all go way back like Earth Shoes and Converses.

Nuance Art, your covers and interior layout are never boring. Keep up the good work. Your moms is so proud of you. Thank you. To the WCP Street Team, I know you guys are gonna go hard for me.

And to all of the WCP authors, especially Ne Ne Capri of the Pussy Trap. Girl, you are a mess!

Last but not least, to the sister who gave me birth, The Official Queen of Street Literature, Wahida Clark. Much love to you and Uncle Yah Yah.

If you haven't read Uncle Yah Yah yet, you don't know what you are missing. That book saved my life.

Enjoy *Baller Dreams*!!

Follow me on twitter @Tasha_Macklin.

# FOREWORD

*Baller Dreams* is not about me and Trae Macklin. No, it is not a part of Wahida's Thug Series. ☺

It is a story that I wrote in fun and for therapy. *Baller Dreams* was written in using some of my experiences. It is about needing a dream to become reality so bad that it becomes an obsession. Being obsessed about something can be a blessing and a curse. The blessing comes with having the heart and mind to work hard to make the dream come true and being rewarded for the fruits of your hustle. The curse comes in when the trappings of the dream is your only focus and you lose your sense of who you are and then you forget about people and being careful. You also forget that karma visits everybody at least once a year.

*Baller Dreams* is about proclaiming you're invincible when you're only just flesh and blood. I hope you can get something good out of my first novel. Much love and enjoy!!!!

# Chapter 1

"Stop that shit before it be a problem," the menacing bully threatened as Dre beat his pencil against his desk in an agitated manner.

Dre peered at the oversized bully and the clock on the wall. "Three minutes left on the last day of school and you wanna take a beat down home with you for the summer," the guy known as Big Mike said.

"What?" Dre replied with a frown.

Everyone in the classroom, including the teacher, shifted their eyes toward the bully with the pair of arms that bulged from his crisp white T-shirt.

"This is a class and it's almost over," the teacher said. "But it is possible to get expelled on the last day of school."

Dre's eyes still beamed at the bulky looking dude, sizing his opponent up. Big Mike outweighed Dre's tall, lanky body by fifty pounds and his frame was as twice as thick. Images of the last two people the beast had knocked out flashed in his mind.

Big Mike tucked his gold chain in his T-shirt. "I'm getting left back again, so I don't give a fuck about being expelled. I might fuck around and drop out."

"Or get *knocked out*," Dre said, masking the fact he was leery about fighting.

The bully smirked, looking at Dre's dusty Air Force ones. "Bum ass nigga," he spat, glaring at Dre. Then he turned to the class and started cracking jokes about Dre's clothes.

"Look at his dusty ass shoes. This nigga wearin' biscuits. Broke, bum ass!"

"All right, this is not a comedy club," the teacher said, gazing at Big Mike condescendingly.

Dre was furious. He grinded his teeth, tightening his jaw while quickly tapping his right foot. It wasn't the first time his impoverished upbringing had become a distraction for him striving to make his way in the streets of Detroit.

The bell rang and the class began dispersing. Dre stood as the bully winked and began cracking his knuckles. As Dre took a step behind the bully, his teacher stopped him. "What's up, Ms. G?" he huffed.

"You've got a brain, so use it," she said.

"Sometime you have to act off of street smarts," Dre replied, glaring at Big Mike's back.

"There are plenty of youth who thought like that. You know where they are now?"

Dre shrugged his shoulders.

"Cells and caskets. There's never a shortage of prisons."

Dre shook his head, thinking of his mother being murdered on the streets and his father being in prison. "Can I go now?"

"You still planning on going to college for computer programming? Your math scores are impeccable."

"I don't know," Dre said. His love of numbers was dwindling, with the exception of counting money. Going to college would be a pricey bill on his back that would only worsen his financial strain.

"Don't throw your life away, Dre." The teacher pointed at his head. "Use it." She stepped from in front of him.

He walked off, happy to be finished with high school and the teacher trying to run his life. If Ms. G was genuinely concerned, she would try and do something to help him and his grandmother overcome poverty. Dre stepped out of class, his eyes roaming the hallway in search of the bully. He elbowed his way through a throng of students who slowed his motion to put school behind him. His sneakers beat against the dark waxed floor as he heard someone call out his name. Dre slowed down and peeped over his shoulder in the direction of the voice.

"I know you weren't planning on breaking out without me," his best friend Nut said, walking through the crowded hall with the confident swagger of a young gangster. The lit Black and Mild dangling from his mouth was proof of how little he cared about school or rules.

Dre smiled and gave his man a pound. As he embraced Nut, he could smell a slight stench emanating from him and assumed Nut hadn't taken a shower. *Damn, his old girl must have let the water get turned off again. He could have taken a shower at my spot.* "I wasn't trying to leave you, nigga. I just ain't used to you being here in the damn first place." Dre shook his head at the foolish scowl Nut wore.

"Pssst . . . whatever, nigga. I'm here now, so let's bounce," Nut said, exhaling a cloud of smoke and walking off to lead the way.

"I got beef," Dre said, staring at Nut.

"What?"

Dre hesitated in telling Nut about the bully, because he knew Nut was going to ride for him. Although Dre wanted to handle his drama alone, he knew he would need help.

"Just point the motherfucker out and we giving it to him!"

Dre looked at the demented sparkle in Nut's eyes. *Damn, I got his crazy ass ready to go in*, Dre thought.

"Where the fuck this clown ass nigga at?" Nut asked, looking around the chaotic scene around them. People scurried in all directions in an attempt to leave the school grounds by any means.

"I don't know." Dre stood on the stairs in search of his target. Students rushed toward waiting buses and filled them up quickly. Used and new cars pulled up and took off after eager students jumped inside. Twice Dre spotted his dream car, wishing he had a whip parked in the lot, so he and Nut could ride out. Although Dre was used to walking, he was ready to ride in many ways.

"You still don't see that nigga?" Nut asked.

"Naw. I still don't know—" Dre's words were cut short by a wild haymaker that collided with his cheek.

Big Mike got off a second sucker punch from behind before Nut landed two quick blows to his jaw.

"Bitch ass nigga!" Dre barked as he followed up with a punch that knocked the bully down the steps.

Nut's foot came crashing down on Big Mike's head and face without remorse. Within seconds he was bloody, and a circle of students had formed around the assault.

"The principal coming!" one of the students yelled.

Dre looked up, noticing the principal in the distance. "Come on!" He grabbed Nut's arm.

"Fuck that!" Nut said, jumping in the air and crashing both his feet down on the bully's face, leaving him unconscious. He continued stomping him.

"We gotta *go*!" Dre shouted, pulling Nut as the principal closed in on them. They ran off through the crowd, leaving the bully with blood dripping down his face and splattered on his white T-shirt.

"Motherfuckers gonna respect us!" Nut declared.

Dre wanted the respect Nut spoke of, but he knew that in addition to issuing out beat downs, it would take money to earn respect on the streets.


Dre was halfway through the next block when he noticed a hottie he had been checking for since he was a freshman. "Come on, man," he said, hitting Nut before making haste to catch up to the pretty girl on the move. He picked up his pace and searched for some surefire game worthy of him spitting at her. Ducking through the small crowd, he found himself a few feet away from the gorgeous brownskinned honey. "Tagier," he called out as he darted behind her, catching her attention just as she stepped off the curb.

Somewhat surprised that he had called her name, Tagier glanced over her shoulder at her boyfriend Dante, who was engaged in a cell phone conversation. The last thing she needed was for him to catch her talking to another nigga. Seeing he was busy, she returned her gaze to Dre as he made his way toward her. She had to admit that his appearance embodied perfection. Tall, slim, with some of the longest, silky braids she had ever seen on a nigga. Those characteristics, along with his flawless brown complexion enticed her.

Dre reached Tagier before he could come up with any lines worthy of using.

"Umm . . . I've been seeing you a lot in traffic for a while now and . . . I . . . um . . . was kind of wondering if maybe we could get together or something," he stuttered, eyeing her short, curvaceous frame.

"I can't, Dre. I'm sorry, but my boyfriend wouldn't like that," she replied with downcast eyes.

As Dre opened his mouth to respond, his words were cut short by the loud outburst indirectly meant to disrespect him. "Tagier, get your ass over here and I don't plan to say it again!" the angry voice blared.

He shifted his eyes from Tagier to the candy painted purple Impala and glaring jewelry of the individual with the ice grill. Tagier nervously jumped at the sound of the command. "I have to go, Dre. That's my man." She turned to leave and then added, "I guess I'll see you in traffic."

Dre watched her sexy frame as she hurried across the street. He couldn't help thinking that it had to be a big, bear-looking nigga's money that had Tagier speeding away from him. She looked too good to be with an ugly nigga. Dre returned the mean glare Dante shot at him. But Dre's jaw dropped when dude's hand connected with the side of her face. Tagier dropped to his feet in shock and a plea for help in her eyes.

"Faggot ass nigga like to hit women!" Dre exclaimed in anger, stepping from the curb on some save-a-ho shit.

"Yo, what you doing kid?" Nut asked, following Dre. "Let that nigga discipline his bitch."

Dre wanted to smack the smug grin off the punk nigga's face. The bear-of-a-man pulled a silver revolver from his waist and pointed in Dre and Nut's direction, angering Dre more as he and his friend stopped.

"No the fuck he didn't!" Nut blared. "That nigga done lost his damn mind."

Dre was silent, engaging the man with an unwavering stare. The thug was far more dangerous than the bully Dre and Nut had just pounded out. So Dre knew his position in relation to him, and therefore, he held his composure as Dante yanked Tagier by the hair and tossed her in the car. The humorous look he gave Dre as he got in the car and pulled off infuriated Dre more. Dre knew if he and Nut were on top of their game, Tagier would be his and no one would have dared pull a tool on them. At that moment, Dre made up his mind that shit was gonna change. He was tired of being just another nigga in Motor City, and he was determined to become someone who would demand respect by any means.

Dre's mind went into overdrive as he and Nut reached their neighborhood. He had been silent, plotting their next move. To take things to the level he desired would require deep thought and an intricate plan. But Dre had always been a thinker.

Dre and Nut came upon a crowd huddled around a

dice game at the corner of their block. Nut jumped into the game, tossing money on the ground and taunting a gambler. "You got something on ten or four, nigga? I'll gladly give you six and eight."

Dre continued walking and scanned the block in a wide sweeping motion. His mind flipped crazily in an attempt to formulate a plan. Then he realized that throughout the years his neighborhood had virtually remained the same. The faces had changed, but his block still held the reputation as one of the country's most prosperous dope strips. It was sad, but Dre had no doubt that the same street he stood on would fuel his rise to power.

The harsh reality of his environment reminded him of his father, who was serving time in a federal prison. Dre experienced a slight tinge of doubt. He had always imagined his father's suffering over the last ten years. The man now imprisoned had become a legend on the same streets his son stood on contemplating an identical lifestyle that could land him in prison.

Dre sighed at the realization of what he had to look forward to if he failed. He took a closer look around him, summing up the scene once more. Crackheads and dope fiends lined the block, while rats paraded through the trash strewn about the multitude of burned-out lots. Dre laughed to himself to ward off the sadness of the situation. But ironically, he loved his neighborhood, regardless of how disheveled its condition. It was the only home he had ever known.

"What up, doe? Holler at your nigga, baby," Jamal said, snapping Dre out of his thoughts.

Dre was immediately reminded of what he loved most about his hood: his niggas. "What up, Jamal?" he responded, thinking that his dog walked, talked, and generally carried it as raw as any Eastsider he knew.

"You know me, baby. I'm just trying to make moves and stack this cheddar," Jamal said, staring up the block.

"Yeah, I feel you. With all these pipeheads running around, cheddar shouldn't be too hard to stack at all."

"That's exactly why I'm out here on the prowl." Jamal grinned. "Have either of my cousins been through here, playboy?"

Even as big as Jamal's family was, Dre didn't have to guess which of his cousins he spoke of. Nut, Gaines, and Jamal were the tightest out of the family. "I just left Nut up the block at a crap game. I haven't seen Gaines though."

"Cool. I'll catch up with you later." Jamal gave Dre a pound before heading up the block.

Dre began walking home, thinking of his own business plans. Succeed or fail, he knew his grandmother would be there for him. Just the thought of the woman who had raised him and given him everything within her means softened his heart. His love for her was indescribable, and he had never done anything to hurt her. She was all he had, and as much as he hated to admit it, his decision to hit the streets would crush her.

Dre wanted to turn away from his block as he reached home, spotting the dilapidated buildings and debris strewn around. He held his breath as the stench of trash dumped in the yard of an abandoned house hit him. Everything he was experiencing on his simple trek home told him he had to act soon to change his living conditions. He leaped up the steps of his house and made it inside.

"Grandma, I'm home," he yelled, heading upstairs.

"I'm in the kitchen," she responded in her usual jovial voice. "Come here, baby."

Dre stopped, backpedaled down the stairs and strolled into the kitchen. The sweet aroma resonating from the oven enticed his nostrils. He gave his grandmother a kiss on the cheek. "What's that in there smelling so good?"

She grabbed a dishtowel and nonchalantly replied, "Oh, it's nothing but some ribs, macaroni and cheese, deviled eggs and some homemade buttered biscuits." She began wiping the counter. "Why you ask? You hungry, boy?"

"You already know I am, lady." Dre quickly reached for the oven door.

"Oh, no you don't. Get out of my food and wash your hands, John, Jr. You know better than that."

As his grandmother began preparing a plate for him, Dre dragged his tall, lanky frame to the sink. It dawned on him that no one but her called him by his government name. He grinned at the thought and then wiped his hands on the dishtowel and reached for his plate.

"I'm so proud of you, John, Jr. Graduating in the midst of all the things you've had to deal with on a daily basis in this poverty ridden neighborhood is no small feat. For you to have stayed focused and never fallen victim to the streets like your father makes me a very happy woman." She reached out to hug him. "Enjoy your meal, baby. I love you."

Dre was tongue tied as he embraced her. After letting her go, he watched her head to the door. Right before she opened it, she turned to him and said, "Ford, Chrysler, or General Motors will be honored to give you a job. But if you decide to go to college I'll gladly find a way to scrounge up the money." She strolled proudly out of the kitchen with a smile.

Dre plopped down at the kitchen table. No longer hungry, he pushed his plate aside, thinking about the truth in his grandmother's statement. One of the Big Three would gladly hire him if all he aspired to do was work on an assembly line making cars like thousands of other Detroit natives. But that wasn't the life Dre had in mind. He needed to control his own destiny, even at the risk of hurting the woman who cared for him more than anyone. Dre had only one life to live and he was going to live it to the fullest, no matter who tried to stop him at home or on the streets.

*Chapter 2*

Dre lay in bed, having spent all evening trying to figure out his next steps toward making his existence more worthwhile. After what seemed like forever, he had arrived at no more of a solution than he had prior to beginning his brainstorming session. Sadly, it became clear that a broke nigga couldn't really accomplish anything. Dre refused to be deterred from his goals. So instead of wallowing in disappointment, he decided to play it by ear and keep his eyes peeled for any opportunities that might arise.

"Dre. Hey, Dre!" a voice called from outside.

Dre rose from his bed and made his way to the window. Practically all of the streetlights on his block had been shot out, but he was still able to see his friends standing on the sidewalk, looking upward.

"Nigga, bring your ass down here and hang out with your peeps," Nut stated, waving his arms in a sweeping motion to show their whole crew was in attendance.

"I'm coming, nigga," Dre responded. "Hold the

fuck up." He grabbed his blue and white Detroit hat and his matching Sean John sweat suit. He got dressed and headed downstairs.

Dre and his crew rolled up on Mack and Grey Streets, amusing themselves with jokes and stories of their sexual escapades. As usual, they had no predetermined destination. For as long as Dre could remember, this had been their life. While they had no idea where they would end up, it was always clear that wherever they ended up there would be fun in store.

Dre watched his happy clique that seemed to have not a worry in the world. But he knew they wanted money just like he did. His mind drifted from what they were saying to their faces, thinking of their unique qualities and the role each man would play in his scheme. Nut was the fly guy. A ladies' man with a mouthpiece that rivaled any true mack. The 5'8", 190-pounder had garnered a reputation among bad boys as a monster, but his dark handsome features certified him as an instant hit with women.

"Don't get your head blown off," Rossi said to Nut, aiming an imaginary gun at him with a sneaky grin.

Dre had always liked Rossi's thug persona. Unlike his cousin Nut, Rossi was a quiet killer. A sneaky goon whose 5'8" frame weighed in at just 150-pounds. Females loved his long braids and light brown complexion that many foolish guys misconstrued as a sign that he was soft. As Dre thought of the sorry victims that learned of Rossi's viciousness through bloodshed, Dre knew he needed Rossi on his team.

The crew was large. Therefore, the list of his future team could easily have stretched endlessly. However, as his eyes scanned past Jamal, Rick, Gaines and his man, Big A, Dre smiled when his eyes locked on Lil Billy. Billy was his first cousin, as well as one of the craziest people he had ever known. Not only was he a cold-blooded murderer, he had a pair of the sweetest hands on the Eastside. The freak out of the bunch, Billy had a lust that bordered on nymphomania. Rumor on the street was that women were afraid to give him the pussy because his dick was humongous and he had an Energizer Bunny in his back. But Dre was not concerned with how his cousin carried it with the ladies. What counted to Dre was how Billy brought drama to men. With the type of money Dre expected to get, he knew that war would be an inevitable reality.

Dre decided his team was in order for when he came up with the scheme to put his game in motion. But he knew that although his hands were nice and he had never had a problem showcasing them, he was far from a killer. Yet, he had heart and no fear of experiencing the lethal drama that came with the streets.

"Ouch!" Dre shouted, grabbing his head and spinning around. He glared at his crew in an attempt to see who had struck him. But he couldn't help but smirk at the laughing mob around him. "So you motherfuckers think that's funny, huh?" he questioned, shooting evil looks in each of their directions. "All right, if I find out who did it I'm whipping somebody's ass."

"Well, since you put it like that, I did it," Big A said, throwing his hands up in a boxer's stance. Beginning to bob and weave, he added, "I guess that means you got to give me that ass whipping, cuz."

Dre smiled. "I'm gonna let you have that one, but cousin or not, next time I'm putting hands on you."

"Whatever, nigga." Big A laughed along with the rest of the crew as they continued walking up the block.

"What's on your mind, player?" Billy asked Dre. "Ever since we started walking you been daydreaming."

"It's a difference between a daydream and a vision," said Dre. "I'm envisioning what I've got to do for the summer."

"Damn!" Nut blurted, drawing everyone's attention. "Look at them cuties parked over there in that sweet ass Lexus."

Dre glanced in the direction Nut had indicated, immediately drawn to the burgundy GS with chrome dubs parked in front of the liquor store. His crew was in awe of the vehicle, but Dre was moved by the vehicle because it seemed attainable since he had made his decision to hit the streets. He followed his crew across the street toward the car and the women perched inside.

"I'm about to bag one of them bitches." Nut went straight at the passenger. "What up, doe, ma? I couldn't help noticing that the two of you are killing shit out here, looking like divas and shit. Damn . . . I swear there are no comparisons to the two of you in the whole city."

"What's your name, little slick talker?" said the cutie with the wicked gray eyes who sported a Coogi dress.

"They call me Nut, baby. And I pride myself on living up to that shit, angel."

Dre laughed to himself as he watched Nut lean into the window and continue kicking game.

"You're definitely a little heartbreaker, but you're a little too young for me, boo," Gray eyes said. "But I'm sure that you're entirely too much for those little girls who got to be going crazy over you in these streets."

Dre laughed, enjoying Nut's conversation until he was caught off guard by the sexy voice that rang out from his blind side.

"Damn, Naiza! I can't leave your ass alone for a minute without you drawing an audience." Destiny laughed along with her girl Coco as they made their way past the ogling group of adolescents.

Dre was speechless. The light-skinned woman who paraded in front of him was too cold. Her shoulder length black curls framed her smooth-looking face, but the voluptuous stripper body held his attention as it shimmied with every step she took toward the car. Dre had an uncanny feeling he had seen her before.

It wasn't until she made her way to the car and reached for the door that she did a double take. She stared at Dre, and then motioned him to come to her.

Dre wasn't sure if the gesture was made for him, so he looked over his shoulder. But no one stood behind him. He turned back to face her. *Damn, she is talking to me. She looks familiar as hell though. Where do I know her from?* From the look in her eyes, he could tell she contemplated the same thing.

"I'm busy and I don't got all day," she said.

Dre grinned and stepped over and extended his hand to her, surprised to feel her palms soaked with sweat as she shook his hand.

"I'm Destiny, and unless I'm sadly mistaken or my mind is playing tricks on me, you're John's son."

"John, Jr. But you can call me Dre," he said, holding her captive with an unblinking gaze. He noticed a slight sprinkle of freckles that added sex appeal to her beautiful face. He licked his lips and said, "It's nice to meet you, Destiny."

Destiny snapped out of her daze at the sound his voice and the light chuckles she heard from her friends. "Ummm . . . It's nice to meet you as well."

Dre released her hand, knowing that she was feeling him. He shifted his eyes to her car. "Beautiful car for a beautiful lady."

Destiny giggled nervously. "I'm glad you like it."

"Destiny. Ohhhh, Destinyyy," Naiza called out in a mocking tone.

"What?" Destiny snapped, turning toward her friend.

"Come on, girl. We got things to do and people to see." Naiza sucked her teeth.

Dre grinned at Destiny's frown. "I can tell by the way you're dressed that you have more important things you can be doing than standing here in the hood."

Destiny grinned as Dre eyed every curve of her Coogi dress. She stood frozen with her mouth half-open.

Dre knew she wanted to end their conversation. Yet, he didn't know why a woman of her caliber was so enthralled with him. The awkward thing was that he was just as surprised and nervous. He had never tried his game on a high maintenance, mature woman like Destiny. But her reaction to him must have had something to do with his father. He would have to find out for sure, but now was not the time.

Destiny reached for her Louis Vuitton tote bag, removed a business card and handed it to Dre. "I've got to go, but these are all of my numbers. If you need anything"—she paused and stared directly into his eyes—"and I do mean anything, give me a call." She flashed her dimpled smile and headed to her car.

Dre watched the Lexus pull off as he glanced at the card in his hand. He blocked out the questions and cat-calls from his friends. He was unable to control the smile that crept upon his face at the thought of Destiny's parting words. Had she truly meant what she said? And how did she know his dad? He had a long list of things she could do for him, but Dre was unsure just how far she was willing to go to make his life easier. He placed her card in his pocket, having no doubt he would be using it real soon.

Destiny chewed on her bottom lip as she thought of her encounter with Dre and the feelings it evoked. She hoped her emotions didn't consume her and get her hurt like they had done so many times in other relationships. She thought, she wasn't just traveling through the East-side streets, but she was traveling back in time. A time when Dre's father held her heart. Young, fast, and impressionable, Destiny fell in love with John Sr. while in search of a strong male figure in her fatherless life.

Back then, Destiny was a seventeen-year-old girl unprepared for the power and position John firmly held in the streets. John was a seasoned hustler who transformed her from a fiery teen into a game tight woman who was as classy as any diva in Detroit. But Destiny couldn't stop John from his womanizing lifestyle that came with being a hustler of his caliber. The pain he caused her made Destiny a cold, calculated gangstress who would stop at nothing to dominate men.

Smiling mischievously at her memories of John, she thought of his son. The revenge she longed for could now be hers. But her run-in with Dre showed her that like his father, he had an aura that commanded power over her. Could he wield the same authority as his father had over streets? More importantly, could Dre sex her with the same dominant intensity and passion?

"What the hell you daydreaming about over there, whore?" Naiza asked. "It better not be that young b—"

Destiny calmly responded, "Don't even ask, 'cause you'll never understand." She turned on her system, cranking Jay-Z's "Big Pimpin'." She was in no mood to answer any questions nor hear any objections her girls had. The only thing on her mind was Dre and the task of meting out revenge against his father, while using Dre to fulfill her desires.

*Chapter 3*

After a normal night of drinking, smoking and running game on unsuspecting women, Dre finally awoke fully clothed in his bed. It dawned on him that he had dropped on his bed the night before with no intention of removing his clothes. Even in his drunken and high state, he had pulled Destiny's card from his pocket and gazed at it for what seemed like much longer than eternity. He had been thinking of her from the moment they met. She was the highlight of his night. Looking down to the floor where her card had fallen as he dozed off in a liquor-induced rest, he picked the card up, staring at the digits. What could he gain from calling Destiny? Was her relationship with his father any different than any of the other countless women John had run through? Dre leaned back and closed his eyes in deep thought. He had a feeling Destiny would play a major part in his plan to lock down the streets of Detroit.

Dre glanced at the clock on the nightstand, seeing it was 12 p.m. He reached for his phone and called the number on the card, wondering what he was going to say when she picked up.

"Hello," Destiny answered in a sleepy voice.

"Yeah . . . umm . . . is Destiny home?"

"Yes, this is Destiny," she replied, now fully awake.

"It's Dre. Did I wake you?"

"Uhh, no . . . no. I was already awake."

Dre grinned, knowing she was lying.

"What's up?" she asked.

"Nothing much, just calling because you've been on my mind ever since last night."

"Oh, have I?"

"I'm gonna skip the small talk. I was wondering if you really meant what you said about contacting you if there was anything you could do for me?"

"I'm a grown woman, Dre. I don't say something unless I mean it."

"I need you then. I need you today."

"Huh?" Destiny replied, clearly caught off guard by Dre's statement. "You need me? Please, feel free to explain that."

Dre laughed. "Nah, ma. I think you may have misunderstood me."

"Then make me understand you."

"What I meant was, if you can swing it, I need to meet with you and discuss something. I'm not going into it on the wire."

"Sounds like you got business on your mind."

"Exactly," Dre replied with more confidence than he felt. Something told him she had dealt with his father in the same capacity.

"Yeah, I can swing it, cutie. Meet me at the Greyhound bus terminal at two o'clock."

"Two o'clock?" Dre asked.

"Yeah, it's a good time for me, so don't be late."

Dre laughed as the phone went dead in his ear. He couldn't believe she had hung up on him. It was an act he had never experienced with girls his age. But Destiny was all woman, and what seemed to be a shrewd businesswoman. His experiences with her were growing more interesting each time they conversed. Dre hopped out of bed and headed to the shower, contemplating what he would wear to what could be the most important meeting with the most important person he had met in years.

After taking his shower, Dre thought about his father. Respect was something that Dre didn't have for him. In his mind, John had abandoned him for the streets and ultimately a prison cell. But meeting Destiny and learning she had ties to his father peaked Dre's interest. Dre had little memories of his dad and knew almost nothing about Destiny. But now was the time to learn exactly who they both were.

Dre had just finished getting dressed when the smell of his grandmother's breakfast greeted him. He inhaled deeply as he stepped into the kitchen with a smile.

"I know how much you like them hominy grits and corned beef hash," she said.

"You know I do," he responded.

"Got some eggs for you too." She ushered Dre to his seat at the table and began preparing his plate.

Dre watched his grandmother, thinking of how committed she had been to him. Dre never knew his mother, and with his father in prison, Dre's grandmother had been the only adult who really seemed to care for him. His grandmother had been long overdue for retirement, but still worked hard to make sure Dre had food, a home, and clothes. Dre knew he owed her.

She deserved so much more than he or her son had given her.

His grandmother brought his plate over to the table. "Thank you," he said.

"No, thank you."

"Huh?"

"Thank you for overcoming this madness out here on these streets and graduating from high school."

"You don't have to thank me for that, Grandma."

"Don't have to feed you, either, but I do." She laughed.

Her smile looked so much like Dre's father's grin. It was one of the few things Dre vividly remembered about his dad. "Grandma, I need to ask you something."

"That's what I'm here for."

"It's about my father."

"Okay."

"Did he ever have a friend named Destiny?"

Her face stiffened. She stared at him without a single blink of an eye. After a long silence, she said, "I don't want to talk about her."

Dre hadn't anticipated her clamming up on him. But he knew she was hard on women, especially women who ran the streets. And Destiny seemed to easily fit the bill. But something about the look in Dre's grandmother's eyes made him more inquisitive. There seemed to be something more than her usual disdain for girls who ran through the hood chasing after bad boys.

"Eat your food," she directed Dre.

"So you gonna do me like that, Grandma."

"I didn't make that food for you not to eat it."

"I'm not talking about my breakfast."

"Excuse me?"

"You said 'that's what you're here for.' To answer my questions. Then when I ask you about my father you brushed me off."

"Correction. You asked me about Destiny and I brushed you off."

"Okay, why?"

"Because ain't no room in my house for bad spirits."

"Bad spirits?" Dre repeated. It wasn't a typical term, but the implication was clear: Destiny was poison, forbidden fruit that didn't blend well with the food Dre's grandmother had prepared for breakfast.

"Now eat up, before your food gets cold."

Dre sighed and shook his head. "That's not fair. It's bad enough I don't really know nothing about who my father is. Now I ask about one of his friends and that's a problem. Why, I don't know."

His grandmother looked at him for a moment. "Destiny was no friend of your father. Remember that."

"All right. Girlfriend. He was messing with her, huh?"

"She wasn't his girlfriend . . . She was the worst thing that ever happened to him." His grandmother stood and then walked out of the room.

Dre was lost. He assumed his grandmother was hating because her son was dealing with a woman outside of Dre's mother. But after the "worst thing" comment, Dre didn't know what to think. How was Destiny the worst thing to happen to his father? And how had she befriended him so easily if she was his father's enemy? These questions boggled Dre's mind as he tried to make sense of his thoughts. He realized that he was going to get little information. He needed to search outside his home to get answers about the man whom he was named after, and the woman who had come into his life with the possibility of changing it.

Dre finished his food and washed the dishes. He called a cab and left out the door. When the cab arrived, he got in and bailed out on the comer of Sixth and Howard, directly in front of the bus terminal. Peering at his watch, he threw his hands up in disgust, hoping Destiny hadn't come and gone. He stood on the curb, staring in every direction, trying to spot her burgundy Lexus. He sighed, hoping he hadn't blown the key to his future success.


"Damn it! People can't drive for nothing. All this bumper to bumper traffic is for the birds. What the hell happened so fast? Must be an accident," Destiny said, banging on her steering wheel once and then glancing at her watch. Starting out on her way from her home in the Farmington Hills suburb to Downtown Detroit, traffic seemed a bit slow, but not as bad as what she was facing now. Destiny had already lost the battle with trying to be patient, being only a block away from her destination. She pressed heavily on the horn. "Let's go, people! I've got shit to do." With traffic quickly piling up, she looked at the clock, which showed twenty minutes beyond the time she originally told Dre to meet her. "It's already 2:20. Damn, I hope he didn't leave . . ." She took a deep breath and then slowly exhaled. Miraculously, and without a clear view of what was going on ahead of her, traffic began moving at a steady pace.

"Yes!" she shouted.

As she turned the block, a smile emerged on her

face because she spotted Dre standing on the corner. *Look at his fine ass—looking like a lost tourist in a big city. But a sexy, well-dressed foreigner that I wouldn't mind getting to know.* His baby blue FUBU sweat suit and matching Air Force Ones gave him a thuggish hip-hop appeal that made Destiny want him more as each second passed. The way his fitted hat cocked back perfectly over his designer shades added to his appeal. Destiny knew that with the right amount of time and her sexual prowess, she could mold him into the shining star his father was. It was an ironic turn of events, considering Dre's father had groomed Destiny to become the woman she was today. Now she found herself in a bind, deciding if Dre deserved her attention to become a star, or if he was deserving of the revenge she wanted to exact on his father.

Dre grew more frustrated and distraught by the moment. As he turned and stepped off the curb, ready to leave, his attention was drawn to the black Suburban and shiny chrome rims that pulled up beside him. The dark tints on the massive vehicle made him nervous. The kind of nervousness that came with street beef and gunplay. But when the windows lowered and Destiny flashed her sexy dimples, Dre felt relieved.

"Hey, stranger," she called out.

"What up, doe?" Dre said, staring at the short, sexy woman. He was amazed at her wheeling such a huge truck, but also surprised to see her in a second expensive vehicle.

"I see you stay on some stunting shit, ma."

"There's a lot bigger things to stunt with in life than this toy." She pointed at the truck. "But we'll save that conversation for another time. Right now I need you to get in, so we can talk business."

Dre wanted to kick himself for sounding like a groupie. But he reached for the handle instead, hopped in and leaned back in the plush seat. The state of the art sound and video system in the dash seemed fitting for a woman who seemed to possess nothing but the best. Dre would be surprised if Destiny was not capable of financing his entry into the drug game.

"Like what you see?"

Dre smiled, realizing his assessment of her didn't go unnoticed. At that point, he didn't care if she knew he was assessing her. He couldn't help but take in the beauty of the dime piece that seemed to be no more than twenty-five, but had the maturity and style of a woman in her early thirties. Destiny donned a Prada sweat suit and matching sneakers. Beneath her Prada hat, her long ponytail hung down her back, giving her an edgier look than the Coogi dress and heels she sported when Dre first met her.

"Earth to John, Jr. Did you hear anything I just said?"

"Huh?" Dre uttered, snapping out of his dream at the sound of her voice. "I'm sorry, I didn't catch that."

"I guess you didn't," Destiny said, pouting her lips playfully. "Anyway, I hope you didn't have anything else to do, because I need you to roll with me for a while."

"Nah, I'm cool," Dre said as she turned onto the I-94 expressway. The way she glanced at him subtly, while handing him a pre-rolled blunt of Ganz made him wonder what she had on her mind.

"Spark this up," she said.

Dre put his eyes on the road as he lit the weed. But

from the corner of his eye, he could see the lustful look in her eyes that focused on him. He had witnessed that same gaze from many young girls who had flocked to him on the streets. Destiny was older and more sophisticated, but Dre knew she had the same itch between her legs that needed scratching.

"You hitting that blunt like a professional," Destiny said.

"I didn't come out the house yesterday."

Destiny giggled.

"That wasn't supposed to be funny," Dre said with a slight grin of his own.

"Don't take it the wrong way."

"I'll try not to."

"It's just that you remind me so much of your father."

"Hope that's a good thing."

Destiny's smile dissolved into an emotionless haze. But the more Dre stared at her, she managed to squeeze out a counterfeit smirk.

"Exactly how well did you know my father?"

Destiny focused on the road in front of her. "You said you didn't come out of the house yesterday, right?"

"True story."

"Then I'm sure you did your homework."

"I didn't know you were taking me to school," Dre said. But the reality was, he had not done any research on Destiny. As much as she had been on his mind since he met her the night before, it hadn't dawned on him to investigate her.

"It's not a matter of me taking you to school. It's a matter of you knowing who you're doing business with. The Feds is filled with guys doing life because of a big butt and a smile."

Dre nodded, and then looked at his watch. "True story, but it's kind of hard to do research on someone you met just fifteen hours ago."

Destiny smiled. "Just like your father. He always had an answer."

Throughout their conversation, Dre learned little about Destiny's ties to his father. What he did find out was that she was witty and observant; the type of person who chose her words carefully—another sign that Destiny was a street vet. Dre hoped he hadn't entered into a situation that was beyond his control.

As Destiny pulled into her gated community, Dre's wide eyes beamed, and the way his jaw dropped said it all. She knew he was a small thinker when he revealed how impressed he was with her Lexus and Suburban. But that just showed that he had not been exposed to the finer things in life. What was important was that he was hungry to gain them. He had only hinted at his business interest, but Destiny knew well that he wanted to come up on the streets. She had seen so many ambitious teens like Dre that she could detect their hunger within a few minutes of conversation. What amazed Destiny about Dre was knowing the same man who had schooled her, had not exposed his son to the intricacies of the streets. She chalked it up to John being incarcerated most of his son's life. But that could work to Destiny's advantage, because the more she watched Dre and thought about him, the more she thought it possible to mold him into the man his father was, minus his womanizing ways.

"This is my neighborhood," Destiny said, breaking Dre's gaze at the mini mansions and townhouses around them.

"Nice hood."

"Neighborhood, not 'the hood.' And yeah, I like nice things."

"Thanks, Teach."

Destiny turned to Dre with her eyes squinted. "Teach?"

"Since you turned this truck into a classroom and you're schooling me, you deserve the title teacher."

Destiny laughed as did Dre. She liked his style. She turned a corner and pulled up in front of an immaculate mini mansion. "If I'm your teacher, then this is my university." She pointed at the three-story steel and glass structure that towered before them as she pulled up in front of the four-car garage near a marble water fountain at the tip of the driveway.

"You doing it, Teach."

Destiny giggled as she parked. "Come on." She led Dre from her Suburban and into her home. She removed her hat and jacket, and then hung them on the gold coat rack in the vast hallway. Destiny smiled devilishly, placing an extra twist in her hips to entice Dre as she led him past exclusive sculptures, expensive paintings, and plush furniture. She looked back and smiled because Dre's eyes on her ass had caused an erection in his pants. Destiny continued walking, certain she had her young student where she wanted him.

When they made it upstairs to her master bedroom, she looked over her shoulder and pointed to her couch and bed.

"Make yourself comfortable."

Dre walked past the elevated bed on its platform and sat on the couch in front of it. Destiny turned to find Dre gazing at her butt again.

"Okay, are you going to keep your eyes glued to my

ass all day, or are you going to reveal the details of this master plan you've been hinting at?"

Dre blushed, giving Destiny a boyish smile. "Nobody can accuse you of not being a straight shooter."

"You need good aim to survive on the streets," said Destiny. She sat and listened to Dre disclose the details of his business proposition. She remained silent the whole time, as if she were contemplating whether she would front him the four ounces of cocaine he needed. But she had already decided he could get whatever he wanted the moment he confirmed he was John's son. And it was rather amusing that he wanted such a small amount of drugs, when she was prepared to furnish him with so much more. The way his eyes darted around the room in an attempt to avert her eyes was adorable. The more time Destiny spent with Dre the more enjoyable she knew her small job would be. She wanted to build him up to the ultimate hustler and lover, but she would take pride in destroying her creation if necessary. It would not only be a lesson to Dre, but it would be the ultimate payback to his father.

Destiny figured he had awaited her response long enough. She sighed, giving him a piercing look. "All right, this is how we're going to do this, big timer. I'm gonna double your request and make it nine of them things. You were trying to get a big eight for $2,500, but I'm gonna do you one better on the price too. Bring me $3,500 for the quarter and we'll work from there. Now is that cool with you, John Jr.?"

The smile that stretched across Dre's face as he nodded said it all. "It's time to get that paper now, ma."

*Chapter 4*

Destiny conjured up naughty thoughts as she stared at Dre. She felt her good business gesture was the perfect door opener to bring his joy to another level. "Can you swim, cutie?" she asked with a sneaky grin.

"Umm . . . yeah," Dre responded. "Why you ask?"

Destiny stood. "I was just thinking that a good swim and a bottle of say . . . Louis XIII would be the perfect way to celebrate a prosperous business agreement. What do you think?"

"I guess a swim and some Louis XIII couldn't hurt. But I don't have anything to swim in, and—"

"There's nothing wrong with improvising some-time." Destiny discarded every stitch of clothing and posed naked before him as if it were a normal occur-rence. She knew she was game tight. It would take Dre every ounce of discipline he had not to react to the temptation she presented.

Her motive was as much a test as it was a move to

fulfill her lustful desires. For the sake of her hormones and ego, she hoped Dre failed.

"Lead the way if we're going swimming," he said, slowly removing his clothes.

Destiny slightly arched her right brow, amazed at how nonchalant Dre appeared. The disinterested look in his eyes was foreign to her. But she had seduced and trapped men far more advanced than Dre, so she knew it was only a matter of time before he submitted to her sex appeal. She smirked.

"Follow my lead to paradise."

Dre ran his tongue over the contours of his lips as she turned and walked off. She knew he was watching the gentle sashay of her curvy hips and the bare skin of her ass jiggle. With each step, her body temperature rose, imagining the best way to exert her sexual experience and power on the youngster. Destiny made her way into her backyard and into the fresh air, not looking back. She wanted Dre to get a good look at her thick physique. Once she approached the ledge of the Olympic-sized pool, she dived into the water, swimming to the other side before coming up for air.

Dre dived in the water as she came up for air. "This is definitely a different way of unwinding after a business deal."

"Different is good," Destiny said, smiling. "Never misconstrue me as some typical person."

Dre swam over near her, leaning his back against the wall of the pool. Just a few feet separated them as her back perched against the same wall.

Destiny's eyes were on Dre's bare chest. She eased over and ran her hand across his chest.

"Somebody's been doing some push-ups in between classes."

"You're not the only one who's not typical." He chuckled.

Destiny slid her hand down his chest and stomach. As her fingers entered the water, headed for his dick, she could feel her clit throbbing.

Dre gently grabbed her hand. "Sex with the connect. So this is what the drug game is about, huh?"

"The game is for the streets." Destiny placed Dre's hand on one of her large breasts, and then the other. "These are for in my home." She closed her eyes as Dre rubbed his fingers over her nipples. They hardened between his fingers while she imagined what it would soon feel like to have a young vibrant man like Dre between her legs.

"What happened?" she mumbled as the satisfying touch of Dre's hands vanished and he slowly swam off.

"Business first." He turned back and yelled to her.

Destiny couldn't believe Dre had such control; she was so open off the youngster. His sexual discipline made her want him more, a sign that she could mold him into the man she needed him to be. If he could control his desire to sex her, she was certain he could control the team he needed to control the streets.

Dre returned home late at night after leaving Destiny's house. Things had turned out far better than he had hoped. Destiny had spent the majority of her time with him trying to seduce him. Still, he couldn't understand how he had mustered the strength to turn down her sexual advances. He wanted nothing more than to spend the night engaged in passionate sex. Dre had always wanted to experience sex with a woman of her age and experience. But he knew he had to set the tone on a business level before they got personal.

Dre tossed the quarter-key of flake on the table. Staring at it, he still couldn't believe his luck. He undressed and flopped down on his bed, closed his eyes, and envisioned Destiny being the key that would change his life forever. He was on a path to riches with his team and a thorough woman. But as he drifted off to sleep, he also thought of the potential bloodshed that would come with his rise to power. One of his worst fears was ending up in a prison cell with his father or in a casket like so many people he had known.

The following day, Dre woke up and strolled outside to the sound of rapid gunfire in the distance that he had become accustomed to. Staring down the block, he noticed Moe's raggedy Ford in front of his shabby house. Dre needed to catch up with him badly, so he descended the steps and headed toward his crib.

He reached Moe's house and headed inside, and then up the creaky staircase. He began knocking on the cracked door with the peeling greyish looking paint.

"Whoever beatin' on my damn door like you crazy had better be the police or I'm bustin' my gun!" Moe yelled as he yanked the door open. His face registered an angry glare when Dre came into view. Going in to game mode, he quickly jumped back and began swinging his arms and shuffling his feet in an animated manner. "Dre, my man, my ace. What's up, baby?"

Dre smiled at Moe's antics, and then slapped his extended hand with an old school handshake. Moe's actions were cool at one time, but looked foolish at the moment. "I'm good, baby," Dre said. "But on some real shit, I need you to perform your magic on this flake I got." He patted his bulging pocket to emphasize his point.

Moe's eyes lit up. "Oh yeah. Well, you definitely came to the right place." He did a poor impersonation of a moonwalk into the house, and then said, "Come in, young blood. Let's get this show on the road."

Dre watched Moe close the door along with a bolt and latch. Then Dre followed Moe through a cluttered hallway into an even more cluttered kitchen scented with the stench of death. Dre tried to hold his breath as he looked around in disgust at a sink overflowing with dirty dishes. The table and four chairs by the dusty window were hidden beneath piles of clothes, opened boxes of food and rusted can goods. Stacks of newspaper and even more dishes were strewn about the floor. Roaches and mice were a given. It amazed him that someone could live in such filth. He removed a bag containing the coke, and then handed it to Moe.

Moe's eyes grew wide as he stared at the coke, and then back at Dre. "Nigga, you done come the fuck up! I ain't seen no shit this pure since the '70s." He started shuffling again and singing "Get Money" as he moved around the kitchen, grabbing utensils to go to work.

"Be sure to bring back at least twelve ounces out of that nine. Oh, and Moe, my eyes gonna be on your slick ass the whole time."

Moe never missed a step as he looked over his shoulders and said, "Come on, young blood. Damn, man! Why should I cross you, lil' nigga?"

"Whatever, nigga."

"All right, you got me." Moe laughed. "I'm a junkie, but I'm a cooking, dancing motherfucker though." He increased his already-erratic movements.

Dre shook his head at Moe. Like the rest of the hustlers, killers, and stick-up men in the hood, he liked the old head. Although the holes in his stocking cap, snags and rips in his silk shirt, and rundown gators proved that he was fucked up in the game, the truth was he hadn't always been that way. At one point, Moe had been the rawest pimp and player on the Eastside. He had once commanded respect, having more hoes and dope than the average nigga would see in a lifetime. But whether fucked up or not, Moe had game. Dre knew that, and he could have taken his product to a number of people to cook. Yet, he respected the player's code that stated the game was supposed to be sold, not told. So this was his way of paying for what he wanted. Dre planned to reign over one of the greatest drug organizations to ever hit Detroit. But he understood that he couldn't afford to leave that segment of the game uncovered in the process. And as he looked at Moe go to work, it was clear he was on his way to success.

"This whole shit is ironic," Moe said, looking up at Dre.

"What you mean by that?"

"Me helping you come up in the game when I watched your pops come up in the game."

Dre nodded. I hear you."

"You know what put your pops on the map in Detroit?"

Dre shrugged his shoulders.

"So you ain't never hear the story about Bobby O?"

"Nah."

"Well, Bobby O was a major extortionist in the hood. He was shaking down anybody who was getting it. Drug dealers, robbers, pimps, you name it." Moe grinned. "Shit, he even shook down some other motherfuckers who was shaking down people."

"So he tried to shake down my pops and . . ."

"No, no, no young blood." Moe shook his head.

"So what happened?"

"What happened is your pops was a hustler with a heart. A dude who truly respected the game, so he didn't like the fact that hustlers was out earning money, just to have Bobby O come around and take their hard earned drug money."

"What he do about it?"

"You ever seen somebody get their head blown off?"

"Shit happens all the time in the hood."

"Not in broad daylight in front of police."

"Damn!" Dre said as his eyes lit up.

"Shit had the police so scared he froze in shock and peed on himself."

Dre sat in awe as Moe told him how his father had shot Bobby O in the face with a shotgun, stunning the nearby police officer so much that he could not move. By the time more officers arrived, the first officer was pissing on himself and too stunned to identify who had done the shooting. The few people who had witnessed the killing were happy to see that Bobby O was no longer around to wreak havoc on the hood, so they remained silent when questioned by the police. From that day forth, Dre's father's reputation as a gangster was solidified on the streets of Detroit.

Destiny and Naiza stood outside the main entrance of Northland Mall surrounded by an array of bags containing their designer purchases of the day. Destiny looked off into the distance, searching for her car and the valet. She paid little attention to Naiza as she rambled on about her newest man of the moment.

"Girl, you have got to meet him," Naiza said. "He is soooo fine. I mean fine like Tyson Beckford." She emphasized her words by closing her eyes and grabbing her chest.

Destiny stared at her red-gold Rolex and sighed as if Naiza's words meant nothing. "I'm tired of waiting on this damn car to arrive, Naiza!"

"You know you're a real bitch at times, don't you?"

"I'm not only a bitch at times, I'm thee Bitch!"

"Shit! You were the one who wanted the valet parking in the first place, and you know it takes them a minute to bring the cars." Naiza shook her head. "Sometimes you can be so spoiled."

"Just in case you didn't already know, I'll never park a car or do anything else for that matter if another motherfucker will do it for me."

Before Naiza could respond, the gray Benz coupe pulled in front of them. Hopping out of the car, the young valet held the car door open for Destiny, and then hurried around to the passenger side to assist Naiza with her bags.

Destiny watched the valet gently placing her items in the car. She was amused, feeling that a man was belittling himself at a woman's expense. She hated that women always did the same thing for men. But men had no other choice than to bow down to her, because she paid her way. Without even a "thank you," Destiny slid in the Benz and adjusted her body in the soft leather seat. She handed the valet a fifty-dollar bill, and then casually placed her Versace shades over her eyes and dismissed the hard worker in a haze of smoke as she peeled off.

Naiza laughed while shaking her head. "You kill me

with that diva shit. But I have to admit that you are something else, hooker."

"It's good to see you recognize." Destiny laughed along with her friend. "You're not so bad yourself."

"While we're on the subject of people being all that, what's the deal with that fine little nigga you gave your number to at the store the other night? Did he ever call you or what?"

"Damn!" Destiny blurted, giving Naiza a "mind your business" look. She wasn't trying to put her and Dre's business on blast. But she was aware that sooner or later she would have to quench her girl's curiosity in some manner. So she defended Dre ahead of time. "For future reference, his name is Dre. And although he may be young, he's by no means little. Trust me."

"Oh, it's like that, bitch?" Naiza shook her head with a smile. "When did you start robbing the cradle, anyway?"

"Girl, ain't nobody hardly robbing the cradle. Now, would you please change the subject?"

"Mmmm hmm . . . if that's how you want it. But we both know that there ain't nothing your freaky ass can do with that little dick, baby." Naiza quickly turned up the volume of the music coming from the sound system, blocking out any response Destiny had anticipated hurling at her.

Destiny smirked. Naiza's little dick comment was amusing. Of all the words she could have used to describe Dre, Naiza had no idea how wrong she was about Dre in the dick department. The bulge in his pants, even the image of it soft in the pool was impressive enough to remain as a permanent image in Destiny's mind. She had been thinking of all the things she could do with him ever since she saw it. Still it amazed her that Dre was able to turn down her advances. Also, it was impressive enough to keep Destiny focused on stepping up her efforts to show him she had the power in the relationship they were building.

Dre stood on the strip, happy to see that Moe had brought back thirteen ounces of crack, while keeping the potency of the drug strong enough to have fiends shamelessly chasing it. Dre had given Moe a quarter-ounce for his assistance. He knew that if his team continued to dump the product like they had for the past few hours since he opened up shop, there would be a much bigger load coming sooner than he initially anticipated.

Rick approached Dre. "What up, doe, homie?" He gave Dre a pound and stuffed a roll of money in his hand. "I need another one of those things." He looked around to make sure that no sales got past him.

Dre knew that he was holding $325 for Rick, and his request was for another half-ounce, so he reached in his pocket for another pre-packaged half-ounce. "Here you go, homie."

Rick took the package with a smile. "Damn, nigga! I still can't believe that you of all people are on the grind." He shook his head in disbelief. "If you keep this good shit here, you gonna come up for real."

"I'm gonna keep this shit from now on, and we're all about to come up. Just stick with me. You'll see I'm not bullshitting."

Rick gave his comrade another pound. "That's what I'm talking about. If it's on like that, be sure to count me in because whatever you're planning, I'm damn sure with you, baby."

Averting his eyes from Dre to an approaching fiend, he told Dre, "I gotta roll, but I'll be back real soon for another slab."

Dre watched Rick take off across the street. In just a few hours, his first package from Destiny was almost gone. The weight of the money had his sweatpants sagging. Dre was certain that things could only get better.

Destiny relaxed on the patio, flipping through a *Glamour* magazine and sipping on her first bottle of Dom P for the evening. The cool breeze blew through her long curls as her phone rang, interrupting her peace. "Hello!" she spat.

"Hello yourself," Dre replied.

"Hey, Dre, it's good to hear your voice."

"It's hard to tell."

"Your call just surprised me."

"Anyway, I got something for you, ma. But I need something as well."

"Umm, is that right?" She leaned back and wrapped a loose strand of hair around her immaculately done fingernail. "Well, are we talking business or pleasure?"

"Strictly business, ma." Dre paused. "If it's cool with you, I need to swing by there and get right."

"Get right could mean pleasure," Destiny flirted.

"It could also mean what it's been meaning with the business that brought us together."

"Yeah, I guess so. When can I expect you?"

"Give me an hour. Oh, and Destiny, I was thinking that tonight would be perfect for a swim."

Destiny anxiously leaned forward, but before she could respond, the phone went dead. "Son of a bitch! I know he didn't just get me all hot, then hang up on me," she mumbled with a smile. Dre was proving to be more like his father by the day. She didn't know which way to take his hard-to-get demeanor followed by his flirting. But she was as ready to fuck him as she had been since the day they met.

Destiny stood and pulled her Chanel dress over her head, leaving on her lace thong and strapless Manolo Blahnik heels. She glanced around the patio to the pool, thinking of Dre before she grabbed a bottle of Dom and stepped inside the house. She sashayed up the marble walkway, figuring her attire was perfect to pave the way to a sexual experience unlike any Dre had had before.

# Chapter 5

The squeaking brakes of the cab signaled Dre's arrival in front of Destiny's mansion. He paid the cabby, stepped out of the car and strolled up the long driveway. He sparked a blunt as he took in the opulence of his surroundings. He was just as amazed by Destiny's exclusive home as he was the first time he saw it. Reaching the huge double doors, he pressed the doorbell.

The door opened. Destiny's camisole revealed every natural curve she was born with. Her seductive smile was as welcoming as her figure.

Dre's manhood rose and the blunt nearly tumbled out of his mouth.

Destiny giggled. "Don't worry, you're not the first guy I've had that effect on."

"I did that on purpose." Dre smiled.

"Yeah, right," Destiny said. "But it's about time you got here. Come on in."

Dre's hormones overwhelmed him as he watched

Destiny's hips switch and her ass jiggle as she led him inside.

She turned around. "Congratulations on your first day in the game," she said, her eyes drifting downward between Dre's legs.

"Thanks." He was embarrassed until he watched her eyes widen—a signal that she was impressed with the huge bulge in his sweatpants. He pulled the $3,500 that he owed her from his pocket. "This belongs to you."

She pointed to the glass table in front of the couch beside her. "Just leave it there. We can talk money later. Right now it's time to talk water."

Dre followed as she headed outside the mansion toward the pool area. There would be no games like the night before. Dre wanted to fuck Destiny. He needed to feel her and for her to understand him on another level. It would be good for his ego, his sexual thirst, and his business. Destiny was a gift unlike any Dre had ever been bestowed. He knew a woman of her age and caliber felt she would dominate him sexually. But Dre was determined to beat the pussy up on a level that would outdo anything he or Destiny had experienced.

Dre watched Destiny stop at the edge of the pool, never turning to face him. She seductively undressed and removed the pin from her hair that kept her bun in place. Just feet away, Dre stood transfixed on the perfection of Destiny's body until she was out of her Manolos and camisole, standing with her curly hair cascading down her back. She was a professional temptress, and Dre knew it would take all he had to maintain his control and showcase his skills during their sexual encounter.

Destiny turned and faced Dre with her nakedness.

She stared into his eyes and uttered, "Pleasure time," before turning and diving into the pool.

"Damn!" Dre mumbled as he undressed and circled the pool. By the time she made her way back in front of him, his boxers hit the ground. Her mouth hung open as she stared at his stiff ten inches. "This is what you wanted, right?"

Destiny licked her lips as she stopped and treaded water in front of him.

Dre smiled, knowing he had her undivided attention. He dived over her, hitting the water and heading back toward her treading feet, gazing directly between her legs. He forced her against the wall of the pool.

"What are you doing?" Destiny chirped as Dre's dick eased between her legs.

They were face-to-face and her back was against the wall. He could see the lust in her eyes as he leaned forward and kissed her.

"Mmmm," Destiny moaned as his dick rested against her and his tongue probed deeper into her mouth while his fingers delicately massaged her wet nipples.

Dre broke free from her kiss while continuing to work her breasts. He dived face first into them, twirling his tongue around one after another, drawing deeper and louder moans from Destiny. He had her on fire and he knew he was only getting started, so by the time he was finished, she would submit to anything he desired. He rose back up, kissing her before reaching down and grabbing two handfuls of her soft ass. "Raise up and place your legs around my waist," he commanded in a seductive, but firm tone.

Destiny placed her legs around Dre, locked her ankles, and leaned back into him to continue their kiss.

Dre grabbed her ass tighter as he wedged his rock hard dick inside her with blunt force.

"Aaaahhh!" Destiny screamed.

Momentarily, Dre closed his eyes to take in the sensation of her soft insides. He tried to shift his thoughts to slow down his oncoming climax. He had to sex Destiny with everything he had.

"Damn, ahh!" she moaned louder. Her eyes began rolling into the back of her sockets. "Oh, God! Dre!" She clamped her legs and arms around him as if she were drowning and her life depended on holding onto him as tight as she could.

"Yeah, take it!" Dre barked. He was taking her to a level that demanded her respect of his dick game. He gripped her tighter as she trembled violently under his furious assault.

"Dre . . . baby . . . plea . . . please be gentle with me," Destiny begged.

Dre felt her inner muscles clamping and releasing his flesh. He slowed his strokes as the pleasure was becoming too much for him. Lowering his head, he took a mouthful of her breasts and worked her nipples with his lips and tongue simultaneously. Dre grinded deeper into her tight center, and sucked harder on her nipples while alternating his strokes from short and fast to deep and slow.

"Huh, huh, huh, huh." Her breaths increased while she tried to keep up with him.

Dre pulled out of her and gazed into her eyes. "Turn around," he said. Seeing the indecision written on her face as she slowly complied, Dre stifled his laughter with a closed-mouth smirk. "Hold on to the ledge." He gripped her satiny cheeks, pulled them apart and forced himself back inside of her heated depths.

Destiny screamed his name like he was beating her. "Please Dre!" she begged as his body smacked against her ass cheeks. The sound grew louder with splashing water from the pool. Her body began to spasm into uncoordinated jolts like she was being electrocuted. "Fuck me harder! Oh Dre . . . Ahhh, I'm cumming, baby! I'm cumming!" She threw her head back and Dre grabbed a handful of her hair as she trembled into an overbearing orgasm.

Dre sped up his pace, pounding harder into her. He looked down at her, realizing he had won the battle. Regardless of the rough exterior and tough demeanor Destiny had flaunted since he met her, she was no match for the young don. "Yeah," he blurted as he felt himself about to cum. He rammed harder and harder until he reached his peak. Then he stared down at Destiny's weary body and disheveled hairdo. She had lost the battle of the sexes. Dre knew he made his mark. Now, the only thing left to do was use Destiny to help him make his mark on the streets.

Destiny tried to catch her breath after their sex session that started in the pool and ended inside her bedroom. She lay in bed on top of Dre, unable to even crawl off his semi-erect penis that sporadically twitched inside her. Destiny could not believe Dre had worked her over so thoroughly. Raising up on her elbows with a smile of satisfaction, Destiny wiped a long strand of damp hair from Dre's face and then placed a kiss on his lips. "Boy, you know you wore me out."

"You're not the only one drained." Dre grinded inside her.

"Uh, Dre!" Destiny snapped. "No more, baby. Not tonight. After the way you ravaged me in the pool, the shower, and every imaginable place and in every conceivable position in the bed, I'm honestly too tired and sore to take any more of that monster," Destiny uttered before realizing that she was actually submitting to a teenager. But she knew that Dre knew his effect on her. To prove she was being truthful, she slid forward, allowing his dick to plop out of her with a wet sucking noise.

Dre burst out in laughter. He kissed Destiny's forehead, tracing his fingers through her hair in a gentle massaging fashion.

Destiny cuddled up against his hairless chest. Still in disbelief at how intense their sex had been, Destiny couldn't get the one question that had been nagging her out of her mind. She braced herself for the answer and asked, "Dre, how old are you?"

"I'm seventeen, ma. And I'm sure at this level in the game, age shouldn't be a problem for us. But if it is, we can gladly continue our business relationship and leave the sex out in the pool where it started."

From the moment Destiny had found out Dre was John's son, she had decided to have sex with him strictly for personal reasons. Revenge was her only thought at the time. But she was no stronger than the average woman whose body had betrayed her. She leaned down and kissed Dre passionately for a minute. "That should answer exactly how I feel about age."

"I like it when you speak with body language."

Destiny giggled like a careless child. She knew she would never live the moment down if her girls were to accidently walk in on her and witnesses her bowing down to a seventeenyear-old. But she knew that at the rate her relationship with Dre was developing they would eventually find out.

Dre kissed each of her ripe 36C breasts, and then stood and began walking off.

"Where you going?" Destiny asked.

"Bathroom."

"Can I come?"

"After you grab that half-a-key. 'Cause I gotta get back to work in a minute." Dre stepped into the bathroom.

"Oh, hell nah! I thought you were spending the night."

"Nope," Dre said, stepping in the glass enclosure and turning on the water. "You know money don't grow on trees, so I gotta make it. But I'll stay next time."

Destiny was ready to explode as she got up to retrieve the coke. She tightened her lips to control her emotions, knowing that showing her feelings would only work against her. But the last thing she was going to put up with was Dre fucking the hell out of her and disappearing in the middle of the night. Pouting as she turned the dial on the safe in her closet, she decided to play whatever cat and mouse game necessary to lock Dre's young ass down. It would just be a matter of time before she came down off her sexual high and got Dre open off the good thing he had in her.

# Chapter 6

Dre couldn't help but feel as though the past few months had been nothing short of phenomenal. What had started with just a thought and a half-baked plan had ballooned into a major operation and mind-blowing sex with an older woman who showered him with all the drugs he needed to regulate the streets of Detroit. Every sex session with Destiny had been unimaginable. The fact that he had continuously made his mark, controlling their encounters made matters so much better.

Dre had just headed to Moe's home to investigate his father's relation to Destiny. He knew that if anyone on the street could tell him the truth, it was Moe.

"Your pops and Destiny were a hell of a team back in the day," Moe said, nodding his head. "I mean, we talking some real live Bonnie and Clyde shit, pimpin'." Moe burst into laughter as if he had heard the funniest joke to reach his ears in years.

"What's all that about?"

Moe shook his head and smiled. "Just reminiscing

on some of the shit your pops used to do to these hos. Destiny included."

"Oh yeah?"

"Yeah."

"Like what?"

"Your father raised Destiny. Had the bitch since she was young. Gave that bitch too much game for her own good if you ask me."

"What's that supposed to mean?"

"It means that bitch will run circles around some of the slickest players in Detroit if they sleep."

"All right, so my pops put her on to game. But what type of shit did he do to her? Whatever it is that had you laughing a minute ago?"

Moe sparked a cigarette and took a long pull as a smile grew wider and wider on his face. "How long have you known Destiny?"

"Just met her."

"What you think of her body."

"Thick. Ass, tits, her shit is right."

"Think you can get her to strip for you?"

Dre chuckled. "What kind of question is that?"

"The kind of question your father answered the day he had that bitch Destiny strip buck naked in the middle of the street to prove she loved him."

"Get the fuck outta here!" Dre waved Moe off with his hand.

"If I'm lying I'm flying, and I definitely ain't got no wings, ya dig?"

"So you for real?"

"It's all I've ever been."

Dre had seen some women do some unusual things for men. But what Moe had just told him topped the list. Dre tried to balance thoughts of what that scene must have looked like with the image he had of Destiny. She seemed to be so in control, confident, and powerful. Not the type of woman who lowered herself in public for a man.

"Your father had a way with women, and Destiny was just one of many that did a bunch of insane shit to prove themselves to him in some form or fashion."

"So at the end of the day, what happened to them? She just broke out when he got locked up?"

Moe let out a deep breath. "That's where the picture gets blurry."

"Well, try clearing it up for me."

"First, your father cut her off before he went in."

"So what's so blurry about that?"

"Some people think she was the reason he went in."

"You saying Destiny snitched on my pops?"

"I'm saying what some people were saying. Only thing for sure is, your pops was making a lot of money and the Feds took it all and took him down."

Dre could now see why his grandmother reacted the way she did when he mentioned Destiny's name. There was no doubt in his mind that his grandmother was one of the people who suspected Destiny was the cause of his father's downfall. But if she had been responsible for setting him up, Dre assumed she would be avoiding him, not going out of her way to befriend him. This was the same woman who approached him, engaged him in a conversation, and then handed him her card and encouraged him to contact her if he needed anything. "This is crazy," Dre said, staring at Moe.

"Welcome to the streets."

"What did my father say about her after he got arrested?"

Moe plucked some ashes from his cigarette in an

ashtray. "I don't know. What I do know is he never had her touched. And we know he could've, because he was running his operation even behind bars before they shipped him off to ADX."

That made sense. Dre knew that his father had been placed on 23-hour lockdown in Florence, Colorado and denied visiting and writing privileges because of his running his drug operation from inside the prison. For the first time, Dre wished his father was allowed correspondence. That would have afforded Dre the opportunity to contact him and inquire about Destiny.

"So what's up, player? You planning on seeking revenge or laying up in that spot in Destiny's bed where your father used to sleep?"

Dre wasn't sure, but he definitely wouldn't tell Moe if he was going to kill Destiny.

"The bed or the burner?" Moe asked.

Dre smiled. "Who knows?"


Later that day, Dre was perched on the hood of Rick's '79 Cutlass, surveying the block. The sky was filled with sunrays, and the streets were packed with fiends who scurried around in search of their next high. Dre smiled, knowing they were in search of not just crack, but his product. Because of the quality of his product, his cheddar had grown astronomically. His life had grown more comfortable than most people in Detroit.

Dre gazed at the crack house he operated further down the block. Runners were moving hordes of fiends through an alleyway in a single file line. Everything was moving in an orderly fashion. Mel and Big A had always run a tight operation. Yet, regardless of how well Dre's people handled their respective tasks, Dre liked to watch his paper from time to time. The spot he watched was not his most lucrative house on the Eastside, but it easily cleared over $20,000 a day. The spot behind him was different. It was a weight house Dre ran alone, with the exception of Rossi and Billy, who held the dogs at bay with AKs. From this building, Dre supplied numerous crews throughout the Eastside.

Dre turned toward the sound of the heavy bass that snatched him from his thoughts. He noticed the driver, Big Juan, the overweight hustler with his diamonds glistening under the sun. But he couldn't make out the individual in the passenger side of Juan's truck. He discreetly reached under his shirt for his .45 Ruger. With all the business he had taken from Juan, Dre had little doubt that dude was salty. So he braced himself as he switched his gun from safety to fire.

The pearly white Navigator stopped beside the Cutlass. Juan turned down the blaring sound system and leaned his head out of the window. "What up, lil' nigga?" he asked with bitterness in his voice.

"What up, doe?" Dre grumbled, not liking Juan's use of the term 'lil' nigga.'

"I hear through the grapevine that you're the reason why my paper been coming up short."

Dre slid his index finger into the trigger guard.

"Streets is talking," Juan stated.

"Everybody got an opinion, and it ain't always good to listen to what you hear," Dre said.

Juan chuckled and his eyes narrowed. "Guess you got a point there, lil' nigga." He glanced up and down the block. "Only the shit is too clear not to believe. So because I like you, I'm gonna give your young ass a piece of good game. Never fuck with another nigga's paper when he had to leave a trail of blood to mark his spot. Don't forget that, lil' nigga. It may just save your life one day."

Dre hopped off the hood of the Cutlass. "I feel where you coming from. But how about you never fuck with a nigga who is on a mission to stack his cheddar and couldn't care less whose toes he has to step on to get his shit right."

Juan gritted his teeth as his nostrils flared.

Dre said, "Also remember that old bloodshed don't mean shit to a young nigga who's prepared to leak niggas about his right now." Dre slightly raised his shirt, revealing his semiautomatic. "If you keep that in mind, it might just save your life, fat nigga."

"What, motherfucker?" Juan jumped out of his truck followed by his man.

Dre yanked the Ruger from his waistband. He nervously began to raise the weapon when a booming voice behind him stopped the two approaching men.

"Juan, my man. What's up with you and your partner?" Billy asked, brandishing an AK back and forth between the two men. "You weren't having a problem with my family, were you?"

"Nah, player," Juan said, putting his hands up as he and his friend began back pedaling. "It ain't even like that. I was just spitting some good game at your cousin, that's all." Juan eyed Dre as he got back in his truck. He flashed a sneaky smirk and blurted, "Just remember what I told you, lil' nigga." He winked and pulled off.

As he watched the Navigator pull off, Dre couldn't help but think he played himself. He didn't fear Juan, but he knew he wasn't to be taken lightly. He was not only a drug dealer, he was a killer. And pulling guns on killers without ending their existence was not the smartest or safest thing to do. It was official. The beef was on.

"You want me to take care of that nigga or what, cuz?" Billy asked, dropping his AK toward the ground.

"Nah, cuz. I'll take care of Juan myself." Dre knew that if he was going to receive the respect needed to run his crew, he had to put in his own work.

"Are you sure you want to do that, man? You know all you have to do is say the word and I'll slump his fat ass for you."

"I got it!" Dre declared, knowing that somewhere along the line someone in the game was going to place him in a kill or be killed position. After only three months in the streets, his prediction had become a deadly reality.

Destiny was lounging on her couch with her head resting on Dre's chest as they listened to Mary J. Blige's *My Life*. His embrace was comforting. She couldn't help but think of the good times she had shared with his father and the irony of her relationship with Dre.

"What you thinking right now?" Dre asked.

"Nothing."

"That's impossible. We're always thinking of something."

"You," Destiny said. "I'm thinking about you."

"What about me?"

"You and me. Where we're going with this."

"We're going wherever it takes us."

Destiny eased her head up and stared into Dre's eyes.

"What's up?"

She answered him with a passionate kiss that lasted over a minute. "That's what's up." She grinned.

"What do you see in me?"

"What kind of question is that?"

"The kind I need you to answer," Dre said.

"Okay." Destiny paused. "I see a star."

"How do you define a star?"

"Somebody who shines. Someone who uses their brain to regulate shit and stay on top. Someone who people recognize and don't hesitate to follow behind."

"So, you ready to follow my lead?"

"Depends on where you plan on going."

"To the top," Dre said. "That goes without saying."

"As your woman, it's my job to help get you there."

Destiny kissed Dre.

Dre was silent for a moment. "Tell me something. What happened between you and my pops? Why did y'all break up?"

"That's a long story."

"All we got is time."

"Well, your father wasn't exactly a one-woman man."

"So he cheated on you and you left him."

"For the most part."

"So what makes you think I'm any different?"

"I never said I thought you were any different than your father."

"So why deal with me?"

"I'm a risk-taker and a thrill seeker, so I go where my heart moves me. When I saw you, I was drawn to you. Just like the first time I saw your father I was drawn to him." From the look in Dre's eyes, Destiny could tell he was hiding something, holding back on what he wanted to say. She wanted to probe his mind, but she decided he would speak what was important to him when the time was right. It was the first time he had really asked about her relationship with his father. She knew his interest would soon be disclosed.

"Just so you know," Dre said, "I'm not my father. I really don't know him and really don't give a fuck about him. I'm just interested in getting to know you better."

Destiny smiled. She reached inside his shorts and began massaging his penis.

"This is what I wanna get to know," she whispered in her most seductive voice before lowering her face toward his growing erection.

Nut drove a black Regal with dark tints while Dre rode shotgun. Dre clenched his fists tight to fight off the nervous jitters that threatened to overtake him as his heart rate increased. It was bad enough they each were carrying an AK as they searched the city in search of Juan. But the fact that they rode in a car that Nut had jacked an hour earlier only increased Dre's nervousness. His fists unfolded, palms sweaty as his fingers began tapping against his thigh beneath the assault rifle across his lap. The look on Nut's face told Dre that his comrade had never thought the day would come when Dre would be joining him on a caper.

"You all right over there, player?" Nut asked.

"Yeah. I'm . . . uhh . . . just fine," Dre stammered, flashing a cheesy smile as he sat up straight. Averting his eyes from Nut to the scenery outside his window, Dre could no longer fool himself. He was scared to death.

"Where the fuck is this clown at?" Nut asked himself.

Dre continued scanning the lit and unlit side streets they passed. He couldn't shake the fear that gnawed at his insides. He was beginning to second-guess his decision to murder Juan. Dre wondered whether it would be wise to give up the search and let Billy handle it. As he decided to do just that, Nut's outburst caught him by surprise.

"There that fat motherfucker is, right there!" Nut pointed, and then slapped the steering wheel.

Dre's heart beat out of his chest at the sight of the Navigator two car lengths ahead of them. Even with bumperto-bumper traffic on Gratiot, there was no mistaking Juan's truck.

Nut popped a clip in the AK. "Get ready, nigga. We're not about to play with ol' boy, so wherever he stops is where he drops."

Dre followed Nut's lead, popping in his clip and pulling back the lever to slide a round into the chamber. Dre knew that the time had arrived to earn his stripes. He tucked his long braids beneath the black hood and pulled his fitted cap low over his eyes. At that moment he saw the blinking turn signal, indicating that Juan was about to enter one of the many establishments that lined the strip.

"We got your ass now, nigga!" Nut shouted. "Yeah, bitch nigga. Go 'head up in the Chicken Shack."

Dre watched the truck pull into the Chicken Shack parking lot in what seemed like slow motion. There was no longer any doubt that his beef with Juan was about to end.

"We're not gonna play no games with this nigga, Dre. When he comes up out of that truck, him and whoever is unlucky enough to be with him get it. You hear me?"

"Yeah, nigga. I know!" Dre responded, nervously watching the doors of the truck open. Dre took a deep breath when he spotted two beautiful little girls exit the truck with bright smiles and swinging pigtails. They couldn't have been more than eight years old. Juan and a woman who the little girls resembled, followed them. Dre knew the woman to be Juan's wife.

"Shit!" Dre sighed, turning to Nut with a look of indecision.

"Hey, it's a dirty game, player," Nut said with a devious smirk.

Dre wasn't surprised. Regardless of how true Nut's words would prove to them, all Dre could do was stare at his friend, speechless and in disgust.

"There's no such thing as fair in love and war, so let's get busy, nigga." Nut pulled into the parking lot of the Chicken Shack.

Dre decided that if he was going to kill Juan he had to be sure that his wife and children remained safe despite what Nut said. "Stay put, I'm gonna take care of dude myself, in my own way."

"What?" Nut snapped. "Stay put? How the fuck in the world I'm supposed to let you bust your shit alone and I'm sitting in the car?"

"Simple. Lay back and watch how I do this."

"Dre, anything can go wrong while you're out there by yourself."

"We not gonna argue about this. I'll be right back." He exited the Regal, noticing Nut's exasperated sigh.

"Be safe," Nut said.

Dre nodded and walked toward the restaurant with the AK concealed as much as possible behind his leg.

He slowed his pace at the sight of Juan exiting the restaurant alone, engrossed in a phone conversation. Dre had never anticipated it being so easy to catch a killer like Juan slipping.

As Dre picked up his pace, his nervousness subsided. He raised the deadly assault rifle into firing position, standing so close he could hear Juan's voice as he argued with someone on the other end of the phone. Dre was empowered by the thought of having Juan exactly where he wanted him. He couldn't believe he had been ready to abort the mission earlier and let Billy handle it.

Suddenly, Juan spun around and a look of utter shock emerged on his face as he stared into the barrel of the AK. His phone dropped to the ground. He threw his hands up.

"What's up now, gangster?" Dre sneered. "You don't look like you did when you rolled up in front of my spot talking reckless."

"Hold up, homie." Juan looked around.

"Ain't nowhere to run to and ain't nobody to help you."

"I don't got no beef with you."

Dre smiled. "You right, because this is about to be over."

Juan's eyes blinked and his lips quivered. "Come on, man, we don't have to get crazy over something as petty as a block. Look . . . Dre . . . uh, I'll retire."

"You're right, I'm gonna retire you." Dre pulled the trigger as Juan covered his face and pled for his life. The 7.62-milimeter bullets tore his hands to shreds and ripped through his face and forehead. Dre took a few steps forward as Juan's body dropped to the asphalt. He fired a burst of bullets from the assault rifle into the remainder of his face. Feeling a hand on his arm at the same time, he noticed Nut's frantic voice.

"Come on!" Nut urged, staring at the faceless frame that lay in an increasing puddle of blood. "We gotta get out of here."

The look on Nut's face and urgency in his voice told Dre that Nut would look at him in a different way from that point on. Dre's street credibility was officially solidified.

Nut tugged at Dre's arm.

Dre turned with Nut and they started jogging back to the car. Halfway across the parking lot he heard a series of screams. He turned back and saw a sight he would never forget. Juan's wife and kids stood over him screaming. But what tore him apart was the look of shear sadness in the eyes of his oldest daughter as she stared at the mutilated remains of her father. Dre realized that he was becoming something he didn't want to become. He was cool with handling street beef. But he had never thought of the damaging effects that street life could have in the homes of family members of thugs and hustlers. His first murder had placed him on a path that would be impossible to turn back.


Dre sat in front of his weight spot surrounded by his crew, smoking a blunt of Ganz and sipping from a cup of Hennessy while laughing at jokes and braggadocios banter. Besides the careless jokes, the guys he had grown up with all his life had changed. The gold chains and diamond pendants sparkling around him were proof. Added to that were the highpriced toys parked in front of them. He always worried about them drawing attention to their organization, but the reality was that just about everyone on the Eastside of Detroit had heard of them.

"Dre, my nigga, what's good with you?"

Looking to his left, Dre's face lit up when he spotted Billy approaching. "I'm straight, cuz. But what's happening with you though?"

Billy gave him a pound. "Congratulations, player."

"On what?" Dre asked.

"Shit, after that move you pulled tonight, it's official, nigga. The block is yours now." Billy winked and then began walking away. "You already know we got your back, baby."

Dre had a blank look in his eyes and searched Nut's face out in the crowd. The devilish smile on his partner's face said it all. Nut had spread the news of Dre murdering Juan.

"Yo, everybody, listen up!" Nut said. "I have an announcement to make."

"Come on, motherfucker. If the shit is that important, let a nigga hear it." The loud outburst from somewhere in the crowd brought a chorus of laughter from the clique.

Nut laughed along with them, and then cleared his throat. "In case you niggas don't already know, next month is Dre's birthday. I was thinking that in celebration of his special day we should do something big for his broke-acting ass. What y'all think about that?" he asked, cutting his eyes mischievously in Dre's direction.

Dre sat as if he weren't the object of their discussion. He smiled, taking in the array of questions and statements that were thrown at him. No doubt. Nut had a big mouth. But it was funny to Dre how the nigga was in the process of free styling a major event in his honor just to make up for his slip of the lip.

Nut blurted, "Okay, this is how we'll do it. I'll holler at my nigga Mason from WJLB."

"You mean 97.9?" Billy asked.

"Yeah," Nut said. "I'll get him to shout out that the Eastside Syndicate is throwing a birthday bash for their man, Dre." Nut paused with a smile. "We can do this real big. Have a concert in Belle Isle Park."

"That sounds all good and shit," said Rossi. "But who the hell is the Eastside Syndicate?" Dre stared at Nut, waiting for his response as did the rest of the crew.

"We're The Syndicate, nigga!" Nut declared. "Like I was saying, we can throw a serious event if you niggas are prepared to kick in your share of cheddar to make it happen. Y'all with me or what?"

Dre looked around at Nut's smiling face, and had to admit that Nut mesmerized everyone with his quick wit. The idea had actually turned out to be damned good. Like the rest of his crew, he too was feeling the notion of them throwing a birthday bash.

"Count me in, nigga," said Billy.

"Me too," Rossi affirmed.

"It's a done deal then," Big A roared. "Let's put this shit in true baller fashion, Syndicate."

Dre locked eyes with Nut and shook his head. Once again, his man pulled off some wild shit. He blocked out the excited rambling around him. At that point, Dre realized the name Eastside Syndicate sounded as powerful as he felt. As their leader, the time had arrived to let the rest of the city know exactly who they were.

# Chapter 7

On that beautiful September day, the sky was clear and the sun sat at just the precise angle allowing its rays to flow through unrestrained. Dre couldn't have been luckier, because the weather was perfect for the celebration of his eighteenth birthday. He rode in the passenger seat of Nut's Cadillac STS, listening to Biggie's "Life After Death" thundering through the speakers.

They pulled up into the confines of Belle Isle and were instantly swallowed up by the huge crowd that numbered in the thousands. Through the rearview mirror, he smiled at the sight of the long line of automobiles driven by his crew. They were in full force. Dre couldn't help but be proud of how far they had come in such a short time.

As they steered through the crowds, Dre could see some of his crew mingling among the partygoers. One of his workers was dancing with a bottle of Moët in his hand, caught up in the raw energy of the atmosphere. It was impossible for Dre to ignore the fact that Nut had a vast power of persuasion. His ability was evident all around him. No one else would have been able to orchestrate such a large gathering in such a short time. Dre felt proud to have Nut on his team.

The STS came to a halt. "The whole hood is out here," Dre said.

"Yeah, baby. They love you," Nut said.

Dre and Nut exited the Caddy, and Dre was bombarded with greetings and Happy Birthday wishes, hugs and handshakes. He had never felt so much love on any of his previous birthdays.

Nut walked beside Dre as they made their way through the Eastside crowd. "I have a big surprise for you later, partner, but . . . " Suddenly preoccupied with the view on Dre's left, his words tapered off. "Ummm . . . I'm gonna save it for when the sun goes down. But check out that little crew of stunners behind you," he added, licking his lips.

Dre had to exhale at the sight of one of the most beautiful women he had ever laid eyes on. He instantly forgot Nut and found it hard to concentrate on anything besides the angelic face before him. "Stacy," he mumbled, when he heard one of her friends mouth her name.

Stacy was conversing with a cluster of young women who were strolling through the park. She seemed oblivious to Dre eyeing her. But from her sex appeal, he could tell she was used to getting attention. His eyes drifted past her Parrasuco T-shirt that tightly clenched her 34D breasts and ended on her matching Parrasuco jeans that clung to her sexy curves. Her seductive bowlegged walk and meticulously pedicured toes peeked through her strapless open toed heels. Her exterior qualities alone made her worthy of Dre getting to know her. If her mind completed her outer perfection in any way, Dre could more than imagine her as wifey material. Destiny was still in his life, but she was the answer to his sexual and cocaine needs. If Stacy had a brain, she could easily be everything a man could want.

Dre and Nut quickly closed the gap between themselves and the entourage of unsuspecting ladies. He towered above her 5'5" frame, reaching out to her and gently grasping her hand. "Hello, my name is Dre, and what might your name be?"

"I'm Stacy."

The way Stacy stepped back, replacing her quizzical look with a smile, Dre could tell she was not used to men coming at her in a mature fashion. "Stacy huh?" Dre repeated with a slight laugh.

"What? What's so funny?"

"It's really nothing," Dre said.

"You have to tell me. You can't just leave a woman hanging."

Still smiling, Dre shyly stated, "I hope you don't find this confession corny, but when I first laid eyes on you, it hit me that you were the most beautiful woman I had ever seen."

Stacy blushed. "Thank you."

"Then no sooner than you said your name, it crossed my mind that you could pass for an identical twin to Stacy Dash. It may sound corny, but next to you, she's no longer the most beautiful woman in the world."

"That's so sweet," Stacy said with a smile, oblivious to her friends snickering. "There was nothing corny about that, Dre."

"So, Stacy, are you from Detroit?"

"Mmm hmm. I'm from the Westside of the city."

"Oh yeah." Dre nodded. "Near what str—"

"Hey, Dre. Happy Birthday, boo," a girl flirted as she walked past him.

"Happy Birthday, baby," the girl's friend said as she exhaled a gust of weed smoke. "The Syndicate made a major move when y'all threw this joint in the park, Dre."

A third groupie put an extra twist in her hips, stating, "You're the man. Holler at me later and I may just have a little present of my own for you."

Dre turned his back to the women, upset that they came at the worst possible time. He could see the disgust on Stacy's frowned up face and on the grimaces of her friends. Clearly, they were not the average hood chicks he was used to dealing with. Dre shrugged his shoulders and said, "Where were we?"

"So you're that Dre, huh?" Stacy said in a sour tone.

"What Dre might that be?" he asked.

"The Dre that they've been blowing up on the radio all month." She sucked her teeth and shook her head. "You really fooled me, because you didn't seem like the type."

"Excuse me for being lost, but what type are you getting me mixed up with?"

In response, she pointed her finger over his shoulder, and then folded her arms across her ample breasts. Stacy cut her eyes defiantly in the direction of the new arrivals.

Dre glanced over his shoulder. His jaw hung slack at the sight of Destiny exiting the cleanest Impala he had ever seen. It was evident by the huge ribbon that adorned it that the car was a birthday gift for him. Nevertheless, she was the last person he needed to show up when he was in the middle of trying to mack on his dream girl.

\* \* \*

Destiny basked in all the attention she received as she cruised through the crowd of gawking spectators enthralled with Dre's birthday gift. She had rescheduled her Chicago trip so she could surprise him. The platinum '99 Impala with light tints, 20-inch rims and state of the art audio and video systems were a surprise that she hoped would help make up for the arguments they had been having over Dre not spending enough quality time with her.

Naiza said, "Your birthday boy sure got him a fine ass friend."

Destiny had been so focused on Dre that she didn't see Stacy standing in front of him.

Her smile dissolved as Stacy's beauty invoked a tinge of jealousy within her. Her mind screamed out, *Who the hell is that little bitch all up in my man's face?* Destiny was determined to teach Dre's female friend a lesson in boss game. Dre belonged to her, and there was no way she was going to allow some whore to enjoy the man she had created.

"What you gonna do?" Naiza egged on.

Destiny sucked her teeth and remained silent. As she parked near them, she noticed the people with Dre honing in on her. She exited the vehicle in all her splendor, flashing her flawless frame draped in a white Dolce and Gabbana body suit highlighted by diamond jewelry. She flashed a phony smile to mask the anger that brought her blood to a boil.

She could see Dre watching her as her crew followed in tow. Her flamboyant girlfriends hopped out of a 6 Series Benz, two 500 Coupes, two Lexus sedans and a Range Rover. Stacy had sex appeal and the appearance of class, but she was still out of her league with Destiny and her team of street savvy vets. Destiny knew she was the shit. But still, Stacy's youthful sex appeal intimidated her.

Destiny boldly walked up, threw her arms around Dre's neck and gave him a passionate kiss. Reluctantly breaking their connection after a matter of moments, she wiped the gloss from his lips and smiled. "Happy Birthday, baby."

Dre seemed caught off guard by her open intimacy. "Thanks. Whose car you got there?"

"It's yours, boo. I thought you knew mama was gonna show her love on your special day," she boasted, dropping the keys in his palm and removing a platinum chain from her neck and placing it over his head. Dre shifted his eyes to the car.

Destiny smiled, eying Stacy, who seemed frustrated that her time with Dre had been interrupted. Already, Destiny made it clear who held his heart. Stacy was young and hot, but Destiny was certain she didn't have the ability to cop a new car for Dre, and the chance of her supplying Dre with kilos of cocaine was nonexistent. So it didn't matter that Stacy was staring at her with a gaze of disgust.

"Damn," Dre said, hefting his keys. He opened his arms, allowing Destiny to cuddle up close to him in a well-deserved hug. Destiny peeped over Dre's shoulder and winked at Stacy.

Stacy stared at her as Dre broke his embrace with Destiny. Stacy sighed lightly in defeat, her slumped shoulders giving her emotion away. When Dre turned around, she said, "I'm glad to have met you." She reached out and delicately touched his face. "If it's possible for your birthday to get any better than it already seems to be, I wish you an even happier birthday." She turned to walk away, and then stared over her shoulder. "And, Dre, remember what I told you. The Westside is where I rest, baby."

Destiny grew heated as Stacy stepped off with her clique. "What the fuck is that about?" she asked Dre.

"What?"

"I'm not stupid and neither are you."

Dre shook his head. "We not gonna be arguing out here, because you jumping to conclusions." He looked around at their friends. "Especially on my birthday."

Destiny gasped. She didn't like the uneasy feeling churning in her belly. She glanced at Stacy walking away. The little bitch's beauty or her confidence reminded Destiny of herself at the same age. But what alarmed her was the brightness in Dre's eyes when he looked at the whore in a way that he had never looked at her. Destiny mumbled, "Don't even think about getting my man, bitch. Keep walking if you know what's good for you."

"One-two, one-two, mic check," Rock's voice barked through the speakers. He was CEO of the local rap group Rock Bottom.

Destiny looked around as crowds of people became rowdy and animated.

"What up doe, homies?" Rock said. "We want to thank you for coming out to show love tonight as we celebrate that nigga Dre's birthday. The big homie from The Syndicate. This whole joint is courtesy of him. Wherever you are in the crowd, happy birthday, nigga."

The crowd went crazier when the loud bass of "We Stay Gatored Up" came on and Rock Bottom began performing. Destiny couldn't help but be happy for Dre as he and his friends began popping bottles and waving blunts in the air. She thought of how she had molded him into a man and made his name known throughout the city. Her only problem now was maintaining a leash on the dog he had become. But she was up for the challenge.

She walked over and stood in front of him, pressing her huge ass against his dick. In seconds, the pair were dancing as if the drama with Stacy had never occurred. Destiny wasn't surprised to spy Naiza and Nut in a similar embrace. Destiny turned and pulled Dre into her arms, kissing him. Then she looked into his eyes, wondering what he was truly thinking. She was thinking how much he resembled his father. The man she hated, but no longer was interested in seeking revenge on through Dre. She wanted the same loving she had sought in Dre's father. At that moment, she decided nothing and no one would separate her and Dre. That included Stacy.

The roar of the crowd was deafening. From where Stacy stood, she was unable to control the swaying motion the thunderous sound of the crowd and the music had her body moving to. Unlike the rest of the partygoers, Stacy's mind and body were working on a different accord. Although the music moved her, she could not understand her constant thoughts of Dre—thoughts that clouded her mind. It became utterly impossible to enjoy the performance, because from a distance she could see Destiny watching him like a hawk. Stacy felt like a hypocrite; she had made a vow to stay away from hustlers and she was tired of guys from the hood pressing her. She wanted more out of life than mediocre living and ghetto drama. But something about Dre told her he was different. He had a style that was acceptable in the hood, but the way he talked made her think he could move in circles far beyond the streets. Stacy had never seen that balance in a man before. Now that she met a man who had it, she was determined to make him hers.

Stacy squinted at the open display of affection between Destiny and Dre. She wondered what an older woman like her saw in Dre? Probably the same things Stacy saw in him. She could tell that Destiny was not the average hood chick. She had an air of elegance in her swagger. And from the way people reacted to her and her materialistic presentation, Stacy could tell she was more powerful than the average hood chick. That was a problem for Stacy that could place Dre out of her reach. But Dre had approached her, despite his relationship with such a powerful woman, so Stacy knew she had a chance at making Dre hers.

She also knew that in the process of making him hers, she would have to make him a man who had no interest in the streets. That would be far harder than taking him from Destiny.

# Chapter 8

"When will you be back in Detroit?" Dre spoke into his cell phone as he exited the black Suburban and moved toward the spot.

"Either tonight or tomorrow," Destiny replied.

"Yeah, alright then." Dre detected the indecision in her voice while he vigorously scanned the large residential street for any possible threat. Dre's free hand lingered inside his pocket, clutching the Ruger that had become a necessity in the last year.

"Look, baby, I just got off the plane. I'll give you a call later," she said.

"Later," Dre said. He hung up the phone, thinking to himself how Destiny had been spending so much time in Chicago lately. His gut told him that it was more than business, which was her rationale for the frequent trips. As much as he enjoyed sex and business with her, his mind battled with maintaining their relationship. Part of him wanted to milk her until there was nothing left. Another part of him wanted to find an excuse so he could leave her and track down Stacy. She had been on his mind since they'd met, but Dre had decided to keep his distance from her for the sake of what he had going with Destiny. Plus, Destiny had been showing him extra attention since she discovered there was a beautiful young woman to compete with her for Dre's attention.

Dre led Big A, Rock, and Mel into Moe's upscale home and gave him a pound. "What's up, Old School?

"You know me, baby. I'm ready to do what I do." Moe stared down at the bags Big A and Rick held, and then looked at Dre and rubbed his hands together. "Holler at your boy, young blood. What we working with today?"

"Fifty birds," Dre answered.

Moe smiled and began walking off. "Follow me. You already know I'm the chef of all chefs, gangster."

Dre laughed to himself at Moe's usual jokes and slick talk. But what was unusual was how far Moe had come since Dre began doing business with him. His worn-out gators had been replaced with fresh Maury's. And his tailored suit had him looking just as good as he did in his heyday. To top it off, he had left the hood. Dre was now inside Moe's exclusive apartment in one of the Westside's nicest upper middle class neighborhoods.

After the keys were removed from the bags, Dre watched Moe go to work inside his makeshift lab equipped with a heavy digital scale to weigh the product and large paddles to stir the drugs. Dre's phone vibrated and he removed it from his waist and answered it. He gritted his teeth and shook his head. "What!"

"We got problems, man, and I need you to handle 'em," Billy said.

"Tell me what's happening, cuz?" Dre began pacing.

"It's that bitch ass nigga Budha from Prominade. He's on some bullshit, and I'm tired of it!"

Dre allowed Billy to vent, knowing the problem would eventually be revealed completely.

"Man, I know we should've took the whole block from them niggas," Billy said. "But nah, we let their punk asses coexist! Psst. Well, now the word on the streets is he put a crew together to roll on us."

"Oh yeah," Dre said.

"They planning to take the whole block back no matter how many Syndicate niggas have to die in order for them to do it. This shit needs to be dealt with, cuz. Like yesterday!"

Dre boiled at the audacity of Budha. He would never allow anyone to take anything from The Syndicate. Prominade was a million dollar block, and he never had any intention of taking their whole block. Enough cheddar came through their strip to keep everyone on both sides eating.

"Talk to me, cuz," said Billy.

"You got the green light."

"That's what I'm talking," Billy said.

"Take a squad along with you. And deal with the nigga in a manner that will send a message through the city for anybody that may want to test us."

"No doubt. I'll get back at you when the job is done."

"Cool, just be careful." Dre hung up, nodding his head. He knew Billy would assure that Budha's death was ruthlessly orchestrated. It was Billy's style. And it was what Budha deserved.

\* \* \*

Billy dropped his phone on his lap. "It's on," he told Nut and Rossi who occupied the truck he sat in. "Now you niggas know what it is! Let's do our thang."

Rossi smiled as he put the truck in drive. "It's about time we put in some real work. Money without murder just ain't no fun."

"Yeah, it's on," Billy said.

"Yo, I got that fat nigga when we get there," Rossi spat.

"Oh, no you don't either," Nut retorted. "I'm doing this one."

Billy shook his head, allowing them to argue. Regardless of what they thought. Budha belonged to him and no one else. He stared in the rearview mirror, watching the caravan of Syndicate members who trailed close behind. Billy reached down for the riot pump in the floorboard, contemplating the best way to accomplish the task at hand. He wanted to strike fear in the hearts and minds of any enemy who may have been lurking in the city. "Motherfuckers gonna get the picture when this shit go down!"

Budha broke the embrace that his young sex goddess had him locked in. He reached for his leather Pelle jacket. He suppressed a laugh at the sight of her standing with her hands on her hips with fury in her eyes. "I'll swing through a little later and holler at you, ma."

"Yeah, sure you will, motherfucker! I'm sick of your shit, Budha. If you think I'm gonna keep putting up with this, you got the game twisted, nigga. Just lock my door on the way out."

Budha reached for the doorknob. "That's cool. Call me when you tired of being mad." He laughed and walked outside into the cold evening air. As far as he was concerned, he didn't have any problems. His mind was focused on The Syndicate being smashed on and him having full control of Prominade Street. With that set to go down before morning, this would be the best day he'd had in a long time.

The sound of Juvenile's new shit floating up the block caught his attention as he headed up the block toward his homies. A caravan of luxury vehicles rolled toward him. Squinting his eyes to get a better look, an alarm went off in his mind when he recognized The Syndicate.

Billy's intention was to alert the whole block to the presence of The Syndicate as they traveled through Prominade with the system in his truck blaring. He didn't want a soul to miss the show they had come to put on for their benefit. He spotted Budha and calmly informed Rossi. "There he is." He pointed up the block. "Your ass belong to me now, nigga."

Rossi sent the Yukon lurching forward in pursuit of their suddenly speedy target. Murder set the mood.

Nut let the sound of him inserting a clip in his AK speak what he felt. Billy heard him click the lever back and load a bullet in the chamber. "Pull up beside him, man." Billy disengaged the lock on the door.

Budha glanced over his shoulder as a truck accelerated toward him. He picked up his pace as his heart accelerated. The thought of running didn't seem like a bad idea. But running would signify guilt, and he was sure there was no way The Syndicate could have gotten word of his plot. Only a few of his closest comrades knew of the scheme. So he nervously contemplated why they were rolling through his block in full force.

Budha gained courage with the belief that he was foolishly allowing paranoia to set in. He forced a hoarse laugh, deciding that with his entire crew nearby, not even The Syndicate would be brave enough to pull a stunt. But the blaring systems and screeching brakes that brought the hulking vehicles to a halt changed his mind. The drama was on. The glare in Billy's eyes left no doubt of that.

Billy hopped out of the vehicle and grabbed Budha by his leather coat, stopping any ideas he had of escaping.

"Yo . . . Yo . . . What's up, Billy?" Budha stammered, throwing his hands up in submission as he gazed at the riot pump in Billy's free hand. "What's going on, man? What I do?" he asked foolishly as the large contingent of The Syndicate members exited their rides with angry faces and heavy artillery.

"What you do, huh?" Billy laughed. "So now I guess you're gonna act like you have no idea why the fuck we're here?" He smashed the riot pump into Budha's brow before he could answer, drawing blood.

"What the hell was that shit for?" an angry member of Budha's crew yelled, leading the crew of soldiers up Prominade.

Nut raised the AK into firing position. "You got a problem with it, bitch?" Receiving no response from the group, Nut raised his voice. "Answer me, bitch . . . You . . . have . . . a motherfucking . . . problem?"

They stopped in unison, beaming helplessly at Syndicate members, who stood in position with their guns trained over the block. The self-appointed leader of Budha's crew growled, and then slightly parted his lips. "Who the fuck do you Syndicate niggas think you are? We don't fear that Mack and Grey shit over here!"

"What, nigga?" Billy said, slamming his shotgun into Budha's face a second time. Budha flinched and cried out.

The self-appointed leader angrily mumbled something as he eyed the rest of his crew making their way from cars and houses on the block. "You niggas might pull this bullshit on them other blocks you be taking over, but we ain't going for it around this bitch."

"Here's the deal for you niggas who don't already understand what's going on," Billy said. ''We tried to show you bitches love and allow you to get money with us, but somewhere along the way that wasn't good enough."

"What the fuck is that supposed to mean?" one of Budha's boys asked.

Billy tightened his grip on Budha and his gun. "This fat piece of shit and some of you other motherfuckers wanted to get greedy. So now we're taking the whole block. Nothing will be sold around here from now on unless it belongs to The Syndicate. And let this serve as a warning." Billy pulled the trigger, blowing Budha's head from his shoulders.

The rest of The Syndicate began shooting, taking out the self-proclaimed leader of Budha's crew with a barrage of AK bullets. The sound of gunfire and screaming lit up the block along with a haze of smoke as the unlucky members of Budha's crew nearby were riddled with an assortment of bullets.

Receiving light gunfire from up the block, The Syndicate opened fire in nearly every direction. Only those who took cover or laid down with their hands in clear view were spared. Billy grinned at the sight of Budha's headless body lying with its twitching feet. He pumped two more buck shots into his torso for the hell of it. Then he nonchalantly strolled over to his truck as the gunfire dissipated. The Syndicate had just made their mark on a major level and staked their claim, but as always, the potential for retaliation was a reality.

# Chapter 9

Destiny's bobbing head worked feverishly between Omar's widespread thighs as they lay in bed. She was working harder than usual, because she was still upset with Dre and wanted to please Omar better than ever. At the forefront of Destiny's mind was Stacy, and the potential for Stacy to steal Dre from her. So Destiny worked feverishly to prove to herself that her sex game was not something that would be the cause of her losing Dre. Sexing Omar was also her way of meting out revenge on Dre for having the audacity to engage Stacy in public.

"Damn, girl!" Omar blurted.

Destiny watched his eyes roll back as his toes began to curl. He grabbed the back of her head and forced it further down on his throbbing tool. But his intentions were shortstopped when the phone rang.

"This shit better be important," Omar yelled as he pushed Destiny off him and grabbed the phone off the nightstand.

She wiped saliva from her mouth and sat up. Reaching for her kimono styled robe, Destiny slightly jumped, surprised by the venom in his voice when he screamed, "They did what!" She concluded that whatever quality time they had planned to spend was ruined. She placed her robe over her sweat-covered body, stepped into her Victoria's Secret heels and made her way toward the terrace. She figured he needed some privacy, plus his call would allow her some time to observe the Chicago skyline from the fifty-story-perch above the city.

She leaned against one of the huge Roman statues at each end of the terrace. Gazing at the shrubbery that reminded her of a rainforest and thinking of the heated Jacuzzi she had been in earlier, Destiny tried convincing herself that she wasn't missing anything if she were to lose Dre. Everything he had, he had made because of her. It was she who showered him with lavish living and loving. But she couldn't deny that her feelings for Dre were strong.

Faintly hearing Omar's angry baritone as he tossed commands to whoever was on the other end of the phone, Destiny exhaled. She was glad that she wasn't on his bad side. Out of all the people she knew, he wasn't one that she would want for an enemy. Omar crushed his opposition, and the Detroit underworld had trembled under his reign for over a decade. Not only was he a supplier, he supplied the majority of the Midwest: Minnesota, Ohio, Michigan and Illinois. He had a dynasty. But Destiny knew that Detroit held a spot in his heart because he had been born and raised in the Motor City. She also knew that Omar was a gangster at heart and not a hustler. He was a risk-taker that had almost sacrificed millions on several occasions because of his emotional outbursts and desire to prove he was one of the few major money takers that could shoot it out with the wildest street thug.

Destiny reflected on her history with Omar. He had been the person who took her to the next level after her life with John ended. She owed him millions. That's why her loyalty to him was unwavering. The fact that he had sex appeal and was a beast in bed only made matters better.

Omar slammed the phone down on the dresser, snapping Destiny from her memories. She stepped from the terrace in the spacious bedroom.

"Who the fuck do these Syndicate niggas think they are?" Omar barked. "If they want war, then I'll end these motherfuckers!"

Destiny stopped. *Please, God. No.* She feared the reality of Dre becoming an enemy of Omar's cold, calculated organization. The Syndicate was no match for an experienced organized body of killers and hustlers ruled by one of the most vicious men to ever emerge from the streets of Detroit. Destiny felt powerless. There was nothing she could do to stop a man like Omar from destroying anyone who opposed him.


The Syndicate made their usual attention-grabbing entrance in a caravan of newly acquired Corvettes. The entourage made its way through the standing-room only crowd at the Brass Key, one of the most elite strip clubs in the city. The Westside club was the spot where most of the truest ballers from all over the city came to showcase their wealth and politic for positions.

Dre nodded his head at the club owner, Sherman, and led his crew to the bar. Sitting at the rear of the establishment, Dre made a mental note to holler at the old school club owner before leaving. He juggled long paper, and there was no doubt in Dre's mind that Sherman would be interested in purchasing his work from them now that the prices could be lowered to accommodate him.

The club was packed, but after hitting twenty bottles of Black Label Moët, room was made for the Syndicate at a number of tables directly below the stage. VIP treatment was the norm for them.

Whistling loudly, Nut exclaimed, "Look at the bitches they got working the room tonight! I don't know who's going home with me, but somebody is definitely going to get blessed."

Rossi rubbed his hands together in anticipation as he eyed an Asian beauty that returned his stare and gyrated her hips toward him.

Dre smiled at his crew, content to see them happy after all the drama they had been through. He watched Billy paying little attention to the half-naked women parading provocatively past them. Billy had always been the mysterious one of the clique. Dre thought of the story he had heard about Billy viciously handling Budha earlier in the day. Everybody in their crew had spilled blood, but Billy killed for the sport. Dre knew he enjoyed the power that came with taking all power away from someone else.

"Yo, Dre, ain't that old girl from the last day of school?" Nut asked, pointing toward one of the strippers onstage. "Damn, baby girl thick as hell."

Dre was shocked to see Tagier. She was indeed thick as hell, and the way she was dropping it to Rock Bottom's "Freak For Dollars," he had no doubt that she would gladly do just that. Life had clearly changed for her and him.

"That bitch is serious!" Nut added.

Dre watched silently, his eyes not blinking. They had unfinished business, and he was going to pick up where they left off. He patiently waited for the set to end, and then waved Sherman over to his table.

Destiny played the concerned act to a tee after Omar finished his heated phone call.

"What's stressing you, baby?"

Omar looked at her and just shook his head. "Street shit."

"Like what?" she probed, stepping over and massaging his shoulders. It had taken her years to gain his trust in disclosing incriminating information about his life on the streets, but she knew how to work him. "Don't let that shit stress you, baby."

"Shit is crazy."

When Omar leaned back into her embrace, Destiny asked, "It can't be that bad, nothing you can't handle. Right?"

"It's definitely gonna get handled."

Destiny probed more, until Omar revealed that The Syndicate had been a problem for him for too long. They had taken over a number of blocks through murder and intimidation, but Prominade was the first that Omar owned. They had disrespected him, and none of his people in Detroit seemed to be capable of handling them, so he was prepared to take a hands-on approach to resolve the problem.

After racking her brain for a solution that would buy Dre some time and hopefully save his life, she asked, "Instead of having to take it to the point I know you're prepared to, why don't you let me go back and do a little investigation first."

"Investigation?" Omar laughed. "Fuck are you, Magnum PI?"

"For real, I'm sure that my people will be able to locate these so-called Syndicate niggas and handle shit without you having to get your hands dirty."

"Why would you want to do that?"

Destiny tried to laugh off her nervousness as Omar turned around with a violent glimmer in his eyes. "Why wouldn't I do whatever I can for the man who raised me up and never let me down?"

"Is that a fact?"

"Can't a bitch do something for her nigga sometimes?" Destiny rolled her eyes.

Omar stared at her for a few seconds. "Alright, Destiny. Since you wanna help so much, find out everything you can about them niggas, and I'll handle it from there. But Des, don't play games with me, because you already know how I get down. You got me?" He reached around her head and grabbed a fistful of her curls.

"I got you, baby," she responded, wanting to scream for the joy she felt over Dre's temporary reprieve. She leaned forward and kissed Omar. As their tongues fought for dominance, she conjured a plan to save her boo. Not only could she save Dre's life, but if she could help him, she would solidify her position in his life on a level that Stacy could not.

Dre and Tagier were engrossed in conversation, oblivious to the strippers who shimmied and shook while giving Syndicate members lap dances. They communicated without interruption, which was a plus because he needed to talk his way into her thong.

Dre watched her finish off another glass of champagne. She flicked her tongue invitingly over her glossed lips to remove any remaining liquid. It was just something else that added to the way she had been arousing Dre since he spotted her onstage. Now, after an hour of them catching up with each other, he kept comparing her to the smart, sweet Tagier he remembered from school. She was now the confident stripper who had proved she could freak for dollars with ease.

"Whatever you were thinking about while you were staring at me, had to be serious as hell," she said.

Dre grinned.

"How about you share your thoughts with me?" she asked, staring into his eyes with a look that said "anything goes."

"I was just thinking about how much you changed."

"Is that all?"

"And I must admit, the whole time you been sitting here, I been thinking about fucking the shit out of you."

Tagier blushed, sitting in silence for a moment. "Come on, I want to show you something."

Dre grabbed a fresh bottle of Moët and fell in step behind her. Her swaying hips were enticing, just as much as her smooth chocolate skin. It was a funny feeling for him being so excited about sexing an exotic dancer, considering he had sexed so many different women. She wasn't on par with Stacy or Destiny or any of the women he usually bedded, but she was more interesting to him at the moment than any of them. She represented a failure that he could make up for. Although she had virtually dissed him the last time they met, tonight he would even the score.

They reached the back of the club and a door that read "Private Personnel Only." Tagier looked over her shoulder, tossing Dre a seductive smile. "I guess you'll get your chance to fuck me after all." She snickered as she led him inside the secluded area that Dre never knew existed. Tagier locked the door behind him and immediately dropped to her knees, fumbling with his sweats, releasing all he had to offer. She leaned back, clearly amazed at his size.

Dre stepped forward, rubbing the head of his dick over her lips, and snapping Tagier out of her daze. She enveloped the head of his dick in her warm mouth as she looked up through desperate eyes. He calmed her fears with soft words. But he planned to fuck her like she had never been fucked before. There would be nothing gentle or loving about their encounter. What he had in store for her was unadulterated lust.

"Umm," she moaned, taking more of him in her mouth.

"That's right, bitch. Do your thing. Do you your motherfucking thing."

Nut was engaged in what seemed like a never-ending lap dance. But he was still thinking of Dre and Tagier creeping off. It was ironic to him that Dre had finally gotten the chance to have sex with her.

"You wanna go in the back, daddy?"

Nut looked at the stripper who was grinding against him. "Nah, get up. I'm good." He needed a break and he wanted to go out and get some air. Nut tossed her a few bills, ignoring the stink look she gave him. He finished his drink and stood up.

"Where you going, man?" Rossi yelled above the music and loud conversations engulfing them.

"I'm headed outside to the car. I got a stash of Ganz out there."

"You ain't going nowhere without me," Rossi responded. He quickly pushed the stripper off his lap, handing her a fifty-dollar bill and snatching up his coat in what seemed like one motion.

Nut shouldered past whoever was in his path. Rossi showed no more respect, following his man with nothing else in mind but reaching the exit.

Having parked their fleet of Corvettes directly in front of the club, they found themselves seated, warm, bouncing to music and high as hell in minutes. If there was possibly another weed more powerful than the Ganz they were smoking, neither of them would have believed it.

Nut eyed the traffic around them. His team had too much beef for him not to keep his eyes open. "Oh, shit!" he said under his breath with a smile. He couldn't believe his luck. After over two years, Tagier's boyfriend, Dante picked tonight to surface. All Nut could think of was the day Dante had flashed his gun on Dre after school. "Come on!" Nut barked, shoving his .45 down the waistline of his Iceberg jeans.

"Where we going?" Rossi asked.

"We're going to have some fun, nigga. Just grab your burner and follow me."

Nut exited his Corvette, followed by Rossi. They weaved in and out of the crowds of partiers that exited the Brass Key. Nut's heart rate accelerated as he followed Dante into a dark alley nearby. Dante had made the mistake that so many before him had made—he was caught slipping in the hood.

"Mmmm!" Tagier moaned loudly, bucking her hips back to meet Dre's powerful thrusts while she gripped the edge of a desk and faced the mirror in front of her. Her mouth was wide open as her head swung forward in ecstasy with each deep stroke.

Dre worked his hips in a circular motion. He could feel her inner walls tremble as the wet sounds of her pussy and her high-pitched moans resonated throughout the room. Gripping her ass cheeks and slamming into her deeper, he ground against the spongy flesh of her Gspot.

"Oh . . . My God . . . Please!" Tagier begged as she threw her head back and closed her eyes. Dre could feel her muscles choking his meat.

"I'm . . . cum—ing!" Tagier screamed, squeezing her ass cheeks around Dre's dick.

"Damn, girl," Dre mumbled as his erection grew. He watched the beads of sweat flowing down the arch in her back. Feeling a climax approaching, Dre quickly pulled out and shot thick globs of his cream all over her ass, back and hair. He grunted in satisfaction as he watched the joy in Tagier's eyes and the smile on her face as he looked at her reflection in the mirror.

"Oh shit!" Her smile turned sour. "Did you hear that? Somebody's shooting."

Dre released his grip from her waist. The gunshots sounded like they were somewhere in the distance. Outside of the club. Gunfire was nothing new to him, but he pulled up his sweatpants and straightened his outfit in preparation to leave. He removed a large knot of Benjamins, slipped a thin layer of bills and dropped them on her body as he turned to leave. Pausing at the door, he said, "That was good, ma. And the money should cover your time and effort. See you in traffic."

Dre strolled out of the room and back into the club as an alarm immediately surged through his body upon seeing his clique standing with blank stares. He searched their faces, realizing that Nut and Rossi were missing. His mind flashed to the sound of gunshots he heard a moment ago. "Where they at?" he asked Billy. "Nut and Rossi?"

"Who knows?"

"You're supposed to know!" Dre declared.

"We were wondering the same thing you thinking," Billy said, falling in step as Dre led his crew out of the club. The comments and pointing of partygoers outside the club indicated where the shooting had taken place. Dre noticed the Corvette that Nut and Rossi had come in was gone. He walked toward the alley where the crowds were pointing. Upon turning the corner, he spotted a purple Impala with a lifeless body slumped over the steering wheel. He knew the car and its dead driver well. Memories ran through his mind of the day Tagier's now dead boyfriend had stunted on him at his school.

"What's so funny?" Billy asked.

Dre smiled at the sweet sight of revenge. He knew the lifeless victim in the car had felt the wrath of Nut. It was ironic to him that he was finally sexing Tagier as her man was being murdered. Dre turned to Billy. "Let's blow this joint, cuz."

"But what about Nut and Rossi? And who that nigga over there with his brains on the dashboard?"

Dre tossed his arm over Billy's shoulder and grinned. "Nut and Rossi are fine. As for the dead man, he was caught in the right place at the wrong time." He pulled out his phone to call Nut to affirm his belief.

# Chapter 10

Stress lines snaked across Destiny's forehead. Finding something worthwhile on the Syndicate for Omar without giving up Dre had Destiny on edge. Having to make continuous excuses was beginning to wear on her nerves. She had no idea what to do next. She couldn't possibly tell Omar that she was in love with their leader. And she had changed her mind about warning Dre. To let him know of the impending danger he faced at Omar's hand would only cause drama to boil out even quicker.

Quickly tiring of pacing back and forth through her spacious bedroom, Destiny laid across her bed. Today, like every other day during the last two weeks since she had returned from Chicago, would be no more productive than the one before. She ran her hand through her long hair, thinking that she was acting unlike herself. Never had she been one to concern herself with the problems of others. The only thing that bothered her about the fact that Omar's army would totally annihilate the Syndicate was knowing there was no possibility of Dre escaping the drama when everything was done. Other than her safety, she had no interest in what became of his crew. In her eyes, they were nothing but a loosely organized mob of ghetto fabulous knuckleheads.

Dre was another story. He was different from the rest of them in so many ways. Thanks to better breeding, his attitude placed him a step ahead of the average street hustler. She credited that mostly with her schooling him. So she was prepared to do whatever she could to keep her creation safe.

But Destiny worried because Dre had been staying out late and rarely coming home lately. The space that she had become accustomed to sharing with him in her home had practically become empty. In the last week alone, he had only slept there once, claiming that business throughout the city kept him away. Destiny wondered if he was seeing Stacy. Though she wasn't sure what was driving him away from her, it was clear she no longer held the absolute power over him that she once possessed. With that thought in mind, Destiny understood that she would have to find new methods of piquing his interest in the near future.


Stacy's image invaded Dre's mind every hour of the day, no matter if he was conducting business or hanging out with Destiny. Their encounter on his birthday raced through his mind repeatedly. When he could no longer fight what he knew he felt in his heart, Dre became determined to locate Stacy. Dre had just finished driving around what seemed like the entire city of Detroit, but he wasn't having any luck. He pulled up at a light a few blocks from Prominade Street when he got a call from his homie Skeet. "What up, doe?"

"Good news."

"Don't fuck with me," he said with a smile. Weeks earlier, Dre had put Skeet on a mission to locate Stacy.

"She lives in Highland Park."

"Oh yeah?"

"Works at a store in Northland Mall; goes to Wayne State University."

"She got a man?" Dre asked as he pulled off when the light turned green.

"Been single for over a year."

Dre smiled. He liked everything he had heard. It seemed unreal that he would actually be soon laying his eyes on Stacy again. He pulled over to the side of the road and wrote down the information Skeet had on Stacy. Then he looked at his watch and decided to head directly to her campus. He typed the address in his navigational system. His Impala leaped forward.

Dre wanted Stacy more than any woman he'd had in a while. Because of Destiny, his life had taken a turn for the better. But because of her overbearing presence in his personal life, he had outgrown her. He cared for her, but he felt she needed someone her age and someone who was comfortable with her dominating their relationship. Even though Dre knew that she loved him; that love was not enough to keep him committed. It was time for change. Destiny represented the old and Stacy the new.

Dre pulled up in front of Stacy's school just in time to spot her exiting a campus building with an arm full of books. She looked just as good as she had the first time they met. She was engrossed in a conversation with two of her girlfriends. Dre exited his Impala and leaned up against the door.

Stacy stopped and stared at him, visibly caught off guard by his presence. She pursed her lips in a look of disbelief, but there was a hint of a smile evident upon her face.

"Girl, who is that?" one of her girlfriends asked.

"Does he have any other friends that look as good as him?" another friend asked.

Dre smiled when he heard her and the other girl make similar comments. But Dre was focused on the woman standing before him. Stacy sported a full-length jacket, jeans and Manolo Blahnik-styled Timberlands. Everything she wore fit her perfectly, highlighting her shapely figure, but allowing her to maintain a sense of class and style that was presentable in any arena.

Dre took a few steps forward, covering the distance between him and Stacy as her friends fell back behind her. He stopped, coming face-to-face with her. "When you said you lived on the Westside, I had no idea that you would be so hard to locate," he said, gently prying her books from her arms.

"Is that so?" Stacy smiled.

"Yes, that's so."

"Well, I don't recall even saying that the task would be easy in the first place, now did I?"

"Yeah, I guess you're right. However, I was always told that anything that comes easily is never worthwhile in the end."

"So I'm the person who brought you all the way over here on this cold day?"

"Nah, I just didn't have anything else to do, so I thought I would come to the campus and just stand here in the cold." Dre chuckled.

"That was a rhetorical question," Stacy said, rubbing her hands together to gain some semblance of heat.

"Come on. Let me give you a ride home," Dre said, reaching to grasp her hand. She shook her head.

"Uh-uh," she stated sternly, pulling her hand away.

"What's wrong?"

"I would rather stand here and freeze than ride in that woman's car." She folded her arms across her chest.

"But I'm sure freezing is not really an option, so how do you plan to get home?" he asked in a concerned tone.

"The same way I've been getting home. The bus."

"How about I call you a cab to take you home and then come back and retrieve my car?"

She took a moment to think about his proposal. Then she reached out to grab her books, winked her eye and said, "No thanks. The bus will work just fine. But, hey, I appreciate the thought."

"It's good to be appreciated."

Stacy smiled. "School ends at the same time for me tomorrow, so who knows, I may just accept a ride if you're driving something different."

Dre watched her confident stride as she switched her sexy frame off. He knew she wanted him, but she was trying her best to make him work. That was something he was not used to. Women usually threw themselves at men of his status. But he respected her "hard to get" mode and liked a challenge.

Stacy was unable to concentrate on anything her professor was saying. She continued to fidget in her seat and glanced at the clock on the wall that seemed to be stuck. Stacy didn't know why, but she was experiencing a nervous sort of excitement. She had been feeling that way since seeing Dre the day before.

What really struck her as odd was that she had not planned to ever see him again after they met the first time. But when in his presence, she couldn't help free herself from him—their chemistry had a strength all its own that weakened her resolve. Now she found herself hoping he had returned to see her. Her thoughts of Dre went against everything Stacy stood for as a goal-oriented young woman from a good family. Dre was a hustler who was also in a relationship with a woman. That made it clear that whether he appeared or not was unimportant. As much as Stacy was attracted to him, she had no intention of going anywhere with him.

Somehow she managed to get Dre off her mind and focus on her schoolwork. She opened her economics textbook and forced herself to concentrate on the professor's lecture. She had come too far to get sidetracked. But as much as she tried, she couldn't help but anticipate what would happen if Dre was outside waiting for her. It frustrated her that she was not in control of how her heart and body might react, despite what her mind thought.

Dre was confident and exhilarated as he whipped through traffic on his way to see Stacy. Not only had he changed cars, he had purchased a brand new Benz so she would be the first female to ever rest her frame in it. He even went a step further, filling the backseats with colorful roses and heart-shaped balloons. He needed to make an impression on Stacy, because she was different.

Turning into the campus entrance, he leaned forward, increasing the volume to Maxwell's crisp, melodic voice flowing through the Bose system. He felt that he couldn't have possibly been more ready for his meeting with Stacy than he was at the moment.


Stacy rushed through the hallway in her haste to exit school. She was on edge, jittery at the prospect of Dre being outside, though she tried to convince herself that her quick stride had nothing to do with her belief that Dre was awaiting her. Regardless of how she wanted to feel about him, Stacy couldn't duck the fact that she liked Dre.

She reached the double doors and hurried through them. Her heart dropped when she looked around and he was nowhere in sight. She was let down at the realization that she may have played a little too hard to get. Stacy stared in every direction in hopes that Dre would appear. After searching for a matter of minutes, she exhaled in defeat. She pulled her coat tighter as she began to ascend the stairs.

Stacy clutched her books to her chest and prepared to wait for the bus to arrive. She snapped out of her reverie at the sound of Maxwell's crooning. Her neck swiveled in the direction of one of her favorite tunes. "Oh, my God!" She smiled when the window rolled down on the Mercedes 430 steering beside her. Dre leaned back in the seat, singing Maxwell's lyrics to her. "He is too much," she murmured, thinking how attractive Dre looked and how much the sparkling white ride fit him perfectly. Stacy couldn't stop smiling.

"I know you weren't planning to leave without me," Dre said.

"I'm walking."

"But you knew I was coming."

"I know what I see."

"And hear." Dre began singing to her again. Stacy's face lit up. Stopping mid-step, she shifted her weight from one foot to the other. She didn't know what to say, but she knew what she felt—overwhelmed with appreciation. For the first time in years she felt special.

"That's so sweet," she said, clapping her hands when Dre popped the driver's door open, stepped from the car and retrieved her books. He placed them in the car, and then grabbed some flowers and a balloon.

"These are for you," he said, handing her the items.

"Thank you so much," she said, smelling the roses. "I guess right now I'm supposed to say, 'You didn't have to.' But I'll save that, because I'm really glad you did."

"I have something to say, and I think I should say it now."

Stacy smiled and remained silent.

He grabbed her hands, and then exhaled. "Stacy, ever since the first time I saw you, I knew I had to have you. The months of not being able to locate you was killing me. For real. Now that I have you here, there is so much I want us to experience together." He gently massaged her hands, and then added, "I'm prepared to take this as slow as you want or as fast as you like. But at the moment, I'm just asking to take you home."

Stacy pulled her hands back and stared into Dre's eyes in silence, obviously trying to gauge his sincerity. From the look on her face, Dre could tell she had been hurt before and feared ending up on the receiving end of a bad relationship again.

"What I'm telling you is the truth. I just want you to give me a shot so we can see where this goes."

"Okay, Dre. I'm going to let you take me home against my better judgment. But I hope I don't live to regret the decision."

"If I can make you no other promise, believe me when I tell you that this is one decision you will never regret."

Stacy sat inside the Benz, sinking into the plush leather seat. It was a feeling of luxury. The look in her eyes told Dre she liked what she was experiencing. She played it cool, casually punching her address into his navigational system. Dre liked her style: calm, but assertive. Not the loud type or extremely high maintenance woman like those he was used to and tired of. Stacy was the type of woman he could take home to his grandmother. He respected that she was taking a risk going out with him despite her instinct. The last thing he planned to do was hurt her. She seemed to be a woman worthy of so much, and if Dre's perception of her was right, she would receive all that she was worth.

"Right there," Stacy said, pointing at her two-story home as Dre turned the corner of her block.

"Nice house," Dre said.

"Thanks."

Dre was telling the truth. It wasn't the mansion Destiny had, but it was clear she enjoyed the benefit of living in a respectable neighborhood. The home had been fully paid for by her parents. It was part of the good living she had told Dre she learned from her father, who was a doctor. No dice games on the corner like the hood Dre grew up in. No gunshots nor clusters of loudmouth hood rats sniffing behind street hustlers. "You've lived here all your life?"

"Pretty much," Stacy said.

Dre eyed her economic books. "I take it you're not following your father into the medical field."

"I got a thing for money." She laughed.

"Me too," Dre said.

"And you're smart enough to make it legally."

"That's true, but how would you know? This is only the third time we've met."

She turned and faced Dre. "I know who you are. Or should I say what you do. For a living, that is. It's the reason I'm so apprehensive about involving myself with you."

"You don't have to worr—"

Stacy cut his words short by placing her index finger to his lips. "That's another story. My point is, the same intellect and ambition you put into overseeing an illegal operation can be put into running a legitimate business. Don't sell yourself short."

Before Dre could respond, she was stepping out of his car. He watched her sexy strut as she walked off. Stacy was the first woman besides his grandmother who had ever urged him to do something productive. More importantly, without even getting to know him in depth, she understood his potential. She was the total opposite of Destiny, who pushed Dre toward his illegal aspirations. Dre knew Stacy was different from the way she carried herself. But she had just proven that she was not just different, she was someone who truly had Dre's interest at heart. But while he was intent on making her his woman, he was not ready to depart from the fastpaced life of money and fame that came with the drug game.

# Chapter 11

Stacy had been on Dre's mind over the past two months they had been spending time together. He contemplated her being his girl and what she said about him leaving the drug game the first day he drove her home. Her "leave the drug game alone" mantra was a normal thing. It amazed him that just a few questions from a single woman had him rethinking how he approached life. He realized that he had really spent little time analyzing anything he did, with the exception of plotting out killings and making money. If nothing less, Dre's time spent with Stacy made him more conscious of where he had been, where he was, and where he planned to go. Reflecting on this, he decided to pay Destiny a visit.

When Dre whipped his Benz into Destiny's driveway, his head began to thump. He rubbed his temples as he put the car in park. Then he grabbed two briefcases off the passenger seat and exhaled, knowing that the meeting ahead of him would be strained. Their relationship had steadily declined the more Dre spent time with Stacy.

Dre exited his Benz with a briefcase in each hand. He knew that eventually he would have to sever ties with Destiny. For them to continue on in this fashion was impossible. Although he still desired her for sexual and business reasons, even he was mature enough to know that such a shallow relationship would not last. Stacy was the only woman he wanted and needed.

Dre reached her door and rang the bell. He didn't even waste his time using the key she had long since given him. It wouldn't have felt right, because he had not used it in so long. Back when he did, he was practically living with her. Most of the time Dre spent now was at his new home, where Stacy was often a houseguest. So much had changed since Destiny opened her door to Dre. They both knew it, and they both were soon to confront it.


Destiny bit down on her bottom lip to control her anger at the fact Dre hadn't used his key. She stopped cutting some collard greens in the kitchen and stomped through her dining room toward the front door. "Calm down, Destiny," she told herself as she stopped in the living room. She slowly walked to the front door and opened it. Flashing a phony smiled, she granted Dre entrance. "I guess you forgot your key, huh?"

"Lost interest."

"Excuse me?" she said as Dre walked past her.

"Later, we'll discuss that later."

Destiny tried to remain calm, but Dre was making her more frustrated by the second. She closed the door and walked over to the table in front of the couch where Dre set the two briefcases and opened them.

"This should clear our tab."

"Yeah, yeah," Destiny replied. "I'm not trippin' over no money, Dre. You know better than that."

"Bills is bills, and I pay 'em."

Destiny rolled her eyes at the briefcases. There were rows of banded stacks in them. She turned to Dre. "Why have you not been answering my calls? And where have you been sleeping every night, because you damn sure ain't been here with me."

"That goes back to what I said when I stepped through the door and you asked me about losing my keys."

"Huh?" Destiny shrugged her shoulders. "What the hell is going on, Dre?"

"Lost interest."

"Lost what!" she screamed. "Ooooh. You're such a big man, now, huh?" Destiny could feel tears welling in her eyes and anger boiling in her blood. The man who she'd made had the nerve to tell her that he had lost interest in her. She felt he had used her, but she was the vet who was supposed to be using him until she fell in love with him.

"What the fuck is going on, Dre!" she barked.

"Can't believe you're resorting to making a scene."

"You don't even know what a scene is." She glared at him.

"You usually seem to have everything under control in every situation. Business, personal, you keep your cool."

"Anyway you were playing your position at one point."

"My position?" Dre said. "What? Young fool?"

Destiny froze. Anger had caused her to reveal herself. To admit that their relations revolved around her being the experienced beautiful woman who controlled the inexperienced.

"Yeah, yeah. Shit. That feels good, Stacy."

"Yes, mmmmm." Dre strained his stiffness into her thrusts. He could feel himself losing control, but he loved it. Stacy felt so good. Every thought he ever had about her couldn't compare to her sexual prowess. "Ahh, shit. I'm cumming."

"Yes, me too." She rocked faster and harder, slapping down her wetness against him until they both climaxed at the same time.

"Damn, baby. Shit!" Dre pulled her close, basking in the warmth of her tender flesh as they gained their composure.

"So you got what you wanted," Stacy said.

"You damn right." Dre laughed. "You did too."

Stacy giggled.

"You got me all sweaty; now I need to shower again."

Dre smiled.

"Me? You're the one who started this." Stacy kissed him, and then got up. "I'm gonna run us a hot bath."

Dre smiled as he watched her nude frame while she walked off. He had finally fulfilled his desire to have sex with Stacy. It was all he thought it would be, plus more. There was nothing separating them anymore. They had explored everything there was to know about each other. Dre had disclosed his life on the streets and she had told him everything from her family issues to school and career goals. Stacy brought out a side of him he didn't know existed. He was used to being so guarded. But with her, he couldn't help but reveal his true self. Stacy was getting to know the person no one on the streets knew.

"Come on, baby, your bath's ready."

Dre smiled at the sound of Stacy yelling to him from the bathroom. He always loved how she catered to his every need. He stood and began heading to the bathroom. Before he made it there, he heard his phone ring, so he stepped into the guest room.

"What up, doe?" he answered.

"I think we need to get rid of Moe."

"What?" Dre said, sitting on the bed.

"We need to get shit cooked and cut, and he's nowhere to be found."

"Again?" Dre shook his head. He stood up and began pacing. It was the second time Moe had been missing when they needed him. Dre was tired of him. He was tired of a lot of things he encountered on the streets.

"You need to look into it."

"Yeah," Dre said. Stacy hugged him from behind and began planting kisses on his neck. Her comforting embrace and hot bath she had waiting for him felt awkward. Because of a dope fiend he depended on, he was being pulled back into the streets. At that moment, Dre realized just how mixed up his life was. "Don't worry, I got it," Dre told Nut, and then tossed his phone on the bed.

Stacy eased around him and looked into his eyes. "You okay, baby?"

"As long as I got you." He smiled and kissed her, allowing his hands to drop down and palm the soft skin of her ass.

She pulled back. "Then come on and let me bathe you."

"I'll be there in one minute."

"Don't let the water get cold."

Dre's dick hardened again as he watched Stacy's ass shake as she walked toward the bathroom. He would have to handle Moe later. Looking at Stacy, he realized they needed some time alone. They had been practically living together, and Dre was planning on buying a new house, so he was thinking of somewhere secluded and far away from the hood. Somewhere he and Stacy could officially call home. Now was the time to also get a break from the streets, and since her semester was coming to an end in a week, she could get a break from school. Dre thought about an ad he recently saw on television for Montego Bay, Jamaica. A sandy beach on Jamaica was the perfect place for them. He decided he would contact a travel agency in the morning and a crooked real estate agent. He had a worthy woman by his side, and it was time to spend some of the riches he had amassed over the past year-and-a-half. He needed a vacation and new living quarters.

# Chapter 12

Dre and Stacy had been on the island of Jamaica for a week, enjoying everything that Montego Bay had to offer. When they weren't in their beachfront cottage, they were out dining, partying or on the beach, among other places.

Dre sat on a beach chair in back of the cottage thinking about Stacy as he fingered the sleek velvet box in his hand. He had outdone himself with the exquisite gift. A day earlier, he had slipped away from Stacy and purchased the five-carat diamond necklace from the premiere jeweler on the island. The bracelet represented something different than the clothes, money and the trip Dre had showered her with.

Dre entered the cottage. He could hear water running in the room. Their personal chef and housekeeper had left. He pocketed the bracelet and strolled out in front of the cottage onto the patio. Dre sat on one of the wicker chairs surrounding the large table that was covered by an even larger umbrella. He removed his

Cartier frames and placed them on the table, concentrating on the view around him. Dre saw nothing but beauty. From the coconut trees perfectly placed along the huge manicured grounds, to the deep blue sea and white sands. The ambiance created was so different than what he found back in Detroit. His life had truly changed as he rose to prominence. Never had he imagined sitting in the comfort of an exotic island with a beautiful woman he loved. To add to that, were riches that had made life comfortable for him, his family, and friends. This was not the type of life that usually unfolded for a child of the ghetto who had a father in prison and a list of dead homies.

Dre removed a bag of weed from his pocket and rolled a spliff with Rizla paper. He sparked the spliff and inhaled. Leaning back as the potent weed quickly brought forth the euphoric feeling he desired, Dre eased further down into the comfortable chair. "This is the life," he mumbled to himself and closed his eyes.

Dre felt Stacy creeping behind him before he opened his eyes to see her peering down at him. "You look so good," he said.

"You too, since I braided your hair and dressed you."

Dre laughed, but he felt good with his fresh cornrows, Armani shorts, and shirt with a tank top beneath it. It gave him a sort of preppy yet rugged look. If it had not been for the diamond Rolex on his arms and the Cartier frames he had just placed on the table, Dre could have easily passed for a vacationing college student. But the irony was that he was one of the wealthiest street hustlers in Detroit who was on vacation with a college student.

Stacy plopped down in his lap and began playfully kissing him.

"You taste good," Dre said when they were done. He wrapped his arms around her waist. She reached for his spliff. "Let me hit that."

"You don't even sound right saying that." Dre laughed as he held the spliff away from her. "Besides, I didn't bring you all the way out here to Jamaica to turn you into a weed head, all right?"

"You better let me hit that, boy." She pouted, grabbing the spliff and taking a short toke before Dre could grab it back. She began coughing and choking.

"See what you get." Dre laughed and took a toke of the spliff. He watched Stacy's eyes grow red and slanted. He knew that she was letting her good girl persona down because of the atmosphere and her comfort with him. He watched the strong weed release her inhibitions as she snatched the spliff and pulled on it again.

"This is good." She exhaled, smiled and placed the weed back between his lips.

"You don't know what good weed is."

"I know what a good man is, and I got him in my arms right now." She began kissing Dre.

Dre stared into her slanted eyes as they parted. He watched a smile emerge on her face as she ran her nails through his braids. "You're high off of them two tokes."

Stacy giggled like a child. "Yeah, yeah. What else is new?"

She laughed again.

"I can't believe you're smoking with me."

"Believe it." She pecked him on the lips. "So where did you go when I was sleep?"

"Um . . . I . . . um . . . had something to do," Dre fumbled his words, trying not to reveal that he had been out to purchase a bracelet for her. "Had to take care of something real quick."

"Oh, you did, huh?" she asked rhetorically, shifting her weight on his lap, purposely sliding her ass over the growing bulge beneath her. He could tell she was horny. The combination of the weed, the scent of his cologne, and the stiffness up against her were all working to his advantage.

She stared into his eyes and said, "Well, what do you think about taking care of me now that you're back?"

Dre looked out at the waves in the water in the distance from them. "Sex on the beach, huh?" He grinned.

Stacy placed his hand on her bikini top-clad breasts. She pulled his face to her own, boldly placing her moist tongue in his mouth.

Dre wasted no time pulling the string that held her bikini top in place. He fingered her erect nipples while exploring the contours of her mouth with his tongue. It still amazed him how sexually liberated she had become since they became intimate.

"Taste them," she said, shifting her breasts into his mouth. She purred, "Kiss them, suck them... Yes, like that. I'm on fire," she moaned as his lips and tongue pleasured her breasts. He placed his free hand between her legs and rubbed her pussy through the wet fabric of her thong. Her breathing increased at the same moment that her legs opened wider to allow further exploration. He hooked a finger in the seam of her bikini bottoms. Dre was in heaven when he pushed it inside her sopping wet depths.

"Ah, ah, ah," she panted, closing her eyes and pulling his head closer to her chest. The combination of his finger working her center and his mouth devouring her breasts brought a deep feeling of bliss, causing her to scream. She reached down and grabbed his erect penis.

Dre released the hold on her breasts and stood with Stacy in his arms. He placed her on the table. Her legs dangled over the side. Pulling the string on either side of her hips, he squinted in lust as her bikini bottoms came loose, leaving her completely exposed.

"Yes, Dre," she moaned.

Dre dropped to his knees and spread Stacy's legs as far as possible. Then he stuck his tongue inside the dark tunnel between them while rubbing on her clit with his thumb.

"Ooohhh, shit. Baby. What . . . are . . . you . . . doing to me?" Stacy yelled.

He gripped her soft ass cheeks in his palms, pulling her closer into his rapid tongue movements. Then he clamped his lips over her clit and sucked while flicking his tongue against it. He could taste her juices as she came.

"Stop, baby! Please stop," she begged as her body shook and she thrust her body against his head. "I need you inside me."

Dre stood and unfastened his belt, then dropped his pants and boxers in one fluid motion. He grabbed his monstrous dick and rubbed the head between her lips.

Just the touch of it drove Stacy wild. "Come on, I need you."

Dre slowly pushed inside of her, feeling her body tense up as it did each time during sex. Both of their breathing became concentrated. Closing his eyes, he groaned because of the tightness that swallowed him.

Stacy gripped his butt, pulling him deeper into her. "You feel so good, baby. Fuck me harder!"

Dre thrust his whole length inside of her and began rotating his hips. He picked up his pace, making sure to come in contact with her clit each time he plunged into her.

Stacy screamed out Dre's name over and over as he built up a fast pace. "This pussy is all . . . yours. Oooh. Don't stop, baby! Don't you dare stop . . . fucking me!" Her body bucked violently against him, her eyes rolling back into the depths of her head and her inner muscles gripping him.

"Shit!" Dre exclaimed at the feeling of Stacy working her magic. He threw his head back and pounded into her faster. "Yeah!" He felt himself about to cum and forced himself in her as fast as he could. Dre gritted his teeth as he released a jet of cum into her, filling her insides with his seed.

"Yeah, baby," she whispered. "I love you."

"I love you, too." Dre lay across her body, breathing heavy. They were both overwhelmed from the intensity of their lovemaking.

Stacy turned Dre's face toward hers and exhaled. She gazed at him with pleading eyes. "Please don't hurt me."

"Huh?" Dre squinted.

"I've been there before, Dre. I know what it's like to place my heart in someone's hand, just to have them destroy it."

Dre kissed her lips, and then her forehead. "I'm not that somebody, Stacy. I wouldn't be all the way out here in Jamaica with you if I didn't feel you were worthy or that I was ready for a real relationship with a real woman like you."

Stacy hugged Dre. When she released him, he reached down and grabbed his pants. He removed the velvet box from his pocket and handed it to her.

Stacy glanced from Dre to the box, and then nervously opened it. "Oh, my God." She smiled. "Baby, this is beautiful."

"Not as beautiful as you are," Dre said.

"Thank you so mu—"

Dre pressed his index finger against her lips to quiet her. He held her gaze and spoke in the most sincere voice he could muster. "I'm aware of how much it took for you to give yourself to me. To trust a man of my background. To break your vow of celibacy. Your trust and faith in me is priceless, but this is the least I could do to let you know that I recognize your commitment to me."

Stacy hugged Dre. "Thank you, thank you so much."

Dre whispered into her ear, "I knew I was for you and you was for me when I made eye contact with you for the first time in the park on my birthday. The only thing different between now and then is you're mine." He looked her in the eyes. "I love you for real, Stacy."

She began crying. Dre wiped her tears away. "I'm gonna do all I can to make you happy for as long as you want me to. I'm yours."


Dre and Stacy entered Pier One, having decided on dinner before hitting Club Wow for a night of dancing. The posh restaurant was known for its classy decor and premiere food prepared by Jamaica's most sought-after chefs. It was an eatery reserved for affluent tourists and island dwellers.

"I should have known," Dre mumbled, realizing there were no empty tables in the establishment. He approached the hostess station and eyed the finely dressed employee.

"How may I be of service?" she asked in a thick Jamaican accent.

Dre said, "I was hoping that you could find me a table for two." When he noticed her smile turn into a grimace, he added, "You see, we just got engaged, and we were hoping to celebrate here."

"Sir, I'm sorry. But unless you have a reservation, there's nothing I can do for you." She shrugged her shoulders as if to accommodate her apology. Then she smiled and gave her undivided attention to another couple.

Dre was ready to flip, but Stacy gently tugged on his hand. "Baby, come on," she insisted. "I'm sure that we can find somewhere else even better to eat."

Dre doubted that they would find a better restaurant. Yet he turned to leave. Before he could take a step, the sound of someone calling out to them stopped his movement. He glanced over his shoulder and saw the man whom the hostess had given her attention to after disregarding them.

"Excuse me," the Latin voice repeated. The older man walked over to Dre and shook his hand. "My name is Torres." He nodded toward his companion. "She is Consuela. Anyway, I couldn't help but overhear of your little situation. If you would accept my humble invitation, you and your lady are welcome to dine at our table as our guests."

Dre scrutinized the stranger before him. He could

sense sincerity in his invitation. The Bulgari watch that peeked from beneath his Ferragamo blazer, coupled with his Gucci loafers spoke of wealth. Dre couldn't think of any reason why they shouldn't accept his gracious invitation.

Cutting his eyes toward Stacy, he asked, "What do you think, ma?"

"It sounds good to me."

Dre turned back to Torres and said, "I'm Dre, and this is my lady Stacy. We accept your invitation, but all I ask in return is that you allow me to pay for dinner."

Torres laughed. "It's not necessary, but if it will make you feel better, be my guest."

Dre gripped Stacy's hand, proud to have someone as beautiful and desirable as her on his arm. They followed Torres and Consuela to their table.

Torres popped the cork on their fifth bottle of champagne. He filled everyone's flutes, spilling some of the Moët on Consuela and Stacy's fingers, bringing forth their drunken giggles.

Dre laughed as well. He found it odd that what had begun as an accidental meeting, hours before, had spiraled into a festive party. They had found common ground in conversation during dinner. Any strain that may have been evident when they met had quickly dissolved. The women began chattering incessantly. It was only natural that Dre and Torres also communicated freely. But Dre couldn't help but notice how Torres seemed to be analyzing his every move. Dre wondered what Torres was trying to figure out.

Torres placed his glass in the air in the middle of the table. "I would like to propose a toast to our new friends, Dre and Stacy. May tonight be the beginning of a fruitful acquaintance." Dre tapped glasses with the other three, turned up his drink and bounced his head to the blaring reggae. Though they had planned to visit Club Wow, they had been persuaded to venture into the newest hotspot called Disco Inferno.

"So we're on for tomorrow? Right, Dre?" Torres questioned loudly above the music.

"Yeah, that's definitely a go," Dre responded. He couldn't wait to see the yacht that Torres had spoken so highly of. "There's no way I'd miss it."

"Okay, my friend. This cruise only comes around once in a lifetime." Torres winked at Dre and turned up his drink. "Let me ask you something else," Torres said.

"What's that?" Dre asked.

"You always this comfortable and trusting around people you don't know?"

Dre wondered what the hidden meaning was in Torres' words. "Guess I could ask you the same."

Torres smiled. "But I'm the one who has essentially pursued you. And now I'm inviting you to a place on a foreign island you have no knowledge of. So if anyone should be leery, it's you."

Before Dre could question him on it, he felt his phone vibrating. He placed a finger in his ear to drown out the loud music before answering his phone. "Yeah, what's up?"

"How is life in Jamaica treating you, my nigga?" Nut questioned.

"Boy, this is how ballers are supposed to do it."

"Is that a fact?"

"This shit is sweet. Believe me when I tell you, you gotta come down here."

"Alright," Nut said. "That's enough. I get the picture, nigga. While I'm freezing my ass off in the city, you're walking around half-naked, fucking in the sand and shit."

"Yep, that's about the size of it, player. But tell me why the hell you're calling me at . . . " Dre looked down at his watch—"three-twelve in the morning?"

"Okay, first of all I miss you, nigga."

"At three in the morning, huh?"

"Plus, I wanted to be the first to wish you a Merry Christmas. And being as though I've been working my ass off for you in your absence, I figured that I would let you know that the house you toured before leaving now belongs to you. All Stacy's things have been placed in storage like you instructed and everything is ready for the two of you to return."

"Now that's what I'm talking about, dog. Good looking, Nut. I owe you one."

"You damn right you do. When are the two of you coming home?"

"I'm not sure yet. The vacation has just begun to heat up," Dre replied, catching Stacy's eye and blowing her a kiss.

"All right, man. Enjoy yourself, pimp. And give me a call before you arrive so I can scoop you up. I'm about to bust up, so I'll holler at you later." Nut hung up.

Dre put his phone away as he noticed the smirk on Torres' face. Dre shook his head, excited at the news of the house and the fact that everything was going as planned.

Torres reached for the bottle of Moët, and then poured them each another glass. He winked, and then clinked their glasses together. "I think we can hold off on you checking out my yacht."

Dre narrowed his brows, clearly baffled. He could see he was being tested by Torres, but Dre had no idea why. The look in Torres' eyes told him there was a lot more to him. And Dre was sure that the mystery would soon unfold.


Destiny felt numb as she sat in her bedroom with the phone in her hand listening to every word Naiza spoke. Naiza had been with Nut and overheard his phone conversation with Dre. She had only gotten pieces of the talk mentioned by Nut. But the basics were covered—Dre was on vacation with Stacy, and they would be coming home to a new home together. Destiny had been pondering if it was Stacy who had damaged her relationship with Dre since his birthday when she saw Dre captivated by the young woman. But receiving a confirmation was devastating.

"Mm hmm, you know I was all ears too," Naiza said. "Nigga had the nerve to be all up in Jamaica, doing it big with another bitch like he's built like that." Naiza sucked her teeth as if she were more disturbed by the news than Destiny. "Girl, you can't let him get away with that shit!"

"I don't plan to, Naiza. He has played me for the last time, and now he'll find out what happens when I become the enemy."

"Yeah, he'll definitely find out," Naiza added. "Now, what do you need me to do? 'Cause you know I got your back."

"I'm not sure yet."

"Shit, you better *get* sure."

"Don't worry, when it comes time, I'll let you

know," Destiny mumbled, feeling overwhelmed by the situation. "Good looking on the info, girl."

"Ain't nothing."

"But until I'm ready to strike back, do me a favor and keep your eyes and ears open for anything they do that may be important, alright?"

"I'm on it. And if you need anything, and I do mean anything, don't hesitate to give me a call."

"I won't. Thanks, Naiza." Destiny hung up the phone before her friend could notice that she was crying. Destiny leaned against the wall for support. It felt like a knife had been dug into her heart. "Ugh . . ." She placed her hand on her belly and winced as the realization that Dre was in love with someone else settled in her mind. "That motherfucker . . . After all that I invested in him . . ." Destiny tried to laugh although the tears kept streaming down her face. She nodded in disbelief. "Motherfucker . . . I still can't believe . . ." Her laugh became a cackle as she doubled over to stop the hurt from consuming her. It was bad enough that he was in Jamaica with another woman, giving away all the good loving that Destiny felt belonged to her, but him purchasing a home to live in with another woman was more than Destiny had fathomed. Dre had committed the ultimate deceit. Regardless of how much she loved him, his actions left her no other option than to bring about his destruction. He had turned out to be just like his father. The revenge she initially had planned because of his father when she met Dre was back in motion. There was no way she should have allowed her feelings to cloud her vision.

Destiny looked down at her jeweled Rolex through her tear-soaked eyes. There was plenty of time for her to get herself together, call Omar and schedule a red-eye flight to Chicago.

It was time she exposed the truth on the Syndicate's operations in the city. Dre would learn the extent of her wrath, just as his father had.


During the two days following their introduction, Torres had called Dre several times. Their conversations were filled with Torres hitting Dre with direct and indirect questions that explored everything from Dre's trust in people to his loyalty. Torres managed to hold back a lot of information about himself as he pried deeper into who Dre was. This peaked Dre's interest in Torres more.

Torres' yacht obviously impressed Dre after he had been given a tour of the 192-foot marvel. Like he had previously thought, his new companion was extremely wealthy. The fact that he owned a yacht that resembled a mansion was more than enough proof to exhibit his riches.

"Intriguing, isn't it?" Torres asked as he watched Dre eyeing the helipad on the deck.

"So you own a helicopter too?" asked Dre.

"Of course. And you could too."

Once again Dre found himself wondering about Torres' innuendos. There always seemed to be some deeper meaning to the nonchalant statements. Was Torres in the same line of work as he was? Torres mentioned that he was into international shipping. Shipping what was the question. The lifestyle that Torres was leading could have certainly been financed by an international drug operation. That thought made having Torres as an acquaintance more appealing to Dre.

"Let's walk," Torres said, placing his arm around Dre's shoulders and steering him away from the women. "Let them relax by the pool and enjoy the view of the Caribbean Sea or whatever else it is that women do. Because I think it's time that you and I had a talk."

Dre was certain now that Torres had been drawn to him by an ulterior motive. He didn't know if it was something good or bad. But he couldn't help but worry as he looked around at the all-male crew that he had mistaken for sailors and ship staff, but who seemed more like a security force strategically stationed in key locations on the yacht. They could pass for the type of goons that made up Dre's crew of soldiers back in Detroit.

"I promise you that what I have to say won't take long at all."

"Oh yeah?"

"And our discussion may turn out to be the most significant conversation you've ever had."


Stacy was still trying to grasp how their vacation had elevated from simple relaxation to something grand and extravagant. Consuela had proudly showed her around, giving her a thorough tour. Stacy loved the richly furnished mahogany wood and gold fixtures that adorned its luxurious interior. Even now, as they lay alone by the pool on the sundeck, she was flabbergasted by what she had seen. Their stateroom alone was more exquisite than her entire house and any other home she had been in. She wasn't the jealous type, but she still wished that she and Dre were the owners of the yacht.

Stacy felt an awkward presence lurking nearby. She

glanced over her shoulder, locking eyes with a member of the crew. The leering stare he gave her made her uncomfortable. She instinctively turned over on her back to hide her nearly-exposed behind. Then she unconsciously sucked her teeth in disgust.

"What's wrong?" Consuela asked, easing up on her elbows and following Stacy's eyes. She received the answer to her question and launched a barrage of Spanish words in the man's direction.

Stacy was surprised at the fire in her voice and the way the powerful man had lowered his eyes, walking off rather quickly. Stacy stared at Consuela with her mouth open in shock. Though she was glad he was gone, she found it hard to believe that someone that seemed as cultured and kind as Consuela could become so mean and explosive. "What did you say to him to make him look so afraid?" she asked.

Consuela returned to her jolly self. "It was nothing."

"That's a lot of nothing."

"I just let him know that we wished to be left alone."

Stacy recognized the outright lie immediately, because she was in her third year of Spanish at school. Now she worried about Consuela being serious when she threatened to have Torres chop the man's penis and balls off, place them in his mouth and throw him overboard for shark bait if he didn't get away from them.

Knowing there was more to her new associates than she expected, Stacy didn't know what to think. Fearfully, she looked around, becoming more afraid because Dre was nowhere in sight. Stacy glanced over at Consuela and scrutinized the carefree smile that languished upon her beautiful face. Could Stacy have read more into Consuela's comment than intended?

* * *

"You actually supplied Dutch Jones?" Dre asked Torres, finding it hard to believe that fate would have placed him in the midst of a man who helped make one of Detroit's most notorious legends. Dutch was rotting in a federal prison with a life sentence for his drug exploits. But that dismal outcome didn't matter to Dre. He only saw the good part of Dutch's life.

"That's correct." Torres smiled. "That look on your face tells me you're surprised."

"You could say that."

"How about if I said you could be bigger than Dutch?"

"I'm listening."

"I've brought you here because I had a feeling about you when we met last night."

"What kind of feeling?" Dre asked.

"I make hustlers, so I know them when I see them."

Dre nodded.

"So after you mentioned you were from Detroit, I contacted someone at the Half Moon Resort where you're staying and got your information. Then I called a few friends from the city to inquire about you."

Dre was astonished how quickly and effectively Torres worked.

"Anyway, after throwing your name around and the name on your chain"—he pointed at the Syndicate medallion on Dre's platinum chain—"I was easily able to obtain everything I needed to know about you."

"Under normal circumstances, I get pissed off when people check up on me."

"But you know this is far from normal circumstances. And under normal circumstances, I would not even be approaching you."

"So what's so abnormal about this?"

"Your father."

"What?"

"Let's just say I knew him very well and have a lot of respect for him."

"Oh yeah?"

"He helped me get to the point where I can help you."

Dre smiled. He didn't need to know more about Torres. Everything made sense now. First, Dre had come up in the drug game through Destiny off the strength of his father. Now he was set to take things to another level thanks to his father's stellar reputation.

"Now, here's the deal," Torres said. "Dutch is no longer with me, for reasons I'm sure you know."

"Sad story, but shit happens."

"People come and go in this game. And if you wanna stay, it's wise to get rid of stuff like that." Torres pointed at Dre's Syndicate medallion.

"I hear you."

"But this is the deal. If you knew of Dutch's reign over the city, you know my resources are unlimited. With that said, I've been looking for someone to take his place."

Dre contemplated the proposition which seemed like a dream. "Okay. So if I'm understanding you right, what you're saying is you selected me to be the candidate for Dutch's old spot?"

Torres nodded. "But you decide if you end up where Dutch is."

"I wanna end up where you are."

"With time, patience, and most of all me, it's possible." He pointed to the helipad. "I told you every man should have one. Remember?"

"I definitely want one."

"But are you ready to walk that road toward it?"

"I've never been more ready."

Torres smiled.

"So what exactly are you willing to offer me?" Dre asked.

"There's nothing I can't offer you. It's about what you want," Torres said.

"I like that kind of talk," Dre said with a smile.

"But there's a lot for us to discuss before we get started." He shook Dre's hand. "Since you're now a member of the family, there's no rush. Let's enjoy the rest of our vacation, then we can concentrate on increasing our riches."

"Makes sense to me." Dre grinned. He had a new alliance, so his thoughts of reuniting with Destiny for business were fading. But he still felt indebted to her. Yet now he could totally concentrate on Stacy and the Syndicate.

Torres sparked a cigar. "Well, partner, our business is done for the moment. So let's not keep the ladies waiting any longer than we have to."

Destiny strutted through O'Hare Airport with her white full-length mink swinging behind her. She was too preoccupied with her jumbled thoughts of revenge to pay attention to the gawking stares and appraising glances of holiday travelers that she passed. Dre had single-handedly shattered her heart, leaving her no other recourse than to make him experience twice the amount of pain she felt.

"Destiny, Destiny."

The familiar voice pulled Destiny from her

thoughts.

"Over here."

Destiny spotted Omar's bodyguard, Max, walking toward her.

"Let me grab that for you," he offered, reaching for her Louis Vuitton carry-on bag. "How was your flight?"

"Pssst . . . You know. The usual. I'm just glad to be here," she said, following the nearly seven-foot giant through the terminal.

"Omar is waiting in the car."

Destiny strolled through the doors and into the blowing snow. She spotted the limousine parked in a fire zone directly in front of the airport. Max grabbed her arm in a protective fashion. She allowed him to lead her to the car and the man who awaited her arrival. When they reached the vehicle, two suited men emerged from inside. She was amused at the two characters as they scanned the busy sidewalk through beady eyes. Then one of them opened the back door, granting her access to the warm interior.

"Well, if it isn't my favorite girl," Omar said, opening his arms for a hug. "Now, you didn't come to the Chi because you missed me, and you sounded like whatever your reason for making the trip was urgent, so . . . " His got a good look at her. "How about bringing me up to speed on what you felt was so pressing that you basically had me drop everything I was doing?"

"The Syndicate," Destiny said.

"Okay." He nodded.

"I have all the information on their top people, enforcers, and the spots they control throughout the city."

"Is that so?" Omar leaned back, somewhat surprised.

"Yep." Destiny leaned her head against his chest and purred in a sexy whisper, "Now that I've got what you asked for, can you do something for me, daddy?"

Omar ran his hands through her silky tresses. "What is it that you want?"

"Once you have crushed them, all I ask is that I'm able to watch their leader die a slow, horrendous death."

"I always knew you were beautiful, but I didn't know you were this devious."

"Depends on how you look at it."

"Yeah, you got that, though," Omar said, pushing her head into his lap. "You can watch him die."

Destiny fumbled with his Ostrich belt. For the first time since she got the news about Dre from Naiza she smiled. She didn't have a problem with satisfying Omar in Max's presence, because Omar would more than repay her by bringing down Dre. Destiny reached for his dick, moving her hair out of the way as she prepared to suck him dry.

# Chapter 13

Nut leaned back on his couch with a smile on his face. He had just got off the phone with Dre. He was happy to hear his best friend was living large with his girlfriend out in Jamaica. It was a sign that they were really doing things on a major level. He sparked a blunt of Ganz and pulled deeply on it.

"What's up, baby?" Naiza asked, stepping into his living room and sitting on the couch beside him.

Nut put his hand on her thigh and began inching it up her miniskirt.

"Kind of frisky," Naiza said, grinning. She grabbed his hand and pulled it further, until he had two fingers inside of her and another on her clit.

Nut exhaled a cloud of smoke as his dick grew hard. He set the blunt in an ashtray on the coffee table in front of him.

Naiza began moaning. "Damn that feels so good."

He watched her close her eyes and bite down on her bottom lip. The more he pleased her, the hornier he became. With his free hand, he pulled down his shorts and boxers. Nut slowly eased his hand from between Naiza's legs and began guiding her face toward his dick.

"No," she said. "Let me ride it." She hiked up her skirt and slid on top of his stiffness.

"Whoa!" Nut blurted as he felt her warm tightness wrap the head of his dick as he steered inside of her. Her muscles slowly gripped him as she lowered her body. Nut palmed her ass, guiding her up and down.

"Gimme that dick!" Naiza demanded as she worked up a rhythm. She laid her arms on his shoulders and interlocked her fingers, grinding her body deeper into him.

Nut tore open her shirt, sending buttons flying everywhere. He planted his face in her bare chest. His tongue roamed everywhere.

"Yeah, baby. Just like that," Naiza moaned.

Nut pulled her closer. As her moans grew, he quickly lifted her up, his hands still palming her ass as she wrapped her legs around him. He shifted her back until she was against the wall.

"God. Yeah. Just like that," she begged as he plunged into her. Her back slid up and down the wall with each of his strokes. "Fuck me, Nut. Fuck me harder!"

Nut dug deeper and deeper with each stroke until his legs almost gave out. He slid Naiza's body down the wall until her feet hit the carpeted floor. Then he turned her, grabbed the bottom of his erection and entered her slippery lips and tight tunnel.

"Ahhh. Ahhh," Naiza screamed. "Please. Yes."

Nut cuffed her shoulders with his palms and pummeled into her harder. Her butt cheeks slapping together aroused him as she clawed at the wall.

"Yes! Ahhh. It hurts so good. Fuck me!" Naiza begged.

Nut felt himself about to lose it. He closed his eyes and dug faster into her. "Yeah. Oh, shit. Whooo!" He cupped her tightly as a tingling sensation developed deep within his balls and resonated through his shaft. He slowed down as his cream burst into her canal. "Damn, girl," he blurted, falling beside her with his back toward the wall.

Naiza faced him and dropped to her knees. "I'm not finished yet." She grabbed his limp dick and sucked it back to life.

"Shit!" Nut said as he palmed the back of her head. He looked down and watched her suck him off while she rubbed her fingers over her clit and into her hot bush. Naiza closed her eyes and moaned while she deep throated him. He knew that she got off on pleasing him orally. It was as much a pleasure to her as it was to him.

Her body began to rumble and she came just as Nut did.

Nut closed his eyes and let out a deep breath. He was drained in a good way. Sex with Naiza was always the bomb. He watched her gain her composure, and then he went off to the bathroom. After Nut showered and got dressed, he stepped into his closet where he opened his safe and removed a .40-caliber Taurus. Nut tucked the gun on his waistline and pulled his Iceberg sweater over it.

"Nut!"

"Yo?" he responded to Naiza's call from another room.

"Call me later," she screamed out. "I gotta go meet Destiny."

"All right." Nut looked in the mirror, making sure his gun was concealed properly. Then he grabbed his keys, stepped out of his bedroom, and walked into the kitchen. He grabbed a bottle of Hennessy from the freezer and took a swig. He put the cap on the bottle, slipped it in his pocket and walked out of his home.

Nut scanned his block before walking over to his car and getting inside. He pulled off, headed to meet up with Rossi. As he turned the corner of his block, he turned the volume of his system up and nodded with a smile as Tupac's "Me and My Girlfriend" cranked. When he pulled up to the curb, he pulled out his liquor and took a sip before putting the bottle away. As Nut nodded to the music, a Crown Victoria pulled up beside him. When the window rolled down he spotted two white detectives.

"Pull over, buddy," the man closest to him demanded.

Nut knew the car's fresh red paint job, chrome rims and booming system had caused the police to racially profile him as the drug dealer he was. There had been no legitimate reason for them to demand he pull over. Nut gripped the steering wheel tighter and mashed his foot on the gas, peeling off. He swerved between two passing cars, leaving the detectives in a haze of burnt rubber. But in his rearview mirror he could see them trailing him in the distance. He turned the corner and switched gears in his new Cadillac.

Sirens began sounding and flashing.

"Fuck!" Nut slammed his hand against the steering wheel as he spotted a police car pulling up directly behind him from what seemed like nowhere.

"Pull the car over now!" a deep voice blared through the loudspeaker on the patrol car.

Nut turned abruptly, nearly hitting an old man cross-
ing the street. "Oh shit!" Nut screamed as he lost control and his brand new car slammed into a lamppost.

The patrol car skidded to halt behind him. Two cops
jumped out with their guns drawn as the first detective
car and then another one pulled up.

In seconds, Nut was staring at six cops surrounding
him with their guns aimed at his car. He looked down
at the bottle of Hennessy on the floor, and then pulled
up his shirt and gazed at the handle of his .40-caliber.
Flashing his eyes back on the police outside, he knew
there was no avoiding his captivity. He tossed the gun
on the floor near the backseat and reached his arms out
of the window.

"Keep 'em up!" one of the detectives yelled.

Nut watched one of the officer's sprint toward him
and grab his hands. Before Nut knew it, he was being
slammed to the ground and handcuffed.


"Naiza, stop the truck!" Destiny demanded. She
turned in the seat to get a better look at Stacy exiting
the Benz.

"What the hell are you hollering for?" Naiza asked
as she pulled her Range Rover over to the curb. "Who
you see over there? Huh?"

"It's that young bitch, Stacy," Destiny hissed.
"Come on."

"You going after that little bitch?"

"And?"

"Since when you start letting little young bitches get
you all hyped?"

"Ain't you the same one who called me to tell me

you overheard Nut talking about this little ho fucking with Dre?"

"Yeah."

"The house he bought for them? The trip to Jamaica? That shit ring any bells?"

"Yeah."

"That's why I'm hyped."

Naiza shook her head.

"What, you got a crick in your neck or something?"

Naiza laughed. "Listen, Destiny. I didn't tell you about Dre so you could go after some young bitch. She ain't rape that nigga. He voluntarily fucking her ass. So get hyped at that nigga, not her."

Destiny sat in silence, contemplating the words of her friend. They were rational and rooted in truth. Yet, she knew that Naiza would have her back whether she was wrong or right. Destiny was moving off sheer emotion. As far as she was concerned, they were both guilty of setting off a chain of events that broke her heart and had taken away the man who had come to be her greatest creation.

Naiza waved her hands in front of Destiny's face. "Earth to Destiny. Earth to motherfucking Destiny."

Destiny snapped out of her thoughts. Her eyes beamed at Stacy as she walked inside City Slickers. Destiny opened the passenger door of the Range Rover and said, "Come on, Naiza!"


Dre parked outside of his grandmother's home. He stared at the old house he had been raised in. Then he scanned the block, taking in the images of a vacant lot and an abandoned building. The same nosey neighbors were sprinkled throughout the block, along with a few crackheads in search of a fix. He thought of all the fist-fights and shootouts he had seen take place there. He was happy to have made it out alive.

Dre exited his car and went into his grandmother's house. As he stepped through the door, he felt awkward. The place in which he was raised seemed foreign. The tattered table, the old floor model television, the plastic-covered couches—everything seemed so far removed from the plush mansion he now lived in with Stacy.

"Look at my grandson," Dre's grandmother said as she stepped into the living room with a rag in her hand.

Dre hugged her. "What's up, Grandma?" he said as he broke her embrace.

"Just doing some cleaning around here."

Dre sat on the couch, staring at the rag in her hand, and then looking around the room. He peeped a roach emerging from a crack in the ceiling.

"Haven't seen you in a while," she said. "How's Stacy?"

"Good." Dre's vision drifted from the roach to his grandmother's eyes. "When you gonna let me move you out of here?"

"When you start making an honest living."

"Come on, Grandma. Let's not get into this again," he said, referencing the conversations he and his grandmother had previously because of his lifestyle.

"I told you before, if you got dreams of joining your father, that's on you. I'm done trying to lead you to water because you don't wanna drink."

"Me and my father are two different people."

"With one twisted way of thinking that leads to one place: prison."

Dre thought about a recent conversation he had with

Stacy, during which she urged him to leave the streets behind. Dre knew he would have to eventually, but the time was not right. He had things to do and money to make before he departed.

"How long do you think you can duck the law?"

Dre sighed.

"And it's really sad that you got Stacy caught up in your madness."

"I would never jeopardize her," he declared.

"So what happens when the police or some gangster invades the home you live in with her? And you know they will. It's only a matter of time, baby."

Dre reflected on the possibility of his grandmother's reasoning becoming reality. He had heard stories of thugs kicking in the doors of hustlers, and his father had been the victim of the authorities invading his home. But Dre had the downfall of others to draw on in assuring that he didn't fall victim too.

"Kind of quiet over there," his grandmother said.

"I'm gonna be okay and so is Stacy."

"I truly hope so."

"I know so."

Dre's grandmother shook her head. "You sound just like your father."

"Oh yeah."

"We had this same conversation when you were a child. He thought he could outsmart the federal government. Unfortunately, it took him a life bid to learn otherwise."

"Don't worry, Grandma."

"How can I not? My grandson is walking into the same hellfire that my son did."

Dre looked at his watch and stood up.

"I have to go."

His grandmother hugged him and looked him in the eyes. "Think about what I said. Please."

Dre nodded and walked out of her home.

Destiny stepped inside the store and immediately scanned the aisles and racks of clothing in search of her victim. Stacy was enthralled at picking out her clothes as she joked with her friends. Destiny laughed. Stacy had no idea she was being plotted on. From one store to the next, Destiny and Naiza followed Stacy's every move.

"Okay. Where is she now?" Naiza questioned as she looked around.

"Over there, standing by the boot rack. Now you can see her real good."

"I remember her—the little fake Stacy Dash-looking bitch."

"Come on, Naiza, that bitch don't look like no Stacy Dash. Not the bitch I'm looking at in that rabbit coat."

Naiza chuckled. "Now we both know that's a mink."

Destiny sucked her teeth and shook her head.

Naiza said, "It's one thing to want to hurt the bitch, but don't hate on the bitch."

"I know Dre better not had bought that bitch no mink." Destiny stormed off with Naiza dead on her heels, heading toward the inevitable showdown.

"Girl, these are definitely cold." Stacy flashed a pair of red boots to her girls, Erica and Kim as they shopped in City Slickers. "I've got a red mink coat that's dying to be worn with these."

"Ouch!" Kim exclaimed as she gazed at the price

tag. "Shit, for $3,200 I'd have to wear them bitches naked, because a coat would be completely out of the question."

Stacy smirked and then said, "Stop frontin', Kim."

"Mmm hmm. Easy for you to say. You're the one with a ballin' ass man who bought you a bad ass crib in Bloomfield Hills with a marble foyer, winding staircase, high vaulted ceilings and a million bedrooms and shit. Not to mention you're pushing a new Benz, too."

"Shit, that mansion is fabulous, girl. The master bedroom is off the chain. Y'all got three damn floors . . ." Erica said, still amazed at how beautiful and large the mansion was. "And to think that it belongs all to you." She shook her head in astonishment. "You're lucky you snatched up a good man, girl."

"Humph . . . you already know I'm jealous for real now," Kim teased Stacy. "I wish Dre's ass would have noticed me first that night."

Stacy gasped and then chuckled. "No you didn't just say some hating shit like that."

All three women burst into laughter. Then Stacy remained silent as her friends praised Dre and reminded her how much she deserved him in her life. Their comments made Stacy realize how rare it was for a woman to find a man like Dre. It also made her realize how special she was, because Dre had chosen her over Destiny and countless other women that he could easily have.

"Nah, I was just playing earlier about Dre finding me first, Stacy. I'm really happy for you though, girl," Kim said. "You've got a good man that takes care of you. As for me, you already know I've got a no good man, so I stay broke."

"Kim, you and I both know your closet is packed to

capacity. Even though your nigga is broke, your sneaky ass always finds a way to use what you got to get what you need."

"Hey, you know a girl has to do what a girl has to . . ." Kim paused, shifting her eyes. "By the way, do either of you know who these two bitches are who keep stalking us? I just saw them at the last two stores we were in."

Stacy looked in the direction that Kim stared in. She spotted the approaching pair, recognizing Destiny instantly.

"Well, well, look what we have here," Destiny said as she stopped a foot away from Stacy, blocking her path. She scanned her from head to toe. Bitterness rolled off her tongue as she said, "I never expected to see you again."

"That's hard to tell when you're stalking me," Stacy replied.

"You caught my attention when you hopped out of my man's Mercedes."

"Excuse me?"

"I didn't stutter," Destiny stated.

Stacy was vexed. She stared at Destiny with every ounce of anger balled up in her. "Whatever." Stacy rolled her eyes.

"Okay, little bitch."

"What!"

"I said, 'okay little bitch.' Find your own man and stay away from mine."

"You're sadly mistaken, talking that 'your man' shit."

"Well, little bitch, just so you know—when you fuck a man, suck a man, and make the man, he is your man."

"Dre ain't nobody's man but mine."

"You, little bitch, are the one that's mistaken, because that nigga belongs to me. And although he tricks the dough that I've made possible for him to have on your young ass, I'm the one he's fucking and sucking when he's not with you."

"Who the fuck do you think you are? Rolling up on me with this stupid shit. Apparently, you didn't realize—"

"You're out of your league," Destiny said, cutting her off. "Just do yourself a favor and find another nigga. Okay, little bit—"

Stacy swung the red boot with all her might, landing it right upside Destiny's head.

"Ow!" Destiny roared. "Little bitch, I'm about to whoop your—"

Stacy had grown tired of the constant "little bitch" reference and the fact that Destiny kept claiming Dre as hers. It was embarrassing to her after all of the praise her friends had given Dre earlier.

Naiza punched Stacy, who dropped the boot and slipped out of her coat. She advanced at Destiny, raining blow after blow upon her face as Erica and Kim jumped on Naiza.

Destiny threw punches in an attempt to thwart off the attack. She had mistaken the young woman for a weakling when she was actually a wildcat. She fell over a chair and covered her face.

Stacy raged, repeatedly pounding on Destiny without mercy. She was talking greasy the whole time. But her fun was shortstopped by the salesman and male shoppers who finally came to Destiny and Naiza's rescue.

Holding them apart, one of the salesmen peered at Stacy. He shook his head with a smile, and then turned to Destiny and blurted, "Damn, ma, you okay?"

Stacy felt bad because she had lost control and allowed Destiny to tick her off. But it felt good silencing Destiny with violence, because it was the only thing Destiny respected and understood.


Dre was experiencing a mix of frustration, worry and guilt. He had just arrived back from Jamaica, and the news of Nut's arrest was still on his mind. Ever since learning from Billy that Nut got locked up a day after they had spoken to each other, Dre began questioning his lifestyle. Nut had not only received a weapon charge for the gun found in his car and a DWI for being intoxicated, but he had been charged with Juan's murder. There had been an ongoing investigation into Juan's murder. A witness had given a description of Nut, mentioning the she did not get a good view of the other man with him. Upon his arrest, Nut was placed in a lineup and picked out by the witness. Since Dre received this news, he contended with the fact that his new connection could elevate his wealth immensely, but Nut's arrest was proof that members of The Syndicate were not invincible.

As Dre drove through Detroit, looking at the streets that he and his crew regulated, he couldn't escape the guilt he felt for Nut's arrest. The possibility of Nut snitching crossed his mind, but Dre easily dismissed it. But that didn't remove the thought of police arresting him. Dre had spoken to Nut and learned that the police were aware there was another perpetrator involved. As Dre pulled up to a light, his phone rang.

"What's up, Naiza?" he answered.

"I just got back from court with Nut. They granted him a million-dollar bail."

"Word?" Dre's eyes lit up.

"I'm going to visit him now," she said.

"Tell him he'll be home by tomorrow."

"Thanks, Dre."

"It's nothing."

"I'll speak to you after I see him."

"Okay." Dre hung up his phone with a wide smile on his face. He had hired a highpowered attorney who had been trying to secure Nut's bail. But it was a long shot. Now that Nut was defying the odds, Dre was beginning to regain the sense of invincibility that came with the wealth and power of The Syndicate. Money gave them access to things average people were not privy to. It was the main reason Dre had got in the game and the main reason he found it so hard to leave behind. And with Torres as his new connect, Dre knew The Syndicate was destined for greater wealth and power.

In a short time things had changed for the better. Nut was home on bail and The Syndicate was on the rise.

"Damn, I never thought I would be sitting in a room with so many rich niggas," Dre joked as he looked around the room full of his most trusted lieutenants.

"You a funny nigga," one of them said as they all laughed.

Dre allowed the laughter to subside. "We've become a major force in a short period of time."

"That's right," Billy cheered.

"But before it's over, we'll run this whole city." Dre peered around the room. From the smiles and head nods, it was evident that his crew shared his sentiments.

"This is our time, player," someone screamed.

Dre noticed some of his crew's gazes had settled on the only outsider among them: Skeet. Dre was proud to have the rich hustler from the Westside among them. He was one of the livest in the game. Dre pointed to him. "You all know this nigga Skeet, and if you don't— I don't know how. With the exception of us, I don't know another crew in the city who balls harder than his Z8 clique."

Skeet nodded and smiled.

"Well, now he's with us," Dre declared. "This means that his crew, although they're not Syndicate members, is with us as well. Consider them extended family members who will handle our business on the Westside. Now, does anyone have a problem with this new arrangement?"

The room went silent.

After Dre scanned the faces of his crew, he turned to Mel. "I need Big A and you to control the coke houses on Mack, Prominade, and Pelky."

"Got you," Mel said.

"With the increased shipments we'll have coming in, you'll both have to set up new distribution bases for the weed and heroin as well," said Dre.

"Not a problem," Big A responded, looking to Mel who shook his head in agreement.

Dre knew that his new deal with Torres would expand them beyond crack, so he had thought long and hard about choosing the right people to facilitate the growth of their operation. He turned to Nut, Rossi, and Billy. "As for you three, since Jane and Flanders are both major weed blocks and you already have people in place down there, I need you niggas to do whatever is necessary to ensure that our shit is the only thing on those blocks."

"We got you," Rossi and Billy replied almost in unison.

Nut grinned and said sarcastically, "That should be interesting."

Dre knew that Nut meant it would not be a simple task and blood would have to spill. But with Billy involved, Dre was more than confident everything would work out. "Make sure you pick your team well, because the show moves tonight."

Billy nodded and winked. Dre took it as a signal of Billy being privy to information that only had been revealed to him, Nut, and Rossi. No one else in the room or anywhere else had known about Torres or his role in the expansion of the Syndicate. Dre had only revealed this information to the three men beside him, because they were the most trusted from his crew. So they knew not only about Dre meeting Torres in Jamaica, but the shipments that were scheduled to arrive from Texas. Two tractor-trailers full of weed, cocaine and heroin would be awaiting Dre in El Paso. His three most trusted comrades would be the couriers for Dre to send Torres close to $8 million for the precious cargo.

Dre turned to the rest of his crew, grabbing their attention with a wave of his hand and clearing his throat. "Well fellows, I think that concludes our business for this evening. But in the next few days, each of you will be contacted with the location of our new warehouse. At that time, I suggest you be prepared to make a major pickup, because shit is about to step up drastically."

"That's what I'm talking about," Rossi said.

Dre leaned toward Nut and whispered, "Meet me at the Bloomfield Hills house in three hours so we can count the money up. Bring Billy and Rossi along with you. We need to go over the procedure one last time. All right?"

Nut gave him a pound. "We'll be there."

Dre patted Skeet on the shoulder. "Let's bust up. We need to take a ride and discuss a few things."

Dre stood in the guest room. He placed the last stack of money inside the bag, and then exhaled and cracked his knuckles. After hours of counting the money, using numerous machines, he along with Nut, Billy, and Rossi had finally tallied up the $7.8 million that Torres would be paid.

"We've got our crew on standby, and we'll be pulling out around midnight," Billy said as he placed a lock on the last duffle bag.

Nut leaned back on the couch, speaking in hushed tones on his phone while Rossi pulled on a blunt.

Dre shook his head in response to Billy's statement. Before he could verbally respond, the thunderous sound of the front door slamming shut startled him. Dre reached for his gun, but stopped short at the sight of Stacy storming into the room.

"What's wrong?" Dre asked. "And why the hell do you have blood all over your shirt?"

"What's wrong is, you and I are about to tear this house up any minute now if you don't have some good answers for what just took place. As for the blood," she said, staring down at her shirt as if seeing the blood for the first time, "it belongs to your little girlfriend. I just whipped her old ass for popping shit."

"Girlfriend? Come on, bay. What are you talking about?" Dre asked.

"Well, it looks like that's our cue to leave," Nut announced. He stood up and glanced at the sudden stand-off between Dre and Stacy. He patted Dre on the back, grabbed one of the duffel bags and said, "I'll give you a call when the transaction is complete."

Dre nodded and watched his crew leave. He turned to Stacy. "Baby, I have no idea what you're talking about, but would you please calm down and explain to me what's going on?"

Stacy shook her head in despair. Tears slowly began cascading down her face as she stared into a pair of eyes that seemed to hold nothing but sincerity. She dropped to the couch and began sobbing. "I was at City Slickers . . . and the bitch from the park . . . you know the one . . . who . . . brought you the car . . . and chain . . . came in."

Dre sat beside her and gently began rubbing her neck. "It's okay, baby. Come on now. Slow down and tell me what happened." He wiped away her tears. "Okay, Destiny came in. Then what?"

Stacy sniffled and cleared her throat. "She approached me and started talking crazy. She said you were her man and all you were doing was tricking with me." She raised her voice an octave as more tears welled in her eyes. "But what really made me whip her ass was when she had the nerve to say that when you aren't with me, you're fucking and sucking her off."

"What?" Dre asked, disgusted with Destiny's lies. He placed his palms on either side of Stacy's face, and then used his thumbs to remove the tears that covered her cheeks. "Stacy, look at me and hear me good."

She looked him square in the eyes.

"I love you like I've never loved no woman. And I mean this on some real shit. There is no other woman in my life, nor do I want or need any other woman than you."

Stacy wrapped her arms around Dre's neck. "I'm sorry, bay."

"You don't have to be sorry."

"It's just . . . I allowed that bitch to get to me."

Dre kissed her, silencing the unnecessary words that she was set to utter. It became clear to him that Destiny had just begun to intrude into his life. She could be dangerous, and he was wondering what her next move would be?

Destiny grasped the phone tightly, while anxiously tapping on the counter in her kitchen. She was awaiting the answer she desired. After her encounter with Stacy, she needed more assurance that Dre and everything she had helped create would collapse. With Omar on her side, she had little doubt in his ability to handle business properly. But Destiny was in no way prepared to chance Dre's possible escape from harm. His downfall had become a personal vendetta that took precedent over every other facet of her life.

"I'm sorry to have you on hold, Miss," the male voice sounded after clicking back over. "Anyway, I'm Agent Perez from the Eastern District DEA Office. How may I be of service to you?"

Destiny realized that she actually had the awesome power of the government on her side. The thought brought a smile to her sore face. It was an extra incentive she had been lacking in her effort to bring down Dre.

"Hello?"

"Yes," Destiny said.

"I said how can I be of service to you?"

"No, Mr. Perez. I can be of service to you."

"And how might you plan to do this? Miss . . . umm, I didn't catch your name."

"I never gave it. But what I'm about to give you is the information on one of the biggest drug organizations in Detroit." She took a deep breath.

"Is that a fact?" Perez asked.

"As sure as the earth is round."

"I'm listening."

"The crew I'm speaking of is called the Syndicate."

"Never heard of them."

"Then you're not doing your job."

Perez chuckled. "So help me do my job. Tell me about this Syndicate."

"Their leader is John Dodson, Jr. aka Dre . . ."

*Chapter 14*

Omar had spent the last few months in Detroit. The information Destiny had given him on the Syndicate and their activities within the city had proven invaluable. He was now preparing to shake their seemingly unopposed reign by hitting them where it would hurt them most—their pockets. A series of attacks would soon cripple their ability to rake in the millions the crew had been generating.

Omar turned to his man, Big Rico, who sat in the passenger seat of the Suburban, staring intently at their target. "Yo, you ready to set this in motion, my man?"

"Can't think of anything I would rather be doing than plotting on one of the Syndicate's drug spots," Rico said. His Dexter Avenue 50 Strong Crew and The Syndicate had yet to have any run-ins, but beneath the surface he had harbored a hatred for them. He saw the Eastside clique as arrogant. They needed to be put in check.

"You don't act ready," Omar said.

"Because I don't act." He removed two grenades from his coat pocket and pulled down his mask.

Omar nodded. "That's what I like to hear." He gave the other occupants of the truck blank stares as he watched them duplicate Rico's actions. Omar punched a number into his phone and then lifted it to his ear. "It's a go on this end, and I want the rest of our teams to move immediately." He shut the phone and told his crew, "I don't want anyone left breathing when we leave." Omar pulled down his mask, thinking he was finally going to let the young wannabe gangsters known as The Syndicate find out how real the game could be. He exited the truck with his crew and headed toward the drug house. Omar knew this was just one target of the carnage that he had orchestrated to take place around the city simultaneously. If things worked as he had planned, The Syndicate would have no members to oppose him.

There would be no Syndicate.


Big A was in a zone as he wheeled his 745 BMW through the Eastside of Detroit. He had just finished a long night of sampling the charms of a slew of women at the infamous Hojos strip club. He was sated and jaded.

Big A reflected on his night as he steered down Grey. The unmistakable sounds of explosions up ahead startled him. Flashes and more explosions took place along with gunfire as he neared his crack house. He smashed down on the accelerator, speeding forward to aid his crew who he assumed were trapped inside. Big A reached for his .40-caliber and prepared to engage the masked men he saw opening fire as they attempted to make their escape from the scene.

The block was dark, save for the sparks of gunfire and explosives that painted the atmosphere as Omar and his crew let loose on The Syndicate's crack house. From the corner of his eye he could see Rico laying down cover fire as their crew backpedaled toward their truck. Omar's heart beat faster by the second as his adrenalin pumped. He always got a rush from the taste of revenge and experience of deadly action. The blood-lust in his eyes and the way he handled his gun gave validity to the war stories people told about him on the streets of Detroit and Chicago. Omar was an OG—a veteran boss who was not afraid to put in his own work.

Rico turned his weapon toward an oncoming BMW and cut lose a barrage of bullets. Omar followed suit, popping in a fresh clip and unleashing slugs in rapid fire, tearing through the windshield and headlights of the speeding vehicle. The driver lost control of the car and crashed into a pole. Omar watched a battered man stumble from the wreckage with his gun unsteady in hand. He recognized him as Big A. The wounded soul tried to raise his gun, but Omar and Rico tore what was left of him to pieces with a volley of hot slugs.

Omar called out to his young crew of assassins. "Let's get out of here."

Rico walked over to another Syndicate member who lay on the ground near a car, his body trembling from the bullets that had torn into him. Rico removed his mask and smiled at the man. "Now you know who killed you." He fired four bullets into the man's head.

"Come one, man!" Omar barked, shaking his head. "Stupid motherfucker taking his mask off." As Omar got into the truck, he looked once more at Big A and grinned. Taking out Dre's cousins and most valuable lieutenant was a power move that would send a strong message. Omar knew it would be hard to find one of the major figures from the Syndicate, so his goal had been to take out all of the minor figures, because they were the people who kept the crew's crack house working. But Big A was a plus. A gift for Omar and a deadly wound for the Syndicate.

Dre was livid as he spoke into his phone. He couldn't believe what he was hearing. It didn't make sense. The type of assault on the structure of his operation was unheard of. It was the type of massive, simultaneous onslaught thugs talked of, but never did. It required the kind of calculated teamwork that most crews were incapable of pulling off. "Who could have hit us in such a precise manner? And exactly how many of our houses did they hit?" He paced his living room.

"Man, they hit every spot we had on the Eastside," Jamal declared in disgust.

"Nah, you can't be serious." Dre shook his head.

"Mack, Grey, Prominade, Flanders and every other spot I didn't name are no more than burnt out skeletal remains from what I've been able to learn so far."

"Did any of our people inside those spot make it out?"

Jamal sighed and shook his head. "Dead. Everybody."

"Fuck!" Dre pounded his fist into his palm.

"From what I've been told, niggas rolled up on the set like a covert operation and shit, tossing grenades in the houses, then cutting down anyone who tried to exit."

"How? How this shit happen? And to us?"

''I don't know what's going on, but we can't take this shit lightly."

"This shit is crazy."

Dre knew that he had lost at least thirty members of his crew. The product was of no consequence, because it could easily be replaced. But he had assembled a tight team of low-level workers that were committed to the Syndicate. The type of loyalty and proficiency they exhibited was rare and integral to his operation. And the spots he had were the result of his ability to find good locations and take established locales through bloodshed. Someone would have to suffer painfully for the blow that had been dealt to the Syndicate.

"This is gonna make shit real hot," Jamal said.

Dre stopped pacing. "I want everyone at the hideout within an hour. And tell them to be careful, because whoever our enemies are, they play for keeps."

"I'm on it, Dre. But you be sure to take your own advice and be careful as well. I'm out." Jamal hung up.

Dre stared through his curtains, seeing the approaching daybreak. He knew somewhere in Detroit his enemies were celebrating their late night ambush. They probably thought they would face no retribution. But Dre had little doubt that he would make someone pay in the most violent manner he possibly could.

Dre quietly grabbed his clothes and left the room in an attempt not to wake Stacy. His phone began vibrating. "Yeah," he answered, knowing that another call after Jamal's couldn't be good news.

"Dre, it's me, Nut." He was choked up. Unlike himself. "These niggas really fucked up now. I'm telling you . . . niggas gotta die!"

"I heard the news. And I'm on my way out the house to meet up with everybody at the hideout." The sound of Nut's sobs tore through Dre. He had known Nut since they were children, and he had never once detected a sign of hurt or weakness from him.

"Yo, fuck a meeting. We gotta murk some niggas like they did Big A and the rest of—"

"Big A!" Dre barked, completely caught off guard.

"Yeah, they killed Big A, man. Fucking Big A!" Nut cried out hysterically, sniffling.

Tears began coating Dre's face and his eyes became cloudy. He dropped the phone. After what he had already heard about the night, he was in no way prepared to receive such information. He had brought his cousin into the game and now he was dead. The more the story of what happened unfolded, the more personal Dre was being affected. If Big A could be murdered, no one outside his crew was safe. For that reason, Dre decided that no one responsible for the drama would be safe. He would carry out the warpath personally, even if he had to die in the process.

Agent Perez made it an early morning ritual to watch every news station religiously as he read the newspaper and drank coffee. Like every morning over the past eight years, today had been no different. Except the report of numerous bombings throughout the night. He found himself focused on the massive attention given to the drama by the media.

He listened intently as pictures were shown of each

location and the casualty count given. Agent Perez was confident that they were his people. This was connected to the clique that he had learned of by the anonymous female caller who had given him names, areas of operation and amounts of drugs purchased. There was a sense of nervous excitement for Perez as he watched the news. He grinned, nodding his head like a happy child. He had taken for granted that no such organization could exist in Detroit without the DEA knowing. Now he knew that the Syndicate was no myth. It was time he took them seriously. It was time that he took them down.

Perez stood, spilling the remainder of his coffee in the process. He reached for his suit jacket, never paying the slightest attention to the coffee that he had wasted on his leg. He grabbed his keys and scurried out the door. Perez cared about nothing but getting to work and having a long talk with his boss. It was imperative that he made his suspicions known. If presented thoroughly, there was a strong possibility that within hours, the whole Midwest Bureau and all the vast resources they commanded would be at his disposal. Perez knew that he had been chasing a long shot, but he followed his gut feeling that it was a shot worth taking.


The noise level in the room was defeating. Dre looked around at his lieutenants engrossed in angry conversations. The tragedy that had befallen them had thrust their crew into utter chaos. He stared at Billy and shrugged his shoulders in a manner that more or less said, "There's nothing left to say."

Billy, the calmest of the crew stood in the center of

the room. "A yo, shut the fuck up!" He removed his gun and slammed it on the table beside him. "What's up, doe? Have you niggas lost your fucking minds? We've taken some major losses over the last eight hours, and with that shit looming over our heads, I can't believe that you motherfuckers would rather sit here and argue with one another instead of putting your heads together and trying to find a solution to this shit."

The room went silent. Dre watched the Syndicate members look around at one another. "We've come too far to allow anyone to bring us down," Billy said. "Now, am I gonna have to start busting niggas in this bitch? Or are we're going to get this shit back on track?" He fingered his nickel-plated .44 and asked, "Is there anyone here who doesn't want to get shit back on track?"

Dre's phone rang and he answered it. "Yeah, talk to me."

"Yo, what's up, lil' homie?" the deep voice responded, adding, "This is Brooks."

Dre recognized the voice and name as his older homie, Officer Jerard Brooks. He was a guy whom Dre had known since he was a child. "What's the deal?" Dre asked.

"Well, I don't have to tell you that this is off the record."

"I got you."

"Well, I was one of the first officers on the scene when Big A's body was found."

Dre stood and headed toward the bar to get some semblance of seclusion. "Alright, you were there, so tell me what you got for me."

"Well, for starters, it wasn't a pretty sight. He took a lot of hits. But that's neither here nor there, because the information I've got for you will pretty much give you what's needed to track down his murderers and deal with them however you see fit."

"Then spill it."

"You know I'm taking a hell of a chance telling you this shit … ummm with my job being on the line and all . . ."

"Look man, I've got fifty grand for the information. Now spit it out."

"Okay. There was a witness nearby."

"Oh yeah?"

"Yeah, a crackhead. He said it was some cats from Dexter Avenue—50 Strong niggas."

Dre soaked up every word Jerard uttered, becoming angrier about the situation, but happy to know who was responsible. "Good lookin' on the information, player. I'll have one of my people drop the cheddar off at your mom's crib."

"That's cool, lil' homie. But on the real, whenever I can be of assistance, just remember that I'm only a phone call away."

Dre ended their call. He couldn't believe it was the 50 Strong niggas off the Westside. But the revelation of his true enemies was a gift that would ensure revenge.

Armed with the newly acquired information from Jerard, The Syndicate would have the element of surprise at their disposal.


Perez burst into the office of the senior DEA agent, plopping down directly in front of his boss's desk.

"Sir, you can't just barge in here like this," the secretary announced as she followed Perez.

The senior agent cradled a phone to his ear, staring

at the pair in his office. He waved his secretary off, and then continued his phone conversation. He signaled to Perez with his index finger that he would be with him in a moment.

Perez made himself comfortable in the plush chair. He scrutinized the office and numerous photos that lined the walls as his boss spoke in hushed tones. The decor of the spacious room was somewhat bland. But the photos that showed his boss with the director of the FBI, CIA and different heads of state defined the power and prestige that the polished agent wielded.

The senior agent hung up his phone. "Agent Perez, how may I help you?"

"Sir, I've stumbled onto something I think may be really big. No, on second thought, I'm prepared to say *huge*."

"Is that so? Tell me more."

"I received a call a few weeks ago from an anonymous female who spoke of a crew by the name of the Syndicate. She gave me a string of names and places where they allegedly had operations set up to provide 24-hour access to drugs. She also gave me a list of the large amounts of drugs they purchased regularly. Anyway, after speaking with her I ran every name she had given me through our criminal database and came up empty-handed. So, it was hard for me to believe that an operation of this proportion could be working and none of the men who ran it never received as much as a jaywalking charge."

"Well, what has changed since then?"

Perez reached inside his pocket. He pulled out a computer printout of all the locations that had been bombed throughout the night, as well as all the casualties that were pulled from the houses afterward. He placed the paper on the desk, stood and leaned on the corner of it, stating, "Every spot that my unknown caller told me about is on this list. Coincidences of this magnitude just don't happen."

Perez's boss glanced up from the printout he had been scanning. "If you're right and this isn't a coincidence, what we have here isn't a major organization. We've got the beginning of a major street war on our hands."

"From the looks of things, the war has already begun, and after last night I hate to imagine what will happen next."

"What do you need on this, Perez?"

"All the manpower and resources you can give me, sir."

The senior agent paused and closed his eyes as if in deep thought. He seemed to be tossing around numbers in his head, before slowly coming to the sum he had been searching for. He opened his eyes and slowly set his gaze upon Perez. "I'm placing fifty agents on this case. You will serve as senior agent, which places you in charge and endows you with full responsibility for the outcome of this entire operation." He pointed at Perez and raised his voice slightly. "If this mystery group does in fact exist, I want their heads on a platter!"

"I've never let you down, sir. And now is not a good time to start."

"Sounds good."

"You can believe I will find The Syndicate and serve them to you." Perez knew that with just a dozen agents at his beck and call, there was no one in Detroit who he couldn't locate if he chose. He couldn't wait to hit the streets in search of his prey.

# Chapter 15

The five occupants of the black tinted Grand National were highly armed and anxious as they quietly waited on their unsuspecting victim. The anticipation of the task ahead weighed heavily on each of their minds. After what had transpired the night before, Dre, Skeet, Nut, Rossi and Billy were left with no option other than gruesome payback.

"We've got action!" Skeet announced, pulling on his gloves and pointing in the direction of the approaching Navigator. "That's the nigga Joe-Joe's truck."

Dre stifled a sigh. He could tell by the slight sounds of movement behind him that Nut, Rossi, and Billy were preparing for the encounter as well.

Dre eyed the truck as it made a beeline into the driveway. The garage door slowly started to fold upward. Dre reached for the door handle. "You all know the drill, so let's handle our business." He left the confines of the warm car before his last words were completely out of his mouth. Dre dashed across the yard, making sure to stay close to the hedges. He ducked under the garage door with a 9-mm in his hand.

Skeet tailed. He was no novice to murder and home invasions. His face lit up when he found the terrified look on the faces of Joe-Joe's woman and two young sons.

"This shit is real!" Dre told him. He could tell Skeet was caught off guard by finding the family inside the truck instead of Joe-Joe. It wasn't until Big A's face entered Dre's mind that he disregarded any feelings he had for the helpless family. He grabbed a handful of the woman's weave and yanked her from the truck. Tears flooded her face when she looked up from the ground into the barrel of Dre's gun. "If you want those two little bastards to live through the night, you had better follow every instruction and order I give you to a tee. Now, do I make myself clear?" he asked.

Joe-Joe's woman shook her head up and down as she sobbed uncontrollably.

Dre pulled her to her feet by her hair. He tossed the command over his shoulder to grab the boys. He guided her toward her house. Dre figured that no woman and children would hinder him from completing the task he had set out to accomplish. Payback was a must, and if Joe-Joe didn't make it home in a timely fashion to answer for the damage that he and his crew had done, his woman and children would have to pay the price for his actions.


Rico, Omar, and Joe-Joe sat amongst the crew of 50 Strong niggas inside a penthouse suite of a hotel. They drank champagne and passed blunts while finalizing plans for when the Syndicate ceased to exist. Rico was a candidate to be Dre's successor in the city. He was well known, and the perfect person to step up after having pledged the support of his crew to Omar.

Omar watched his young accomplice intently, wondering exactly what went through his mind. Rico took a deep toke from the blunt and exhaled a small cloud of smoke. He smiled, not having the slightest idea of what Omar had planned for him when they were finished with The Syndicate. The last thing he would be was happy. Even though he recognized the fact that Rico was a soldier, the young nigga's persona screamed snake. By having similar characteristics, Omar was aware that in the long run Rico would be a hindrance to him and his business.

Omar put on a false smile, patted Rico on the back and said, "Drink up and enjoy yourself, man." He pointed to the legion of strippers in front of them and added, "Take your pick of the ladies as well. I had them all sent from Chicago just for your pleasure."

"You sure know how to celebrate." Rico smiled.

Omar nodded toward Joe-Joe, who was engrossed in getting a blowjob from a dime piece. He looked at Rico. "Ain't no use in you missing out on all the festivities when your man's and them are living it up."

Rico licked his lips at the tasty array of gorgeous women parading around. "But before I get off into the enjoyment side of this little get-together, I need you to pull my coat to something."

"I'm all ears, pimp."

"I was just thinking that with my being prepared to hold you all the way down and shit, where do we stand when those Syndicate niggas collapse? I know you got a nigga straight and all, but I just need you to put me up on game. You feel where I'm coming from, right?"

Omar took a sip of champagne. He made eye contact with Rico, thinking that if he didn't need him and his crew to finish up the mission they had started, he would put a bullet between his eyes. He recognized game and having too much of it; he swallowed his drink and gave Rico his most sincere smile.

"I'm just asking," Rico said.

"If you know me and how I get down, then you already know that I've got big plans in mind for you and your crew."

Rico smiled. "I like that."

"Pimp, I'm gonna make sure that after this, all you niggas go down in history with a bang. You hear me?"

Rico nodded.

Omar said, "Rico and the 50 Strong niggas will be talked about for the next fifty years. So to pull your coat to the future, nigga, let's just say I'm gonna make you a legend."

Rico bumped his fist with Omar's. Then he reached out and grabbed one of the thickest white girls present. Pulling her onto his lap, he began to whisper in her ear, receiving an immediate smile and giggles in return. He ran his palms over her body.

Omar watched Rico intently, along with the rest of his crew. What he saw around him were a bunch of young fools who could easily be persuaded to do his dirt through weed, women, and alcohol. He felt nothing but contempt for the whole bunch. But he would keep his word by making them all legends when the drama was over. Only instead of making them all rich and powerful beyond anything they could imagine, he would throw another event like this one and plant a series of explosives through the room. He smiled at the thought, deciding that would definitely send them all out with a bang.

Dre took a long hard look at his watch. The reality that Joe-Joe wasn't coming home had sunk in. The time was after 5 a.m. and they had been there over five hours. Dre's patience had worn thin. The sun was about to come up, and although it hadn't been spoken on throughout the night, he and his crew understood that whatever they were going to do had to be done before it arrived.

He glanced around the room. His eyes traveled from the figures tied to chairs in the middle of the floor, to Skeet and Billy, who were holding a silent vigil as they peered out the window. Nut sat on a sofa, glaring at the terrified woman as if he was prepared to pounce on her at any moment. Rossi snored lightly on the recliner.

Ready to carry out the only other option they had left, Dre made the decision that he had been dueling with ever since he arrived. "Alright, listen up," he announced, instantly garnering the attention of his crew. It had been hours since any of them had spoken, so it was evident that something important was about to be said. "The sun is about to come up, and as you can see, this nigga ain't coming home. We have about thirty minutes left to do our thing. So with or without him it has to go down." Dre heard low sobs from Joe-Joe's woman, but he continued speaking.

"Nut, go to the kitchen and round up five of the biggest, sharpest knives you can find."

"Noooo!" she cried out, fighting against her restraints in an attempt to break the bonds. "Please . . . don't hurt us. We've done nothing," she screamed.

Dre cut his eyes dismissively. Yet, the fact that they were truly innocent of the crime they were being punished for touched Dre. He shook off his thoughts of indecision at the sight of Nut approaching. The glint of the stainless steel knives in his hand pretty much sealed their fates. Turning a deaf ear to her pleas, he allowed himself to transform into the cold heartless killer that Joe-Joe and his crew had been when they slaughtered the people in his spots.

He accepted the biggest knife, and then locked eyes with each of his partners. In each of their eyes he saw nothing but cold, piercing looks, which only aided in spurring him along. Thus, with no words needed, Dre moved behind the frantic, screaming woman. Pulling her head back to expose her throat, although she put up a valiant fight, Dre quickly overpowered her, digging the razor sharp knife in her flesh and dragging it in a perfect arc from her left ear to her right. Observing the shocked look in her eyes, Dre watched her life slowly slip away. Not even the stifled cries and fearful whimpers of the two young boys could compete with the loud gurgling sound and torrents of blood that spewed from the gaping wound each time she fought to breathe.

Skeet said, "We don't have much time, so let's tie up the rest of these loose ends and get going." However, at the completion of his statement, the look he gave the young boys as he and Billy headed toward them was unmistakable.

"Oh, okay . . . let's do that then," Dre stammered. Feeling as if he were in some sort of trance-like state, he plopped down on the couch and watched his crew as they diligently began to work. However, what happened next was utterly unbelievable. Dre stared at the mutilation taking place around him, powerless to stop it. He dropped the bloody knife in his lap, the only thing going through his mind as he watched was, he had set this all in motion.

Joe-Joe navigated his new Cadillac CTS through the city streets. His phone and pager were full of unanswered messages from his woman. He'd get to her later. Right now he raised the volume on his prided Bose system. His girlfriend knew how he got down in the streets. Regardless of what he did or how many women she found out about, she wasn't going anywhere. He knew she loved him unconditionally.

Joe-Joe had just finished freaking two Chi-Town strippers. He was jaded, ready for the comfort of his soft, warm, queen-sized bed and some well needed rest. But he knew his girlfriend was probably waiting for him at home with an argument about him staying out all night. Although she would not leave him, she had no problem beefing with him.

As Joe-Joe turned onto his block, he waved at a group of females who were gathered at the bus stop with their children. Straining his eyes in an attempt to locate his own sons, he concluded that they had yet to leave the house. If anything, he decided they were more likely running through the house like two tyrants, driving his woman crazy. It may have been the reason she had been blowing up his phone and pager.

He whipped into the driveway and exited the vehicle. Then he hit the alarm button on his key ring and strolled across the grass. In his hurry to get into the house, he hadn't even grabbed the morning paper off the porch step. He chose instead to leave that task, as well as any others that dealt with manual labor, to his woman. Reaching out and turning the doorknob, Joe-Joe was surprised to find it locked. "Damn kids," he mumbled. His children had a habit of leaving the door open.

He stepped inside expecting to be met by loud, excited children and his angry, beautiful wife. But what Joe-Joe saw was a gruesome scene beyond his imagination. He vomited as he fell to his knees with a torrent of tears pouring down his face.

Just a matter of feet away, the severed heads of his woman and two sons sat side by side on the table, wearing wide-eyed looks of horror. The blood that covered the floor, walls and furniture told the story of the anguish they had suffered. But Joe-Joe was spared the mystery of their deaths due to the large sign that sat at the base of the table. In bold letters, it read:

> *You thought we wouldn't find out who was responsible for last night? Well, this is proof that you were wrong. Although this is only the beginning of the price that you and your accomplices will pay for your stupidity, we only hope that you found your one night of fame worth the lifetime of pain you will spend, knowing that you were responsible for the death of your family.*
> *Signed,*
> *You know who we are . . .*

Joe-Joe screamed and moaned incoherently. Loud sobs racked his body as he remained rooted to the spot he kneeled upon. Like the note stated, he was responsible for the deaths of his loved ones, and for the remainder of his days he would be haunted by the realization that he may as well have been the one to deliver their final death blow.

Dre crept in the house, discarding his clothing and showered to clean away the blood that covered his torso. Then he headed to his office, needing the solitude it offered him instead of his bed where Stacy awaited his arrival. He dropped down in the high-backed leather chair behind his desk, reflecting back on the events of the night. He couldn't allow himself to have any regrets on how things had taken place. But Dre would have only been lying to himself if he said he wouldn't have rather beheaded Joe-Joe instead of his family.

Sighing as he dropped his head in his hands, Nut's past words fluttered into his thoughts. Almost two years had passed since he killed Juan, and Nut had been prepared to kill his woman and daughters along with him. His justification had been: "It's a dirty game and only the strong survive." Tonight had proven that Dre too felt that way. Like Nut had said, it was a dirty game, and Dre was ready to raise the stakes. From this point on, things would only get worse.

*Chapter 16*

Perez addressed the contingent of agents who lined the room of his headquarters. He stood at the podium giving off an aura of confidence and pride that elevated him above the rest of the group. A chalkboard that he had spent the day before and half the night preparing flanked his right side. He had aligned a makeshift chart that detailed the hierarchy of the Syndicate. Most of his information had been compiled from the mysterious female caller. Yet, he had made contact with numerous DEA informants in the streets and come up with intelligence to back up the data she had supplied. Local police also informed Perez of the murder charge Nut was facing and their belief that he was a member of the Syndicate.

He peered over his shoulder at his team of agents. Perez pointed a thin stick at the bottom of the chart. "This is where we need to begin in order to reach here," he added, lifting the stick to the top of the chart where it landed on the picture of Dre.

Placing the stick back on the bottom of the photo, Perez stated, "The man you see here is only a low level dealer who more than likely works in one of the many houses they supply throughout the city. However, in order to shake the top of the ladder, we must destroy their foundation. Therefore, this man and many more like him will be where we concentrate the majority of our efforts."

Perez moved the stick back to the picture of Dre. "The man you see in this photo is John Dodson Jr. Known on the streets as Dre. Ladies and gentlemen. He is the person we want. From what we have compiled so far, he is the leader of the feared Syndicate. Thus, he is the first and foremost on our takedown list. You will find a brief bio on him in the packet you were given before the meeting . . . "

His personal secretary fidgeted on the sidelines as she nervously inched toward him. Perez waved her over, excusing himself from the meeting. "What is it, Robbin? As you can see, I'm in the middle of a very important briefing."

"I know sir, and I'm sorry," she stated, sincerely apologetic. "It's just that I have some news I felt you may be interested in hearing. It arrived from the Bureau's telecommuter a few minutes ago." She handed a sheet of paper to her boss and gave him room to read in peace.

A grimace distorted Perez's features as he read over the fax. But a tremor of excitement traveled through him with the realization that the beheading of a woman and two children could only have been orchestrated as retaliation for the bombings. Adding to his gut feeling was the attached rap sheet of the boyfriend and father of the deceased. He was a known drug dealer from the Westside of the city. Joe Ramsey had a long list of convictions that included everything from theft in his younger years, to selling drugs and murder as he aged and increased his criminal dealings.

Perez folded the fax and placed it in his pocket. The investigation they were about to embark on had turned out to be even bigger than they expected. And in light of the new developments that seemed to be popping up on a daily basis, he had no doubt that when they got to their man, a death sentence would be easy to obtain. Perez saw this investigation as a means of elevating himself to a cushiony high-level position within the Washington D.C. branch of the agency. He would give operation Syndicate Takedown every bit of skill and expertise he had acquired in his eight years as an agent. There was no room for failure.

Destiny had just arrived at Naiza's home. They were in her bedroom chatting. "Girl, have you heard the news?" Naiza questioned animatedly.

"News . . . what news might that be?" Destiny retorted. Just by the excitement in Naiza's voice, she knew that whatever her girl spoke of was something she needed to hear.

"Pssst . . . I don't know where you've been lately, but the streets are buzzing with talk about somebody trying to take over the Syndicate's spots . . . "

"Oh yeah?"

"Mmm hmm. Word is, the other night about ten different crews hit every spot they had on the Eastside. I mean . . . they really got hit up, girl. They say they set that shit off with grenades, then killed everyone who tried to run up out the houses. It was all on the news too."

"What?" Destiny blurted, trying with all her might to mask the exhilaration she felt. "How many people got killed?"

"Girl, it ain't no telling for real. But I will say this though, from the news and picking up little bits and pieces of Nut's conversation the last two days, I heard they took *major* losses." Naiza shook her head in sympathy. "Ever since that went down Nut's barely here, and when he is, it seems like..." Looking up at the sound of the door opening, Naiza grinned at the sight of Nut entering the room.

"Hey, Destiny." He leaned down and placed a kiss on Naiza's lips.

Destiny waved her hand in response to Nut's acknowledgement, and then watched her girl attach herself to him. She cuddled with Nut as if trying to smother him. Destiny glared at the two with a mixture of jealousy and disgust, wondering when they became so cozy with one another.

She felt like Nut sensed her jealousy. He began giving Naiza more attention. Destiny knew he wasn't in love with her, but he did like her. Destiny was that chick. And she had detected that Nut had imagined himself with her. But not with Dre in the picture. But Dre was gone and now Nut's eyes roamed from her low cut gator boots, past her slightly muscled calves to where her Coogi dress began to rise. She shifted her legs, giving him a perfect view of her white lace panties and the forest of dark hairs that sat behind them.

Nut smiled and licked his lips. Destiny opened her

legs and inched up her dress, smiling at the way his eyes and dick instantly bulged out. Wiggling her hips to scoot the dress back down before Naiza noticed, she gave Nut a knowing wink as she glanced upward with a smug grin. Destiny wiped the smile from her face, deciding that her girl was living in fantasyland if she thought that Nut belonged to her. Destiny knew she could easily have him.

Naiza turned to Destiny, who was getting up. "I know you're not leaving."

"Yup, I'm afraid I have to be going. Business calls," Destiny replied, sighing as she stretched, placing emphasis on her every curve. "I'll see you two lovebirds later."

"Okay then. Give me a call later and I'll handle that move for you," Naiza stated.

"I sure will," Destiny said over her shoulder, putting an extra twist in her hips for Nut's benefit as she headed toward the door. She enjoyed the little game she was playing with him, and decided that he was a rather interesting prospect.

The two phones that Rico carried hadn't stopped ringing all day. The pleasure he had enjoyed since they dealt the Syndicate a major blow a few nights before seemed to fade more and more with each call. In only forty-eight hours, Dexter Avenue had become a war zone. Niggas were dying all over the Westside, and the bodies that were turning up were so horrifically mutilated that it could only be the work of the Syndicate.

Rico lay in bed listening attentively as one of his men babbled on about the latest series of murders. Due to the extreme circumstances they now faced, the only direction he could see fit to give was, "Strike back. Put the word out that for every one of our people that gets hit I want two Syndicate members to die."

"I hear you, Rico. But umm . . . niggas are shook around this bitch, man. I don't mean no harm, but them fools are on some other shit. They ambushed Cam, PeeWee, and Fletcher early this morning on Fenkle. They wet the whole car up with .308s and ARs, and then took the time to cut their dicks off and put them in their mouths."

"Fuck that! Them niggas bleed too, so don't tell me nothing about them being on some other shit. Deal with them bitches!" Hearing the news of how Joe-Joe's family had been butchered was bad enough. Now to make matters worse, his soldiers were getting slaughtered all over the city.

Rico frantically explored his brain in search of a plan that could rescue his crew from the Syndicate's steadily tightening noose. Although he feared no man, he was aware of the powerful team they were up against. Rico knew that the streets were about to become a whole lot deadlier.

He punched Omar's numbers into his phone, wondering how the Syndicate had found out they were responsible for the bombings. He figured that it was too late to worry about it. War was the only thing he needed to be concerned with at the moment.

When Destiny pulled into Naiza's driveway, she noticed Nut's BMW was the only car parked in the garage. She turned in her seat and scanned the residential street in both directions to make sure her girl hadn't doubled back. Finding no trace of Naiza's Range Rover on the horizon, her face lit up with a devious smile.

Destiny cut off the ignition and flipped down her vanity mirror to appraise the flawless reflection before her. More than just mildly aware of her beauty, thus, she knew the task she had in mind for Nut was in the bag. Blowing a kiss at the mirror, she said, "Do your thing, Destiny." Filled with devious intent, she grinned at the thought that she was irresistible. She closed the mirror and exited the car. Destiny couldn't help biting down on her bottom lip, recalling some of the wicked tales Naiza had shared with her about Nut. If he was anywhere near as freaky as she had been told, they were in for a long night. Although she realized she was wrong for going at her friend's man, Destiny figured that had Naiza not put her private business in the streets, none of this would be happening. She was only making an excuse for her actions. Her mind was set, so she rang the bell, prepared to do whatever was necessary to accomplish her goal.

Nut turned the shower off and reached for a towel. He barely stepped out of the stall when he heard the doorbell. He sucked his teeth, in no hurry to get to the door before he dried himself off. Hearing the chiming sound once more, he wrapped the towel around himself, grabbed the .40 cal he kept under the sink and stepped out the bathroom.

Nut held the weapon tightly. With all the drama going on in the streets, he couldn't allow himself to get caught slipping. He reached for the door, seeing Destiny on the other side. Just the sight of her standing there looking like a fashion model gave him an instant erection. He glanced down at the rise underneath his towel, thinking about her flirting with him earlier. Nut had had a crush on her since hearing Dre's first story of how she had laid her sex game down. He licked his lips.

Destiny eyed his bare muscular chest. Water rolled off his partially naked body as he opened the door with a smile. She raised her brow and grinned. "I see I caught you at a bad time," she said, lowering her eyes to the towel and the erection that strained at the material.

"Depends on how you look at it."

Destiny's eyes remained transfixed on his erection.

Nut shrugged and stared downward as well. "I was in the middle of taking a shower. What up, doe? Naiza ain't here," he added. By the way her eyes were glued to his private parts she hadn't heard a word he had said.

"Destiny!" he exclaimed, breaking the hypnotic trance she seemed to have been locked in.

"Huh?" She giggled, pushing past him to enter the house. "It's cold out here, and I need to use the bathroom."

Nut closed the door, watching her parade into the living room with a fluid sway of her hips. He had become even harder as he followed behind her, thinking that the bathroom was the other way.

Making her way across the room, Destiny leaned against the white baby grand piano and leered at Nut seductively as he entered with a gun in his hand. Her eyes scanned from his gun to his bulge. "Damn Nut, I had no idea you carried such a big gun." She emphasized gun by running her tongue over her bottom lip.

"So I see you got a thing for guns, huh?"

She giggled. "Not just guns . . . big guns."

Nut grinned.

Destiny unfastened the belt that held her coat together and locked eyes with Nut. She gave him the type of stare that asked and stated powerful messages without a word. Her coat opened just enough to reveal her lack of clothing. Her voice was calm but full of intensity when she instructed, "Come closer. I've got something I have been dying to show you."

Nut stepped forward, anxious to get inside her.

"That's right, come to mama," she prodded in a sultry voice, shrugging her shoulders to remove the coat and let it fall in a heap around her Jimmy Choo boots.

Nut was mesmerized by Destiny's thick, curvaceous frame. The perfectly proportioned frame he saw was nothing short of a dream. He reached out to grab her ass and pulled her to him for a long, hungry kiss. Kneading her round, silky ass as their tongues dueled for supremacy, he pushed his hips forward, feeling her hand as it moved beneath the towel and grasped his swollen erection.

Destiny pulled away, breaking their kiss and the grip he had on her ass. "What's going on?" Nut mumbled, hoping she hadn't changed her mind.

"Ssshhh," she said, placing a finger on his lips to quiet any complaints he may have had, while controlling the tempo of the session. Taking a step back, she hooked her fingers in the thin spaghetti straps on either side of her hips and began to lower her silk and lace G-string. She ran a finger between her legs, dipped it in her juices, and then placed it in Nut's open mouth. After he had sucked her fingers, she reached out and pulled his towel, letting it flutter to the floor.

The look in her eyes told Nut she liked what she

saw. "You taste delicious, but I want you to taste some of this," he said. Holding himself tightly at the base, he shook his dick, taunting her with the length and girth, before confidently stating, "Nah, maybe it's a little too much for you."

She grabbed his stiffness, spat on it, and used her hand to coat it with her saliva. Then she opened her mouth wide, making sure to fold her lips over her teeth before engulfing the head. Squeezing the base as she slowly began to work up a rhythm, Destiny swept her long hair out of her face, taking the dick so deep that it touched the back of her throat. Hearing him groan as she moaned and increased her loud slurping sounds to a feverish pace, she relaxed her throat muscles and allowed his whole length to slide down her throat.

"Oooh shit, Destiny!" Nut cried out, feeling his nuts bang against her chin. He blinked his eyes to clear his vision, and then grabbed a handful of her hair to steady himself. He rose up on his tiptoes with each downward stroke she made.

Destiny expertly deep throated him, alternating her deep suction with licks around his circumcised head, and then kissing and licking the thick vein that traveled along the underside of his dick.

Nut was about to cum, and as he used her hair to force himself deeper down her throat, he hissed, "That's it . . . suck it harder. Umm hmm, suck this dick, Destiny." Tensing up, he held her head flush against him and erupted in her mouth with a loud squeal.

His juices crashed against the back of her throat, but she continued to suck, milking him dry. Slowly pulling his deflating erection from her mouth, Destiny licked any traces of juice she may have missed from him. She ran her tongue over her lips to retrieve any that might have escaped her mouth. She smiled, reaching for one of the pillows lying on the couch, and then positioned it beneath her ass. Lying down on the floor, she said, "I guess it wasn't too much for me after all." She spread her legs, presenting her moist folds in the process. "Now it's time for you to come taste some of this, since you liked it so much on my finger."

Never one to turn down an invitation, Nut dropped to his knees between her legs, wondering how Dre could have possibly gave up something as sweet as the goddess that stared up at him with a look of anticipation in her lust-filled eyes. What he did know was after the way she had sucked him off tonight this would only be the beginning of their union.

He gripped her satiny thighs and spread them as far as they would go. Nut placed his hands beneath her perfect, plump, heart-shaped ass and eagerly lowered his head between her legs.

"Damn," she moaned as Nut's tongue penetrated her lower lips, forcing her eyes to flutter closed.

Nut loved the way she submitted to him. He had never dealt with a woman as old and experienced as Destiny. He had expected her to be more domineering, but she was calm. Yet, her sexual skills spoke louder than anyone could. Nut had tried to remain cool during their session, but the reality was he was open, thirsty to go at it again and do whatever it was she wanted to keep growing their relationship. He didn't understand how Dre had given up such a woman. But he was happy Dre did.

# Chapter 17

Stacy pranced through her huge master bedroom in a baby tee and matching panties. She danced erratically, while mouthing the words to Bravehearts' "Oochie Wally" that blared through the room. Having completed her daily workout, she made her way around the room, gathering the necessary articles for her shower. But the view she caught on the sixty-inch television interrupted her process, making her grab the universal remote, turn off the stereo and raise the volume on the news broadcast. Stacy listened closely to the newscaster.

"We are at the scene of a gruesome triple homicide that took place in the wee hours of the morning," the pretty reporter spoke. "From what we have been able to ascertain from neighbors and the police, three males who authorities have yet to name were found decapitated."

The news reporter pointed behind her to the yellow

tape that surrounded the home. She paused for a beat. "In the last month alone, over twenty bodies have been recovered all over the Westside fitting the exact manner of execution. It is unclear at the moment as to what is happening in Detroit, but the police are asking for any assistance the public can lend in bringing the assailants of these horrific crimes to justice."

Stacy lowered the volume at the completion of the reporter's plea for help. She couldn't help the gnawing feeling that ate at her insides. Stacy could no longer deny the truth. Somewhere, somehow, she realized that Dre and the Syndicate had a hand in the mayhem taking place. Even though he had her tucked safely away in their little Bloomfield Hills enclave, she was neither dumb, deaf nor blind. In fact, through the conversations with her friends and short snippets of phone calls she had heard Dre engrossed in, it hadn't been hard to see the truth. If that hadn't been enough, his quiet, aloof behavior in the last few weeks had undoubtedly proved that he was experiencing the pressure that came along with his position.

Stacy dropped her head and shook it in disgust. Although she loved him, she wasn't prepared to relive the horrors of losing another loved one to the game. She refused to stand by and watch Dre destroy his life. She would rather walk away without taking a second glance behind her. Yet, her love made her decide to give it just a little longer before resorting to such a drastic measure.

Stacy would keep her eyes peeled for any other signs that would give credit to her belief that the Syndicate was behind the events taking place. If by chance it was so, Stacy knew that it would take every ounce of strength she possessed to leave. But it was necessary to do so to retain her morals and sanity. No matter how much it would hurt her, she would be left with no other recourse but to leave Dre.

"Yo, I must admit you really did one when you purchased this, boy!" Skeet complimented Dre on his new Maserati as they rode through Detroit. "This shit is too hot, and no one else in the city is riding like this."

"Psst . . . it ain't nothing big." Dre chuckled.

"Ain't shit big when your money is as long as yours, nigga."

"I know your rich ass ain't talking, all that money you're sitting on."

"Damn, when you put it that way I guess you got a point," Skeet agreed.

"Umm hmm," Dre teased, switching to business mode. "Well, we got all the houses on the Eastside back in operation with a lot of security. That, I must say is a good thing, but it's your operation that really interests me at the moment. Man, you're bringing in some astronomical numbers. I mean . . . how can you possibly be moving the millions of dollars worth of heroin that you do each week?"

"Moving mass amounts of dope is what I do, my man. In fact, I pride myself on being able to infiltrate any dope market in any state and pop my shit off."

Dre recognized that he was telling the truth, but Dre wanted specifics. "Yeah, yeah, I hear where you're coming from and all but spare me the heroics and tell a nigga how you're really moving all this shit."

"I'm politicking, nigga. Not only have I opened up a bunch of new spots on the Westside, but our shit is now in Highland Park, Grand Rapids, Flint and Lansing. But that's only the half of it because my dude, Tito, out of Columbus and Marl out of Youngstown are flipping birds by the dozens."

"Okay, okay."

Skeet added, "At this rate, we'll be moving shit throughout the whole Midwest before the year is out."

Dre shook his head in agreement while reaching for his vibrating Motorola. He raised an index finger, informing Skeet to hold that thought as he spoke into the receiver. "Okay, you've reached Dre, now talk to me."

"How's life treating you?"

Dre instantly recognized Torres' voice. "Shit could always be better, but hey . . . who's complaining."

"I hear that," Torres replied. "However, I'm calling because I've also heard that you have been experiencing some difficulties in the city. Is there anything I can do to make your problem disappear?"

"Nah, I'm cool. I appreciate it, but I think I can pretty much handle any opposition that comes my way."

"All right. If you're cool, I'm cool. But just so you'll know, I'm only a phone call away."

Dre figured there was no better time than the present to inquire about the next shipment.

"Umm . . . I was thinking that I . . . uh, need to come down there and see you real soon."

"Whoa!" Torres said. "I'll call you back."

Seconds later, Torres called Dre on his burn out phone. He chastised Dre for speaking recklessly over his other phone.

"Okay, back to business," Dre said.

"Umm hmm," Torres replied, somewhat surprised

that his young protégé was ready to purchase another shipment so quickly after the last. "I assume that you will be wanting the same amount of fruit as the last two times. Am I right?"

"Even on the burn out, you're nervous?" Dre asked, listening to Torres speak in his fruit code.

"Just kind of leery after that last call. It'll blow over." He laughed.

"Cool. But as for business, I don't quite want the same thing," Dre answered, calculating the figures for what he wanted in his head. "People in the city seem to be devouring your fresh tropical fruit, so add an extra fifty percent of everything to my order."

"I guess they are devouring it if you're in need of such a large order. Nevertheless, I can have it packed and ready for you within a week's time. Will that be soon enough for you?"

"Yeah, that will work out just fine," Dre said, pulling aside next to Skeet's candy apple red 911 Porsche.

"Look Torres, I'm in the middle of something at the moment, so will it inconvenience you if I call back?"

"No, no, my friend. You handle your business and at your convenience we can pick up where we left off."

After a few last minute pleasantries, Dre shut his phone and turned to Skeet. "You know what?" he stated, grinning as if he had come upon a mind-altering discovery.

"Hell nah, but whatever it is I'm hoping that it's good the way your ass is cheesing," Skeet teased.

"We haven't had any real fun since all this beef shit began. I was thinking that tonight would be a good time to gather up our people and stunt like only we know how. You know, we can show our faces and pop mad bottles of Cris and shit. What you think?"

"Dre, I don't know, man. Shit ain't all the way dead yet, and you know that those 50 Strong niggas took a whole lot of losses in the last few weeks."

"Man, fuck them niggas! If anything, their losses should give us more of a reason to show our faces. Ever since we set our murder game in motion, they haven't been seen or heard of on the Eastside." "Yeah, I guess you're right. But, I'm only saying that we're taking a hell of a chance."

"That's life. Especially the street life."

"I just don't think it's in our best interest—"

Cutting Skeet's words short, Dre said, "I'm not going to let them or any other niggas keep us from going to a club or anywhere else. I say we turn the Network out tonight and that's all to it."

Three suited figures who sat in the dark Caprice Classic half a block away, spotted their target inside of a baby blue Maserati. One of the agents clicked the long-range camera, running through another roll of film. They each wondered who the tall, light-complexioned man was who exited the Maserati.

It was apparent by the vast array of sparkling jewels he wore and the expensive Porsche he got into, that he was a major player within The Syndicate. What was peculiar to them was how he had eluded their surveillance up to this point.

Agent Peyton snapped the last of an array of photos of the mystery man and his red Porsche as they pulled off in the direction of the Maserati.

"Did you get any pictures of the license plates?" another agent asked Peyton.

"I made sure I got those."

Peyton was confident they would have the identity of their mystery man within the next twelve hours. He was the ranking agent, but he liked being hands-on to assure things were done correctly. Peyton logged in the information they had just received from the wiretap on Dre's phone and continued to tail him at a distance. They hadn't gotten any incriminating information from any of his phone calls so far. But Peyton knew that it wouldn't be long now.

Dre entered the house and found no sign of Stacy. He removed his vintage heavy leather Al Wissam coat and draped it over the banister. He ascended the long spiral staircase in haste to locate her. For the first time in weeks, he found himself in good spirits. He realized that she had been experiencing the brunt of his attitude, so he wanted to share his high spirits with her.

"Stacy," he called out, entering the third floor where their room was located. "Baby girl, where are you?" Receiving no response, the sound of running water and the sight of discarded panties and a T-shirt lying on the floor near the bathroom door immediately disclosed her location.

He removed his shoulder holster and placed the matching P89s on the entertainment center. Dre then disrobed. Tossing his clothes in a pile on the floor, he strolled across the thick carpet in the direction of the master bedroom. He instantly caught sight of Stacy's soap-covered body through the foggy glass stall. Dre's dick quickly grew hard.

"Aaaah, boy, you scared me!" Stacy proclaimed, breaking her train of thought at Dre's unexpected entrance.

"I'm sorry, baby. I called you a few times when I came in the house." He reached out to remove the soapy sponge from her hands and stepped behind her. "But when I heard the water running, I just figured that I would join you."

"Okay," she stated.

Dre guided the sponge gently over her shoulders, down her back and between the crack of her ass as she closed her eyes. He knew she had been longing for her man's undivided attention for weeks; right now all she wanted to do was enjoy his touch.

Dre smiled at the way her body swayed with slow roaming strokes of the sponge. He figured that now would be a good time to break the news about their night out on the town. With the throbbing between his legs and the sighs that escaped her slightly parted lips each time he ran his hands between her ass, it was clear to him that in the next few minutes they would be going at it like wild animals.

"Baby, you game to hit the club with me tonight?" he asked, reaching around her to slowly encircle each of her D-cup titties.

"Umm . . . yea . . . yeah," Stacy answered, subtly grinding her ass against the hardness he had placed directly between the cleft of her cheeks. "I'm . . . down for whatever," she stated, breathing heavily.

He dropped the sponge and any pretense of washing her soft body at the sound of her voice and the swirl of her hips against his dick. Dre hefted her firm titties in his palms and began to squeeze them as he placed soft kisses down her spine.

Stacy bent forward, bracing her palms against the marble walls, spreading her shapely bow-legs in the process. "It's been so long, baby. Plea . . . please . . .

fuck me!" she exclaimed, surprising herself with the intensity of her outburst.

Dre raised her right leg, cradled it in the crook of his arm, and then duplicated the process with her left. Locking his arms over her thighs, he positioned his large pole at her opening and slowly began to immerse himself into her molten glove. He bit down on his lip as he felt her insides tighten around him. The low groan he heard escape his throat was lost in the loud sequence of whimpers that erupted from Stacy.

"Uughh, oh . . . uughh," Stacy cried out, feeling Dre's abundant shaft invade her tight hole. She loved the feel of him inside her. And even after all the times they had made love, she still seemed to find it hard to take his unusual size. Although he brought her unfathomable pleasure, the pain that came along with it was a constant price to pay.

"That's right, baby . . . take this dick like I taught you!" Dre grunted, watching her fat ass jiggle back like Jello to meet his very deep pounding.

"Yes," she screamed.

"Whose dick is this?" he slurred, moving his hips. "Huh? Answer me. I said, who this dick belong to, bay?"

"It's . . . mine," she whined. "All mine. Ooooh. Dre . . . Dre . . . give it to me, daddy."

He pounded into her suspended body. Feeling her tighten around his dick, Dre's pace quickened, knowing that her orgasm approached. In an attempt to consummate their brief separation of sorts, he spoke in a strained voice. "I'm ready to explode." Coaxing her on as her moans became labored, he huffed, "Come on, baby. Cum with daddy . . . " Breaking his statement short, he buried himself to the hilt, feeling her walls spasm, signaling her orgasm at the same moment that his own seed spewed forth. Dre spurted jet after jet of cum inside her. As usual, sex with Stacy had been the bomb. However, the gripping muscles that milked him and the erection he still sported stated that their afternoon had only just begun. Not to mention, the hand that reached between them to massage his sack let it be known that she too was ready for the next round.

Dre licked his lips at the thought of what was to come. He allowed Stacy to stand, dropping down on his knees behind her. He quickly pulled her cheeks apart and ran his tongue down her crack, wasting no time getting back to business.

Destiny carted the last of her numerous purchases in the house, and then dropped down on her living room couch. She was exhausted. The shopping trip had been exciting and spending Nut's money had made the venture even more enjoyable. She hit the button on her answering service and his voice quickly snapped her out of her reverie.

"Hey, rna. Look, I know you're not there, but I just wanted to drop you a message and let you know that last night was the bomb." Pausing to give an order to someone in the background, he added, "Hit a nigga later, 'cause I'm trying to schedule a repeat performance of that shit tonight. You know I need—"

"Yeah right," Destiny stated in a stink voice, pushing the button to play through the remainder of her missed calls. She came across a message from Naiza. There was urgency in her tone. She picked up the phone and dialed her girl's number. Naiza picked up on the second ring.

"Hello," Naiza said, sounding sullen and unlike herself.

"Damn!" Destiny snapped. "What the hell is wrong with you?"

"Girl, everything is fucked up around here," she replied. Naiza's voice cracked, making it apparent that she was on the verge of tears.

"Oh shit! What the hell happen now?" Destiny mumbled, silently wishing she hadn't called. As far as she was concerned, Naiza's problems were just that: Naiza's problems. In no way was she trying to spoil her mood.

"It's Nut, girl. I don't know what's happening, but he's changed since the last trip I took to Chi-Town. He's never here anymore, and it seems that when he is, everything I try to do for him and to him is wrong." Sighing, Naiza said, "I don't know what to do, Destiny. I love his trifling ass, but he's seeing someone else and I just know it. Girl, give me some advice, please."

"I . . . I . . . don't know what to tell you," Destiny replied, at a loss for words. She momentarily experienced a slight twinge of guilt because it was she who stood at the root of her best friend's problem. The worst part of the whole situation was that she was only fucking the nigga for sport, with a portion of revenge thrown in for good measure, while Naiza was in love and experiencing heartache. Destiny was wrong and she knew it. But what had been done could not be taken back.

"Yeah, what could I possibly expect you to tell me after you went through the same situation with Dre. Damn, I sure hope Nut doesn't pull off with a young bitch on me too."

Any guilt Destiny harbored had instantly been replaced with a cold indifference. "Thanks a lot for re-
minding me, whore."

"Oh, I'm sorry," Naiza said.

"Anyway . . . there's no sense in you sitting around
the house moping, so you may as well let me treat you
to a night out on the town. I'll call the rest of the squad
and see if they're down to stunt along with us. You with
me? Or would you rather sit there and wait on a nigga
who's more than likely waiting on another bitch?" Destiny knew her words would cut like a knife.

"Umm hmm, I'll roll with you," Naiza hissed barely
above a whisper. "Where are we going?"

"Who knows . . . River Rock, Platinum, Chocolate
City, Network. What difference does it make when
we'll be the stars wherever we end up at?"

"Now that is something we agree on."

"Okay, it's a go then. I'll call you back with the time
and mode of transportation, but I have to get a spa
treatment, manicure, and pedicure in preparation."

"It's not hardly that important," Naiza blurted.

"Humph! Speak for yourself, whore. I'm a hot girl,
so for me the small things are always important."

# Chapter 18

Dre entered the Network and strolled through the sea of people. He tightened his grip on Stacy's hand. The crowd around them moved frantically to the heavy bass of Little John's "B.I., B.I." Yet, the twenty or so Syndicate members who surrounded them as they headed through the congested mass of partygoers easily cleared the lane. Dre caught sight of Skeet and his Z8 crew holding a large spot for them in the rear of the club.

He nodded his head in the direction of a large group of Puritan dudes as they passed. It dawned on Dre that no sooner than the chance arrived he would sit down with one of their top dogs, Lil' Dave. Their crew represented one of the strongest armies in the city, and with all the power and prestige they possessed in the streets, there was no doubt he needed the Puritan mob aligned with him.

Stacy lightly ran a manicured finger over his palm. He winked an eye in her direction, receiving a heart-warming smile in return. He instantly flashed back to the pleasure she had brought him earlier in the evening. Dre couldn't help having lustful thoughts as he unconsciously allowed his eyes to travel over her splendid form. She was a beauty, but the skin-tight Gucci jeans she wore plastered to her perfectly plump, heart-shaped ass was enough to make his mouth water. Her long hair hung in a single braid, swinging midway down the back of her waist length Chinchilla coat. Diamond encrusted frames covered her eyes.

"It's about time you made it, nigga," Skeet teased, standing to give Dre a pound.

Appraising Stacy with amazement, he handed her a flute of champagne. "And you, beautiful, already know that it's always a pleasure to be in your company."

Stacy blushed and accepted the champagne and compliment. She took a seat on Dre's lap instead of on the chair that had been pulled out for her.

"Nigga, back up off my lady!" Dre snapped in a threatening tone, rendering a sly defeated look from Skeet that brought a roar of laughter from The Syndicate members and Z8 clique within earshot.

Immediately getting into the party mood, Dre, Stacy, the forty or more soldiers who surrounded them and their lady friends popped bottles of Cristal like water. They danced, conversed and relaxed in an attempt to enjoy themselves. But Dre kept his eyes open in case beef surfaced.

Destiny noticed Dre and his entourage from the moment they stepped through the door. Her happy demeanor instantly disintegrated. She no longer enjoyed the club or her Remy Martin that suddenly left a sour taste in her mouth. She glared in the direction of their little gathering with hate in her eyes and larceny in her heart.

What she really felt was a consuming jealousy as she watched Dre with Stacy. Even after all the months of neither seeing nor hearing from him, it irked her to find that he looked even better and more prosperous than he did the last time she had laid eyes on him. How he had possibly continued to advance in the game without her was beyond Destiny's realm of understanding. What really had her stumped was, even after contacting DEA, along with all the chaos Omar had orchestrated, Dre still managed to stay on top of his game.

Destiny turned to Naiza. "Look!"

"What you want, hooker?" Naiza joked, nursing her drink and swaying to the music.

"Peep out the ho ass nigga and his bum ass bitch over there frontin' like they the shit," Destiny hissed, pointing her finger toward the far corner of the club. "Umm Umph. That nigga's gonna get his." Destiny sneered, slamming her drink down on the table and reaching for her Armelio Pucci purse. She fumbled around inside, quickly located her phone and began to punch in Omar's number as she shot fleeting glances in Dre's direction.

"Hello!" Omar's deep voice boomed through the receiver.

"He's here."

"He who?" Omar questioned in a high pitched tone. Although he had instantly recognized Destiny's voice, the blaring music that resounded through the phone made it hard to decipher her words.

"Dre! I'm telling you, he's sitting right across the room from me as we speak."

"Oh yeah?"

"This is the chance we've been waiting for . . . he would never expect it right now."

"Where are you and how many people are with him?"

"Look . . . I have no idea how many of those groupie ass niggas are with him. However, we're at the Network, and Omar"—she softened her voice to a more seductive tone— "We may never get another chance as sweet as this."

"I agree with you. We're going to take them by storm while they're least expecting it. But Destiny," he said in a flat piercing tone, "when we arrive I want you and everyone with you to be long gone!"

"But, Omar, you said that when the time came I could be there to see—" Destiny protested in a whining voice, only to be cut off mid-sentence.

"Don't but me, bitch! Just have your funky ass in the wind when I arrive. Now do I make myself clear?"

Normally, Destiny wouldn't have put up with any disrespect that remotely compared to how Omar had spoken to her. But when it came to him she made an exception. She knew that he played no games. Thus, with that particular thought in mind, she meekly answered, "Yes, you made yourself clear."

"Alright. We're cool then. Have another drink for the road, then smoothly make your exit because all hell is going to break loose in the bitch." Laughing at his own words, he said, "I'll give you a call later."

Destiny rolled her eyes and sighed angrily at the way she had just allowed herself to be belittled. She tossed her phone back in her purse and snatched the glass of Remy off the table, draining the remainder of the liquid in a rapid series of gulps. She slammed the empty glass down on the table, receiving stares and questioning looks from her entourage as well as people who sat or stood nearby.

She was ready to explode and couldn't care less who saw or was aware of her intentions. Destiny stood and ordered, "Let's go." Although her mind replayed Omar's instructions, she had decided that before leaving out she would make a slight detour. It would be rude to leave without first sharing a few words with her old friend.

"This is it," Omar stated as he stood in a stash house.

Having already picked up on snippets of Omar's conversation, Rico said, "If this is it, then fill me in on how we're going to handle our business. I'm ready for whatever."

"Where is Joe-Joe? And how long do you think it will take to round up four more of your deadliest shooters?"

"Joe-Joe's on the block. As for the shooters, any one of my people are qualified to pull off whatever caper you have in mind. Give me half an hour to locate everyone, and we'll be prepared." He eyed Rico as he punched in Joe-Joe's digits. Omar's excitement increased, knowing that after what had happened to his family he was still a live wire. Joe-Joe had become a killing machine with no regard for his own life, much less anyone else's.

Omar grinned at the thought of Dre being massacred along with anyone else who happened to be near him. Though he wouldn't be the one who actually pulled the trigger, the exhilaration of knowing that he had caused the young nigga's demise would suffice.

Omar listened as Rico spoke to Joe-Joe in code. He couldn't help thinking that he had linked up with a crew of half-wits. Although they had the hearts of lions, it was obvious they possessed very little sense. They had lost countless friends and family members to The Syndicate's wrath, yet no one had ever had the common sense to question why they were even dying. Concluding that their ignorance was a good thing, Omar shook his head, smiling at the idea that without flunkies such as the ones he controlled at the moment, all the wealth and power he had would be unimportant. He loved the game for those reasons alone. As long as it remained in his power to do so, Omar would continue to call the life and death determining shots that he lived for. Tonight's mayhem would fall into the long category of death and destruction that he had orchestrated, or for that matter, executed during his reign at the top. Dre's death was of little importance as far as business was concerned. For Omar, the collapse of The Syndicate and their leader had become personal.

"I was thinking that maybe after we leave here . . . we could drop by my house and have breakfast, take a dip in the hot tub and spend the rest of the morning exploring one another's bodies." Nut looked into the big dark eyes of the beautiful young groupie. He could tell by the way her luscious mouth twisted into a bright smile that she was game for whatever. His eyes unconsciously roamed around the club. Doing a double take upon noticing a group of familiar women heading their way, he almost spilled his drink, recognizing Destiny leading the pack with Naiza close on her heels.

"Oh shit!" he mumbled in a panic, hearing nothing

his young conquest replied to his prior suggestion. At that moment he wasn't sure whether Destiny had given him up to Naiza. Any thoughts he may have had about conquering the young girl no longer existed.

Nut cleared his throat loudly in an attempt to get Dre's attention. Even in his state of unease, Nut appraised Destiny as she moved across the room. Though he would rather see her in a state of undress, the Vera Wang suede form-fitting bodysuit she wore with a white mink and thigh high stiletto gator boots enhanced her beauty while giving her an alluring look. Nut's eyes, like every other man she passed on her way across the room, were instantly drawn to her full breasts that all but poured out of her perfect v-shaped top that plunged all the way down to her belly button. Exhaling as he held her with an unblinking stare, the lust he felt just then was beyond any other reaction he had ever experienced with another female.

However, as he watched her walk up on Dre and give him a sour look, Nut realized that the feelings he harbored for her were nothing more than what she felt for his man.

Feeling Naiza's intense gaze, Nut ignored her, choosing to observe the interaction between Dre and Destiny. He was not sure what would take place next. He, like everyone else around them, patiently awaited the drama that was to erupt.

"Dre . . . Dre . . . Dre, so we meet again, huh?" Destiny asked, standing just a few feet away from the table. She took up a wide legged stance and placed both her hands on her curvaceous hips.

"What up doe, Destiny?" Dre said in a cool, calm voice.

"What up doe!" Destiny repeated in an agitated

tone, shooting her friends an amused look. "Do y'all believe this ho ass nigga?"

Stacy flinched at the disrespect directed at her man. She attempted to raise up off Dre's lap, only to feel him tighten his hold on her waist.

Destiny ignored Stacy, hoping for a chance to even the score between them. She raised her voice an octave, more to annoy Stacy than anything. "What's up is, your ass has been a no show for a few months now. Also, ever since you hooked up with this low budget bitch here"—she recognized Stacy's discomfort—"you seem to have forgotten who the fuck made you."

"Bitch!" Stacy roared, tossing her glass of champagne in Destiny's face before Dre could respond to her venomous words.

The whole scene had Nut bugging. It was live entertainment. Destiny fought to wipe the burning liquid out of her eyes. She yelled obscenities as her girls erupted in a fit of violence around her. Destiny halted her forward motion in Stacy's direction at the sight of her wielding the broken champagne glass as if it were a knife.

"Let me go, Dre!" Stacy yelled, trying to wrestle out of the submission hold he had her in. Flailing her arms as she twisted and squirmed in an attempt to get to Destiny, she screamed, "I'm sick of her damn mouth, and I'm slicing her old ass up tonight. Get the fuck off me, Dre!"

"Grab the hos and get them the hell out of here," Dre commanded loudly, keeping an eye on Destiny and her crew as they attempted to get past his men.

Nut jumped out of his seat no sooner than members of their clique began to follow Dre's orders. He moved quickly at the sight of the women being manhandled.

His fellow Syndicate members were in the process of dragging the cursing and screaming women away against their will. Nut locked eyes with Naiza. He witnessed her distress as he rushed in her direction. He could tell she felt relieved at the sight of him coming to her rescue. However, her look of relief quickly disappeared at the realization that it wasn't her that he had come to save.

"Get the hell off her!" Nut hissed, snatching the hand of one of their soldiers from around Destiny's waist. Receiving no argument, he shot a knowing glance at her, stating, "Come on, ma, I got you." Loosely grasping her arm, more to lead her through the gawking partygoers than to put her out, Nut never even gave Naiza or his own crew a second glance.

Nut knew Nazia was somewhat numb by what had just taken place, unable to understand what would make him go to Destiny's aide instead of her own. He didn't know how much he was open off of her until he saw her being manhandled. His response was emotional. It was a move that could cost him far more than he could gain from Destiny.

# Chapter 19

The MPV was packed with Omar, Rico, and four gunmen. Omar surveyed the scene outside the club through the tinted glass of the minivan. He watched the group of women they had brought along to transport their weapons into the Network. Each of them were from Dexter Avenue, and their loyalty lied with the 50 Strong clique. Yet, as an added incentive, they had each received $1,000 for their troubles. They entered the establishment, Coach bags swinging, spitting game at the bouncers. Omar found it amusing that the bouncers didn't see anything unusual in the women donning large handbags instead of clutches as most women in the club did. But Omar chalked it up to men thinking with their dicks instead of their brains. He turned and focused his attention on the young soldiers who were more than prepared to carry out his orders. "It's a go. They're inside there," Omar stated.

Though he spoke to the whole group, his words were really directed to Joe-Joe as he looked into the cold, red eyes that stared back at him. Omar had witnessed the look he saw in Joe-Joe's eyes on many other occasions in the eyes of others. Like Joe-Joe, the others had been time bombs. Although they would easily kill without hesitation, due to something traumatic in their lives, it was apparent that they had each carried an unspoken death wish.

"Joe-Joe, you're the leader on this mission. I want you to make those niggas suffer like never before!" he blared loudly in a menacing voice.

"That goes without saying."

"No one receives a pass, and I mean no one. None of those motherfuckers had a drop of sympathy for your friends or family. Remember that!"

Joe-Joe shook his head up and down in rapid succession. "Let's do this shit! I'm all talked out, nigga. It's time to bring it." He reached for the door handle, exiting the MPV in one quick motion.

Omar nodded his head to the other four shooters as they exited behind their friend and closed the door. Joe-Joe sped toward the club, strolling quickly without taking a second glance behind him. Omar leaned back in to the comfort of his seat, beaming with the knowledge that The Syndicate was in for a big surprise, courtesy of him. But he was still amazed that he was placing himself this close to the drama. He knew he was too emotionally tied to revenge, but his only hope was that it didn't cost him.


Joe-Joe quickly found their home girls. They huddled in a corner as if they were dancing, but Joe-Joe and his crew were retrieving the mini Uzis they concealed inside their bags. He handed them out to his crew and ordered the females to leave immediately. He turned to his men and began to deliver the necessary orders, scanning the dimly lit club in search of their targets the whole while he spoke. "Ty, I need you and Mario to come up on the left side of their position . . ." Catching sight of The Syndicate's entourage in the back corner of the club, Joe-Joe paused and pointed in their direction. "That's them over there!" he snapped, never taking his eyes off the group of extravagant figures, adding, "Pooh, you and Cliff will hit them from the right side. I'll come straight through the middle with my shit, so wait for my signal before firing."

Ready to set their plan in motion, each of the shooters removed the safety from their weapons, and the long-sleeved shirts that covered them. A second set of black shirts also wrapped the guns, leaving access to the opening once discharged. They masked their guns and headed off in the direction of the club they had been assigned to.

Joe-Joe watched his boys as they took up their positions. This was the moment he had awaited ever since finding the severed heads of the only people he had truly loved in the world. He moved through the crowded dance floor with the Uzi in open view, hanging beside his right thigh. He neither noticed nor cared that the partygoers eyeballed his every movement and cautiously sidestepped out of his path and rushed away in the opposite direction. Joe-Joe had slipped into a murderous zone, no longer conscious of anyone else except his targets. Almost upon them, his smile broadened.

\* \* \*

The club was jumping and The Syndicate was party-ing hard. Their entourage had returned to their prior festive mood after disposing of Destiny and her crew, but Stacy still had a sour attitude. Dre understood whole-heartedly how her evening could have been ru-ined, but he wanted the night to be special. He was pre-pared to do whatever it took to bring a smile back to the beautiful face that now sported a frown.

"Baby girl, brighten up," Dre whispered in Stacy's ear. He poked his lips out in a teasing manner that matched the look she wore. He smiled, hoping they could get back on track.

Stacy rolled her eyes, took a sip from the glass she held and blurted, "I'm sick of her shit, Dre."

"Don't let her stress you."

"Bay, that old silly ass bitch isn't going to be happy until she makes me hurt her ass real bad. Ugh . . ." she groaned. "I just hate that she can't seem to get it into her thick skull that you're my man now."

Dre gently grasped her face in the palms of his hands and gave her a soft, loving kiss. Trailing his thumbs over the swollen contours of her succulent lips, he spoke in a sincere voice. "Ma, what you and I have is beyond anything Destiny can ever begin to imagine."

"I know."

"I love you more than life itself, and nothing that she or anyone else says can change that. You're my everything, Stacy. All I want is for you to be happy. Right now I just need you to get Destiny and any drama attached to her out of your mind."

Stacy granted him a bright smile. Her attention was instantly riveted to the sound of the Eastside Cheddar Boys newest tune "Pop Your Collar" that resounded through the speakers, driving the crowd nuts. "Ooh baby, that's my song!" she announced, grinding excitedly on his lap.

"Oh yeah?" Dre laughed, raising his brow at the pressure her movements created in his groin. "Well, if you promise to try and enjoy the remainder of the evening, I'll take you out on the dance floor and steal your shine."

"Never could you steal my shine, man. You've got a deal, though. So being that the night isn't as young as I would like, how about we get to enjoying ourselves?"

Dre rose from his seat with Stacy's help. She seemed to be in a rush to get to the dance floor by the way she pulled at his hand. Dre's smile immediately vanished upon viewing an array of red beams shining in their direction. Time suddenly stood still. He saw a sea of smiling faces around him. And as she followed the bright red beams to their source, it quickly became clear that the hooded figures holding the weapons were executioners.

The moment the deadly weapons erupted, he became a human shield for his woman as glass and bullets exploded all around them. Dre watched in horror as members of his crew who stood closest to the spot he and Stacy had just occupied were ripped to shreds. Their bloody bodies littered the floor. He held her even tighter, shutting out the cries and screams of the wounded and dying around them. Dre fumbled beneath his Chinchilla and grabbed the German Luger from his waist. Stacy's loud racking sobs and the reality of the fact that he had placed his people in harm's way brought the enormity of the situation down upon him with the force of a sledgehammer. At that moment he realized he could never join the foray and leave his boo to fend for herself. If it meant giving his own life in exchange, Dre would gladly die so that Stacy could live.

The fully automatic weapons fired slowed to short sporadic bursts. Dre peeped out just in the nick of time to spot one of the hooded figures stepping from behind a beam that had protected him throughout the ordeal. Dre took aim and squeezed the trigger, surprising himself when his first shot found its mark. It exploded through his target's forehead, spraying brain tissue against the wall as the bullet exited the back of his cranium.

Dre noticed Skeet nearby. One of the assassins collapsed with the force of a bullet that had come from an undisclosed source. Skeet locked eyes with Rossi and Billy who had been returning fire from their own semi-hidden positions. Skeet ran out in the open busting his gun like a madman. Billy and Rossi came out as well, firing their weapons fearlessly.

Bullets whizzed by Joe-Joe's head. He ducked as three members of his crew were cut down.

Dre shot fleeting glances around the room at his men. He paraded back and forth through the room in a vile mood. He replayed the earlier events through his mind. Although he attempted to put up a demeanor of being in control for his men, the nauseating feeling rumbling in his stomach at the memory of his people lying dead around him haunted his thoughts.

"I don't believe they pulled that Kamikaze shit, man." Rossi sighed, cradling his head between the palms of his hands.

"That shit was unexpected though," Billy agreed, staring off into space. "Where the fuck is Nut at? Has anyone located that nigga yet?"

Skeet shrugged. "Who knows, dog? From the looks of it, he has disappeared off the face of the earth."

Halting his step at the mention of Nut, it suddenly registered to Dre that he had never returned after escorting Destiny from the club. The thought of him leaving with her instead of holding his people down when they needed him most, angered Dre. On the flip side, Dre unselfishly felt relief at the knowledge that his best friend had remained out of harm's way. As it already stood, they had suffered more than enough losses. Adding Nut to the list would have only increased the deep feelings of responsibility that already weighed heavily on his heart. However, just to make sure that he was safe, Dre decided that once Billy, Rossi, and Skeet left, he would continue to try and contact him.

Skeet stood and grabbed his mink coat, draping it over his arm. "I'm about to be out. We've been up all night and there's nothing we can do to change what's happened, so I'll get at you niggas later." Giving Rossi and Billy pounds, Skeet grasped Dre's shoulder on the way past. He stopped at the door to study the scene, giving Dre a look filled with compassion. "Though we chose this life, this is a dangerous game we're playing, baby boy."

Dre understood firsthand that the game had rules of its own that didn't always fit into the scheme of the players. Yet, even as he shook his head in agreement of Skeet's words, nothing could justify the mistake he'd made when he forced his people to drop their guard. They had been lulled into a false sense of safety, when in all actuality danger had been lurking in the shadows. As Dre watched Skeet exit the room, he knew that although time had been rumored to heal all wounds, the hole that now occupied his heart due to his lapse in judgment would remain.

\* \* \*

Perez pulled up in front of the crime scene with three DEA agents. They each exited the unmarked Crown Victoria as a second unmarked car containing four more agents pulled up behind them. They donned latex gloves as they made their way toward the roped off entrance of the club. Perez scanned the area. City police patrolled the perimeter, while detectives moved about speaking amongst themselves in hushed tones. The multitude of coroner vehicles and ambulance personnel that sat around with bored looks on their faces gave Perez the understanding of just how dire the situation had been. It was apparent that no one was in a rush. But there was no reason for them to do anything besides relax. The dead bodies that littered the floor as they entered the club were in no rush to go anywhere.

Perez gave orders to the agents who surrounded him. He noticed a news van and a reporter who exited it in a hurry. However, his attention was immediately diverted from the new arrivals when an authoritative voice boomed behind them.

"Hey! This is an unauthorized area. Clear out of here!"

Perez turned to face the hostile male voice, giving the approaching officer a blank stare, disregarding him just as quickly as he had noticed him. He removed his palm pilot. "I want you each to go through this club with a fine tooth comb, and regardless of who likes it or not, we're now in control of this crime scene."

The agents quickly dispersed to handle their separate tasks, yet it was obvious by the bewildered look upon the angry officer's face as he approached, that he in no way appreciated the suited men converging on the crime scene.

"What the hell is going on here?" the big African American officer barked, shooting a spray of spit along with his question. "And who the hell gave you permission to come in here?"

"I'm Agent Ramon Perez, and I'm representing the Eastern region DEA office." Giving the officer a smug grin, he added, "I guess that means I'm basically able to come in here without permission." Shrugging his shoulders in a mocking fashion, he reached an arm out in greeting.

The officer glanced down at the offered hand defiantly. The other officer reached out and grasped it in a short half-hearted shake. Making his introduction as short and straight to the point as possible, he blurted, "City Homicide Division, the name's Reynolds."

Perez released his grip and pulled his hand and eyes away from the detective. He looked off in the direction of a forensics expert hard at work in the rear of the club. "Damn! It's a mess in here," he announced, stepping on the shards of glass that littered the floor. "What the hell happened? And how many casualties do we have on our hands?"

Reynolds said, "Eleven killed and another eight were badly injured. Other than that, from what we know so far, five men, three of whom are now deceased came into the club, split up into teams and converged on an unsuspecting group of partygoers with automatic weapons."

He pointed around them wearing a look of disgust. "And this, Mr. Perez, is the aftermath," Reynolds stated.

Perez quietly peeked around him at the death and destruction for the first time since walking into the club. The stench was unbearable. Yet, what really weighed heavily upon him was the fact that prior to this happening he knew that it was possible for the massacre to take place. Too many monitored phone conversations on both sides had all but given them the heads up. However, Agent Perez was aware that regardless of how badly he wanted to make the greatest bust of his career, straddling the fence like he now found himself doing wasn't the way to accomplish his task. Through surveillance, they were clearly aware of the identities of each assailant involved in the attack on the club. The only problem was, in order to trap and prosecute Dre and The Syndicate, they would be forced to look the other way for fear of letting it be known that DEA was involved in an operation as immense as the one that had grown to over 100 agents.

Perez snapped out of his thoughts at the sound of Detective Reynolds' voice. Perez concluded that if nothing major happened within the next week, he was going to tighten his noose around the city. Although he had failed to acquire any real evidence against Dre, they had compiled an adequate amount on the higher ranking members of his clique. Thus, Perez was aware that when the axe fell, if past trials and convictions were any indication of how the streets operated, then the rest of Dre's crew would quickly scurry to make the necessary deals with the government needed to bury him. Regardless of how slick Dre thought he was, Perez had no doubt that when it was all said and done, Dre, and all those who chose to side with him would rot in prison for the remainder of their lives.

# Chapter 20

Stacy rushed around the bedroom. Her eyes were red-rimmed and bloodshot as she tossed articles from her dresser drawers and large walk-in closet all over their huge platform bed. Furs, shoes, designer jeans, dresses, pantsuits, perfume and lingerie all fought for space on the bed. Moving with the speed of a cheetah, the only thought in her mind was making her escape. After what had transpired in her attempt to escape with her life thus far, Stacy had no unreal expectations that she would be so lucky the next time. Though she loved Dre unconditionally, and the thought of living without him broke her heart, she realized that staying under such unstable circumstances would be unhealthy.

"Stacy, what's going on?" Dre stood in the doorway with a faraway look in his tired eyes, gazing from the suitcase and clothing strewn all over the room to Stacy.

"Dre, I . . . I almost—I almost just lost my life. And I can't . . . I can't do this any—" She nodded her head from left to right. " . . . umm . . . I was just thinking that maybe

I should . . . Maybe I should just um . . . " She averted her gaze from his unblinking stare.

"Damn!" Dre exclaimed, slumping against the door-frame for support. He spoke barely above a whisper, "You leaving me, bay?"

Unable to stop the tears cascading down her face, Stacy shook her head up and down.

"Why? Why now . . . make me understand, ma? I'm . . . I'm lost."

Stacy cleared her throat, wishing she could have taken the cowardly way out and left without his knowledge. At a loss for words, she opened her mouth to respond, but dropped down on the bed and broke out in loud racking sobs instead.

Dre inched toward her. He dropped down on his knees between her open legs and waited for her to set the pace.

Though Stacy prided herself with being strong, out of all the things she had to do, leaving Dre for some reason was proving to be the hardest thing she'd ever done. She wiped her eyes in an attempt to pull herself together. Stacy sniffled and then bit down on her bottom lip as she stared into Dre's desperate eyes. She removed a long wisp of hair that found its way into her face.

"Talk to me, Stacy. Whatever it is . . . I promise . . . I'll fix it," Dre begged.

"I have to do this," she whispered. "Just let me go, Dre. Please!"

"I can't just allow you to walk out of my life, baby. You're all I've got in this world. Without you I'm nothing."

Immediately, Stacy felt her resolve evaporating at a steady rate, and the longer she stayed it would be even harder to exit. With that thought in mind, she averted her gaze from Dre and tried to rise up, only to feel his hands grasp her tightly around the waist. Finding herself rooted to her spot and unable to escape his scrutiny, she was forced to reveal her fears in their entirety. "Look Dre," she snapped, "If you just have to know why I'm leaving, here it goes . . ." Taking a deep breath, she said, "Last night brought back a nightmare that I've been trying to run from for years, and the realization that I can be killed, or for that matter lose you at any moment . . ."

"Baby, I . . ." Dre said.

Stacy gently placed a finger over his lips and quieted him with her piercing stare. "Listen, because you need to hear this. As I was saying, I'm not strong enough to relive this nightmare again, bay. I've never told you this before, but when I was a little girl I hid in a closet and watched as my mother was raped at gunpoint by three men who had come to collect an overdue drug debt that my uncle hadn't paid." Seeing the sorrow in his eyes brought tears to her own. "Afterward, I was treated to the sight of my mother, father, and younger brother as they were tied up, doused with gasoline, and burned alive. Just to send a message to my uncle. I was only nine years old at the time," she added, blinded by tears.

"Why didn't you tell me before now?" Dre asked her.

"It doesn't matter at this point." She allowed him to wrap his arms around her waist and lay his head upon her chest.

"I'm so sorry, baby. Damn, I hate that you had to go through that!" Dre said.

Tracing her fingers through his braids, Stacy closed

her eyes to brand the memory of their closeness into her mind. Choosing her next words wisely, she concluded that his answer would determine whether they remained a couple or she completed her journey alone. "Baby, did you mean it when you said that I was all you had in the world, and without me you're nothing?"

"Of course I meant it. Every single word of it to be exact." Looking up into her eyes, Dre held her gaze in a silent questioning sort of way. "Why do you ask? Do you doubt me?"

"No, the last thing I can possibly have is any doubt in you. But what I'm about to ask you will prove to be the ultimate confirmation of just how deep your love really is for me."

"I'm waiting," Dre stated.

"Dre"—she paused, searching for the right words while making an effort to control her emotions. "I can't live this way any longer. And after last night, I'm aware that regardless of how hard you try to keep our life separate from your business, it's just not possible."

Dre gave Stacy a dim look—a worried stare that created ridges in his forehead.

"I guess what I'm saying is . . . it's either me—no, on second thought, it's either us or the game." Sighing as if a mighty weight had been lifted from her shoulders, Stacy said, "You have more money than one man can ever dream of possessing, and to be perfectly honest with you it was never about the money as far as I was concerned. All I ever really wanted was you. So now that you know, what's it going to be?"

"Uhhh . . . I . . ." He hesitated, contemplating her words.

Stacy tried to read his thoughts. She knew he loved the game and the prestige it had afforded him. And she was aware he loved her more than any mortal word or phrase could define. The more he weighed his choices, there was honestly no getting around the fact that all the money and power he possessed couldn't compare to the joy he experienced having her in his life.

Raising her brow at his lack of response, Stacy's heart began to beat erratically as she took notice of the faraway look in his eyes. A short breath escaped her slightly parted lips at the realization that he had more than likely chosen the game over her. She couldn't believe her ears when he blurted out his reply.

"I choose you, bay. Ever since the first time I laid eyes on you I knew that you were the woman I was destined to be with. Contrary to the saying that men pick while women choose, that day in the park I did both." Dre dropped the one clause that had to be understood before they could put everything behind them and start fresh. "There's one problem though."

"What is it?" she questioned. The smile she had worn only seconds before was now a blank mask.

"I have to make one last move before I call it quits, ma. I have no choice. I gave my word, baby, therefore I must see it through." He reached upward to cup her chin. "Give me one more week, and I promise you that this life will be no more than a past memory. Can you do that for me, ma? Huh?" he asked in a syrupy tone.

"Don't you see that this is real, Dre?" she asked and then raised her voice. "We could have died last night."

Dre paused. "It's gonna all be over soon. One week."

"You can be dead today, judging from last night."

"I got a lot of living to do, Stacy. Living with you." He kissed her, and then stared into her eyes.

She decided she wanted nothing more than to be with him. Although she would have rather he made a clean break right now, Stacy concluded that if only one week stood between them living a trouble-free existence, then one more week was worth it. "Okay, you've got a deal. But please be careful. I'm begging you."


Destiny peeped over her shoulder at the sleeping form snoring lightly behind her. She gently removed the arm draped over her waist and slowly slid from beneath the covers. She reached for her short silk robe as she exited the bed. Destiny covered her nakedness, looking over her shoulder to make sure Nut hadn't roused from his slumber as she crept from the room and descended the long spiral stairs.

After the night's events and the argument with Naiza that followed, to Destiny's horror, Nut coming to her aid instead of her girl's had opened a can of worms that she would have rather kept sealed. Thanks to his reckless bravado, along with his nonchalant attitude, once the accusations were thrown, it immediately became obvious that something foul had been going on between the two of them. At a loss for any explanation at that point, Destiny avoided any further confrontation, choosing instead to let Naiza think whatever she liked.

Now it was the next morning, and Destiny couldn't figure out how Nut had ended up in her bed, much less let the cat out of the bag that they shared more of a connection than them both being a part of Naiza's life. She figured that after Nut's award winning performance last night, however long it took her girl to come around, it would be worth it. Only until she did come around, Nut would continue to fulfill her sexual purposes, if nothing more.

Destiny grabbed the phone and quickly disregarded

all thoughts of Naiza and Nut. She concentrated on Omar and the news of his encounter with Dre once she left. Although Nut had proved to be a sweet distraction throughout the night, she had been dying to find out what had transpired in her absence. Absolutely. Upon hearing the voice on the other end, she quickly got her emotions.

"Mmm hmm," Omar growled in a sleepy voice. "Wh . . . what time is it, Destiny?"

"It's 11:40 a.m." Though she still spoke in a jovial manner, Destiny immediately ascertained by Omar's tone of voice that he was in a foul mood.

"Okay, it's 11:40. So you mind telling me what the hell you want so I can get back to sleep."

"I didn't mean to wake you up, bay. I was only calling because I knew what was supposed to go down last night and I was worried about you."

"Yeah, sure you were," he replied sarcastically. "All right. Look, I'm tired, and as far as I'm concerned it's too early for this cat and mouse shit. So now that we've gotten all the pleasantries out the way, ask what you need to ask so I can go back to sleep."

"All right, all right," Destiny retorted in a stink voice. "What happened after I left? Please tell me you got that nigga, Dre."

"Well, first of all, niggas lit that shit up when you rolled out . . ."

Hearing those words instantly brought a smile to Destiny's face.

"But I swear that young nigga has got to be the luckiest motherfucker in Detroit. He's still alive, and although their crew took a serious loss, I'm starting to believe that dude has nine lives or something." Omar switched gears, asking, "What's the deal with you and him anyway? It's beginning to seem like you have a personal interest in him."

Destiny let out a fake laugh, and then replied, "There's nothing between us. You know how it is . . . I just want him out of the way like you do," she lied.

"Yeah, I'm sure you do, ma . . . I'm sure you do."

She could tell he was suspicious of her motives. She hoped he didn't discover the true nature of her relationship with Dre.

Dre was in a zone. He inhaled a perfectly wrapped blunt of Ganz as the loud music reverberated through the four 15-inch woofers of his newly purchased Nissan 350Z. He rode through the Eastside streets in disguise. Though he saw numerous individuals in his clique as he cruised through, due to the brand new whip and dark tints that covered the windows, no one saw him. Being seen was the last thing Dre was trying to do. For the first time in a long time, the only thing he wanted was the chance to be alone and put his thoughts in perspective.

Though he had promised Stacy that he would leave the game behind and he meant to fulfill that obligation as he toured the many streets and spots controlled by The Syndicate, a portion of his heart broke at the realization that everything he had worked hard to create would soon be out of his grasp. With that thought in mind, Dre began to wrack his brain, thinking of who would inherit his position when he no longer held it. He broke his deep contemplation at the sight of a group of young boys standing in front of one of his dope spots with Mac-90s draped over their shoulders.

Dre abruptly came to the conclusion that only one person personified the strength, intelligence, and respect needed to fill his shoes. There was no better candidate than Billy, thus, he was left with no other option than to install his cousin as his successor.

His two-way pager vibrated on his hip. Dre reached for the small box and read the message. The transmission was from Torres. He lowered the music and grabbed his burnout cell phone from the console between the seats.

"Dre, how are you, my friend?" Torres questioned, knowing that no one else could be calling on their private line.

"I can't complain," Dre lied, keeping his adverse thoughts hidden.

"Okay, I know this isn't a personal call, so what can I do for you, my friend?"

Allowing his eyes to linger on the burned out lots as he passed on his way through the Eastside, Dre's heart suddenly became heavy. He realized that although what he gazed at wasn't much of a vision to many, these streets represented his rise to a position that he never realized was attainable.

"Dre, what's wrong?" Torres' tone had switched from one of excitement to concern.

"Ummm . . . I'm sorry. I kind of got lost in thought. But to be perfectly honest with you, there is something of importance that I need to share with you."

"Speak freely then, my friend. There is nothing we can't discuss."

Exhaling, Dre said, "I'm out after this last move, Torres. As much as I want to stay, I know that doing so will only bring about my downfall."

"Is that so?" Torres asked, hearing the sadness in Dre's voice. "Well, when did you make this decision, and is there anything I can do to change your mind?"

Dre knew his decision would affect Torres, however, he hadn't planned for his friend to sound as stunned as he now was. "Yep, this is it. And although I appreciate your concern, my mind is made up."

"Well, if I can't stop you from leaving my family, then what can I do for you?" He let out a half-hearted laugh, but he spoke in a voice that resounded with sincerity. "I'm going to miss having you with me. And if you ever need my help in any way, don't hesitate to give me a call."

"I won't hesitate. I promise. Now, I've got a few ideas that I want to throw your way so that things can continue to roll smoothly even after I make my exit . . ."

"Oh, you do, huh? I should have known that you would have an exit plan prepared and ready for execution, my friend."

"Okay, first and foremost I'm going to elevate my cousin, Billy, into my position. Believe me when I tell you, he can more than handle the job. Therefore, when he comes to bring the money for the next shipment, the two of you can get properly acquainted."

"Billy," Torres said, pausing. "Oh yeah, he's the quiet one who came along the last two times with the couriers. Sure, I recall him well. In fact, I actually liked his style. However, if I recall correctly, his quietness had an eerie presence attached to it."

"That's him, and don't let his quiet nature fool you for one minute. Billy will explode if the situation calls for it. Now that that's out the way, when will you be ready for my people to arrive?"

"I don't know, Dre."

"He's family. What's not to know?"

"Your father was family I knew and worked with. It's why I reached out to you. People usually come to me. But I don't know about this Billy."

"So you're questioning my judgment?"

"No. Protecting my interests."

Dre paused, disgusted that Torres was giving him a hard time.

"If you don't understand that, maybe you should think it over and get back at me about this last shipment," Torres said.

"Whatever." Dre hung up, but soon realized he had dismissed Torres pretty abruptly and disrespectfully. But as far as he was concerned, Torres had disrespected him. Dre wasn't sure what would happen as a result of their debate. But he was prepared to handle anything that came his way.


The following day, Dre called Torres back and smoothed things over. He humbled himself and gave Torres a final proposition for some drugs.

"Let's see," Torres said, thinking out loud. "Send your people as usual out here in another two days. By your order being so big, it will take precedent over the other shipments that were headed down South and up the East Coast. Therefore, in another forty-eight hours, three tractor-trailers containing tons of my best smoke, 750 keys of Fishscale, 150 keys of dope, and 400,000 ecstasy pills will be packed and headed your way."

"Whew!" Dre whistled at the amount of product Torres had quoted. Nevertheless, for the $11.6 million he would be sending as soon as he got word the convoy was Detroit bound, he had no qualms about capitalizing on his investment. But he raised a brow at the mention of 400,000 X-pills. "Coke, dope, and weed is good. Eleven-point-six-million for you for the shipment. But I didn't place an order for any pills."

"I'm aware of that," Torres replied. "The pills are a gift. They're the next big thing, and believe me when I tell you, you don't want to miss the Ecstasy explosion that is brewing. This shipment will make The Syndicate Detroit's premiere distributor of pills within the next six months."

"That's cool then," Dre said. Only with his upcoming retirement, he was aware that he would never witness their growth in the Ecstasy market, or any other market for that matter once he had profited from this last shipment. "The money will be sent when you call to alert me to the convoy's exit, so I'll speak with you then."

"Okay, I'll await our conversation. And Dre . . . I want you to know that you have my blessing for your retirement. Whether you're aware of it or not, you're the son that I never had . . . Adios, mi compadre."

Hearing the phone go dead, the irony of Torres' words filled Dre's subconscious. Throughout their short relationship, Dre had never suspected that the wealthy Mexican had become so fond of him. The reality of the situation was, although it had gone unsaid, Dre shared a fondness for Torres that made it hard to sever their relationship as well. However, what was done could not be changed. The wheels of retirement had been set in motion.

"Yes! We got him now!" Agent Peyton yelled victoriously. He quickly reverted back to his prior all-business demeanor after taking notice of the looks directed at him from the other two agents in the car. Peyton cleared his throat as he averted his gaze away from his underlings. "Drop back and let the other car take over from here," he snapped. Eyeing the driver intently, he added, "The only direction we need to be going in at the moment is headquarters. Agent Perez needs to hear this phone conversation ASAP."

He made himself comfortable in the backseat of the Crown Victoria as it careened through the city streets. Peyton had one thought on his mind, and it intensified his smile. Although drug dealers thought they were the smartest people on earth, to him and other members of the law enforcement community, they were stupid. Staring toward the front seat and the recording apparatus with a foot long padded microphone, he wondered what made criminals think that any conversation they had could be safe from monitoring. With the invention of machines such as the one in his view, dials could be set that made it possible for agents to filter out any other noise with the exception of the conversation they wanted to hear. While Peyton couldn't get what was being said on the other end of the phone, he got everything Dre said. Him ordering an assortment of drugs was enough to bury Dre on a conspiracy charge. The corner office and secretary Peyton had spent years dreaming about suddenly seemed attainable thanks to Dre's recklessness.

*Chapter 21*

Dre peered down at his Cartier watch, pausing to take notice of the fact that once again Nut had been a no show. He set his sights back upon Billy, Skeet, and Rossi, concluding that whatever kept Nut from making their meeting was undoubtedly more important to him than business. "Rossi, you already know the drill," Dre said. "I need you to leave immediately. So I take it that you can have your crew picked and ready to go in the next few hours?"

"No doubt. My people are already on standby," Rossi indicated with a nonchalant wave of his hand. "This shit is easy, pimp. We'll be in and out of Texas with the quickness."

"Yeah, I have no doubt that you have your end covered, but this will be our largest load ever, so supply each of your men with the heaviest artillery we've got. We can't afford to tolerate any mistakes," Dre advised, turning toward Skeet.

"Got you."

Dre said, "Although I've never thought to bring you into this phase of the business due to you running your own family on the Westside, right about now you're about the only other nigga besides Rossi and Billy, who I can really trust."

Skeet said, "Holler at me. You already know I got you."

Dre sighed, knowing Nut was supposed to be handling the task that he was now forced to entrust Skeet with. Dre felt a wave of disappointment wash over him as he began to explain to Skeet what was on his mind. "Man, I need you to go with Billy when he carries the dough to Texas. Nut was supposed to be going, but as you each can see, the nigga is too engrossed in whatever the fuck he is doing to join us." Dre frowned. "There's really nothing to it. The two of you will meet my connect's people at a hotel directly across from the airport. Once they count the cheddar, you can hop back on the plane and come home."

"Shit, I ain't got no problem with that. In fact, I may just decide to spend me a few days out there soaking up the sun," Skeet said.

"I appreciate that, player. But on the real, I already knew that I could count on you." Skeet shook his head in agreement. Then his attention was drawn to his two-way pager and the message that quickly seemed to peak his interest.

Dre stretched his arms over his head and yawned. He did this more so to indicate that the meeting was over than to impress the belief upon his associates that he was tired. Now that the organization's business was taken care of, it was time that he and Billy held a separate conference.

\* \* \*

The lips that held him within their grasp were truly unbelievable and Nut heard the loud, wet sucking sounds as he closed his eyes as tight as possible and shot his load down her throat. Trembling under the pressure of his climax, he groaned, frantically pushing her head away. He retreated up the bed in his haste to escape the tongue that lapped greedily at his private parts.

"Tha—that's enough," Nut whimpered breathlessly. "I can't take it anymore, Destiny." Feeling his dick slip from her mouth as he tried to bring his breathing pattern back to normal, he blinked his eyes repeatedly in an attempt to clear his hazy vision. With sweat pouring from his body, Nut couldn't believe that she had been able to extract another load from his loins after the endless series of climaxes they had shared in the last two days. He had met the one woman who surpassed him in the sexual arena. Nut had no qualms admitting Destiny was a tigress he had neither the strength nor endurance to tame.

Destiny rose up from between his outstretched legs. She used the back of her hand to wipe the sweat from her brow and forehead. A mischievous grin was pasted on her face as she leaned toward the nightstand, retrieved the glass resting on the surface and spit the remainder of the ice she had in her mouth inside it. She closed her eyes. Destiny inwardly smiled, knowing that she had broken her prey down completely. However, even though she was happy that her scheme had been successful, in the back of her mind she couldn't help feeling disgust. It honestly repelled her that the majority of males were so weak that they lost all sense of reality when they were treated to a steady dose of good loving. And good loving was one thing that Destiny was aware that she possessed in abundance. Nevertheless, it angered her that the one man she had found who wasn't weak to the flesh, or anything else for that matter, couldn't care less about her.

"I see this dick got you daydreaming and some more shit," Nut foolishly stated, oblivious to the sour look she gave him.

He kneaded the soft flesh of her ass, adding, "You give it to a nigga so good that I'll slaughter a motherfucker if you try to give my shit away."

*Yeah right!* Destiny thought. She smiled at his ignorant belief that he possibly had any ownership over her or any of her body parts. "Get a hold of yourself, bitch ass nigga," was what she would have said in response to his stupid statement had she not needed him. But she did. So Destiny cuddled up closer to him and replied, "You don't hardly have to worry about me giving this pussy to anyone else, but you. Just keep putting it on me the way you do and this shit will always belong to you."

"Yeah, that's what I thought," Nut retorted arrogantly, running his tongue inside her ear for a moment.

She subtly leaned her head backward disengaging herself from Nut's grasp. She spoke in a whining voice, "Hold up, boo . . . don't do that. You know that's my spot, and before we get started again we need to talk."

"All right, all right. What up doe, ma?"

"I was thinking that maybe you might want to do your own thing out there instead of being in Dre's shadow."

Nut was silent, staring at her.

Observing the sudden look of indecision on his face, she began to gently massage his penis. "From what I hear . . . you're the muscle out there that keeps niggas in line."

"True that," he affirmed with a smirk.

"And I'm sure that if you decided to run the show, those same niggas would follow in whatever direction you chose to lead them in."

"Nah." Nut chuckled, averting eye contact. "Dre's my dude, and we have an understanding that . . ."

She increased her grip and movements on his steadily hardening member. Destiny raised her voice a decibel. "Understanding or not, no one can feed you like you can feed yourself. It's your time to make your mark in the city, and if you're as smart and as strong as I think you are, you will take control of the situation while it's yours for the taking."

"So that's what you really think, huh, ma?"

"It's not what I think, it's what I know. I believe in you." She slid her tongue in his mouth for a moment, and then pecked his lips.

"So you ride for your man, huh?"

Destiny nodded. Seeing that Nut no longer attempted to argue her point, she stared directly into his eyes and caressed his dick. "If you're going to be my man, I won't accept anything less."

"Is that a fact?" He palmed her ass.

"True story," Destiny responded. "I have a connect that will provide any and everything you'll need to support a team of your own. And I trust and believe that you can make this shit a success. Believe me when I tell you." She kissed him. "So what do you say? Is it a go?" she asked, and then lowered her face and gently bit one of his pecs.

"You may be right."

She could tell he had never really taken the time to look at things in the light that Destiny had explained them. And she knew from conversations with Dre and Naiza that a lot of The Syndicate's success had been due to him. Even though he was being paid well, he could easily increase his own wealth and status to the legendary proportions that Dre was now experiencing. At least that's what Destiny wanted him to think.

"You can do it, baby," Destiny said.

"Yeah, I think that's a good idea after all," he said, pulling her on top of him. He gripped her hips. "You need to get in contact with your connect, and I'm going to set up a meeting with Dre as soon as possible to announce my departure."

"It's done," Destiny explained as she allowed his erect tip to slide back between the folds of her sore mound. She leaned back to grab his ankles, letting out a hoarse whimper as Nut penetrated her in one swift motion. She clinched her teeth and closed her eyes tightly to black out the discomfort she experienced with each of his deep, probing, strokes. Nonetheless, even with the pain that surged through her, she was excited at the prospect of coming out on top. Now she would have to trick Nut into telling her the location and time of their meeting.

Perez looked out into the group of agents seated around the room. He adjusted his tie and motioned toward the far wall, alerting his assistant to dim the lights. The low conversations taking place within the group instantly came to a halt as the projector came to life, lighting up the screen that covered the area behind him. He paused in order to allow everyone's attention to be directed toward him. Perez cleared his throat for emphasis and began to address the contingent of agents. "First and foremost, I'd like to thank each of you for taking the time out of your otherwise busy schedules to join me. I'm sure that you each had a million other things to do besides coming to this briefing. Thanks to your diligence and fearlessness, we're about to embark on one of the largest takedowns of any urban crime family in Detroit's history, and this man," he said, pointing his index finger directly between the eyes of Dre's image plastered upon the screen, "is our main goal. As you're all aware, ladies and gentlemen, he is the leader and undisputed 'shot caller,' as they say, of the feared Syndicate."

The room erupted with low murmurs that signaled Perez had grabbed their attention. The gravity of the case had set in. The reality that the agency was on the cusp of closing it was revealed.

"Now, I need everyone to pay the utmost attention because I only plan to go over this once," Perez said. "Through phone conversations that Agent Peyton and his team were able to catch through our electronic surveillance, we now know that this man"—he stabbed his finger back toward Dre's picture— "is in the process of smuggling a large amount of narcotics from another city. He's paying 11.6 million dollars, so that's a street value upwards of 100 million dollars."

The group of fifty or more agents seated around the room were seasoned professionals, but the amount of money that was quoted brought a low gasp from many. Perez was banking on the fact that they would be caught off guard by the vast number. In fact, he wanted the agents to be riled up when the time came for them to move. Because he recognized just how dangerous the Syndicate members were. The last thing he wanted was a bunch of dead agents on his hands.

"Additional surveillance reveals that the deal is taking place in Texas," Perez said.

"Must be a Mexican supplier," one of the agents interjected.

"That's what we think," Perez said. "So some of our agents have already been sent out to Texas to coordinate operations with our Dallas branch. All the train stations, bus stations, and airports in our suspected strike areas have already been placed under airtight surveillance. We have no doubt that the shipment will never make it back to the city." He pressed down on the remote and a new group of faces appeared on the screen. "These people are the top brass in their organization. Due to the numerous briefings and man hours you're each putting in throughout this investigation, you should already know who they are."

Pointing to the board, Perez placed a finger on each of their faces as he gave their alias names. "Here you have Nut, who happens to already be facing a murder case. This is Rossi. Right here you have Skeet, who also heads the Z8 clique on the Westside. And last but not least, this is Dre's cousin, Billy. The streets call him Billy Guns, and word has it that he obtained that name for obvious reasons. If by chance one of you happens to encounter him, don't hesitate to use deadly force because he most definitely will."

"Now, these will be our strike zones," Perez indicated, clicking the remote to change the frame on the screen. "Most of you are team leaders, so as I go through the locations, your particular target will be familiar to you." After clicking past an array of drug spots and fabulous homes, Perez paused at a shot of a large, gated estate. The outer view of the home was exquisite. However, the string of exotic cars that lined the circular driveway added a certain ghetto flair to the overall scene.

Turning to face his fellow agents, Perez stared around the room with an expressionless look. After scanning each face in attendance, he spoke slowly, "The picture you see before you is Dre's home in Bloomfield Hills. This, ladies and gentlemen is the prize. When we drop the net on his operations throughout the city, I will personally lead a team of agents through the gate to pay him a visit." These words brought a smile to his face, because Perez understood that within twenty-four hours his name would be synonymous with the many other legends in the law enforcement community that had made their mark before him. Therefore, with nothing or no one to stop him from obtaining his goal of catching the Syndicate with their pants down, Perez wondered where Dre was and whether he was prepared to spend the remainder of his life in prison.

"Cuz, niggas been ghost ever since they pulled that stunt in the Network," Billy said, cutting his eyes at Dre in the passenger seat. "I'm telling you, our people have been hunting the streets for any signs of them cats, and with the exception of a few stragglers here and there, they haven't been able to get any real retribution."

Dre's only reply was, "Oh yeah." Due to the thoughts that clouded his mind as he peered through the heavily tinted Dodge Viper window as they sped up the interstate, he was at a loss for any other response.

"Damn, nigga! What's with the short answers and shit? You good over there or what?"

"My bad, cuz. It's just that shit is crazy right now. But uhhh. Have our people make sure that all of the Syndicate members that were murdered have lavish funerals. I'm footing the bills, and I don't want none of them to get any short shit, you feel me?"

"Yeah, I feel you, and I'll handle it personally as soon as I return from Texas. But enough of talking about funerals and shit. What's really good? Something's on your mind, and I'd appreciate it if you would just go ahead and throw it out there instead of holding that shit. And don't say you're good either, 'cause I've known you all your life, so I know when you're perpin'."

"Nigga, I don't do no frontin' and you already know it," Dre retorted, cracking a fake smile. "But on the real, though, I do got something to tell you."

"Well, holla at me then," Billy countered.

"It's over, man. I'm out."

"It's over? You're out! Cuz, what the hell are you talking about?"

"You heard me, Billy. I'm out. I've had enough, and I finally realize I can't do this shit no more!"

"What!" Billy exclaimed in disbelief. "You can't be serious, cuz. Man, we got this city under siege. Yo, don't get soft on me now, Dre."

"I could never be soft, and you need to check yourself before you get reckless with your wordplay," Dre replied in a no nonsense tone, glaring angrily at Billy.

"I don't believe you're actually gonna walk away from

a dynasty." Breaking their tense stare and looking straight ahead, Billy chuckled, shaking his head in denial.

"Believe it," Dre emphasized, but he still had a hard time coming to terms with his own decision.

"I hear you."

"Hear me clear. It's over. I've done what I started out to do, and now I just want to enjoy my dough in peace." He observed the gloomy look on Billy's face. "However, being that the show must go on, I need you to step into my shoes."

Jerking his head in Dre's direction, Billy said, "Step into your shoes? Explain that for me!"

"You heard me. Unless you have a problem with it, when you return from Texas, I plan to turn over the Syndicate to you. No one else is capable of handling the responsibility but you." Dre glimpsed the sudden glimmer in Billy's eyes.

Dre had been thinking hard about his conversation with Torres over the following day. He decided to tell Billy about it.

"That's fucked up," Billy said after Dre revealed that essentially Torres didn't trust him.

"It shouldn't matter that he don't know you as well as I do. He should give me the benefit of the doubt based on our relationship."

"Just like he did with your pops."

"Exactly, he put me on based on who my pops was."

"I say we set up one more drop off, then rob the nigga blind."

"What?"

"You leaving the game and the nigga shittin' on me, so let's give him a reason to shit."

"Nah." Dre shook his head. "You're talking about beef with an international hustler."

"No, I'm talking about handling a motherfucker that don't give a fuck about us."

"I'm leaving the game. Don't bring me back in it." Dre raised the volume on the stereo and slouched further down into the leather bucket seat. In another twenty-four hours he would be free to enjoy life anywhere in the world with Stacy by his side. There would no longer be any fear of police, stickup men, or rival crews attempting to murder him at every available opportunity. In one more day he would go from being a well-known drug kingpin to a law-abiding citizen. But this could only become a reality if Billy respected Dre's wishes to leave Torres alone.

*Chapter 22*

It was finally going to be over, and Destiny was ecstatic as she moved through the house putting her thoughts in order. She would use Omar to handle the dirty work, allowing him to take the reins. But Destiny realized that in order for things to move like clockwork, she would have to plan the mission. Having contacted him as soon as Nut left, she was able to gauge the excitement Omar had fought to hide. She heard it in his voice with each question he had asked as she relayed the specifics of the scheduled meeting between Nut and Dre. It was only a matter of time before their reign was over.

"How were you able to obtain this information?" he had questioned with a deep stare, somewhat skeptical.

Amused at the recollection of the question even now, her only response had been, "I got it, and in the end that's all that really matters." She took the golden opportunity to conquer his mortal enemy on face value. Thus, with the impending ambush set to take place in just a few hours, Destiny found herself experiencing a form of anticipation like nothing else she ever endured.

Placing an extra pep in her step as she gathered her clothes, Destiny decided that regardless of how many times she had witnessed it, she would never understand how dudes could be so careless and dumb when it came to letting down their guard around beautiful women. She was the perfect example of the danger that lurked in the shadows, waiting to pounce on her unsuspecting enemies. And little did Nut know his failure to speak with Dre in privacy had cost them.

Destiny contemplated the deaths of her present lover, along with her lover from the past. She had no regrets. They would be dead soon, and then everything she'd had to suffer at their hands would be worthwhile.

"Ugh. Where you going?" Stacy moaned softly, stirring from the gentle kiss Dre had placed on her lips.

"I got to make a few runs, baby girl. But being that you seem to want to sleep the day away, you won't miss me anyway." Dre smiled, glancing down at his glimmering watch.

"Shut up, boy," she whined, pulling the thick comforter back up around her neck. "Don't forget we have reservations for dinner tonight, boo."

"I know. I won't forget," he promised, winking his eye and blowing her a kiss on his way out the door. "You just make sure you're ready."

Dre took the long circular stairs three at a time in a hurry to descend them. Though he would have rather spent the remainder of the day in bed with his boo, he was forced to tend to business.

He exited the house and sunk into the plush seat of Stacy's Mercedes. Nut's phone call entered his thoughts as he sped through the tall, iron gates of their estate. For some reason that he couldn't quite put his finger on, Nut sounded strained and unlike himself. It was as if he had been speaking to a stranger instead of his best friend, and Dre was somewhat baffled by the whole scenario. Nevertheless, he sounded adamant about meeting with him as soon as possible. Putting everything else aside, Dre figured that he would soon find out what was eating at his man. Dre lowered the volume on the stereo and phoned Rossi.

"Yo, what up?" Rossi answered.

"What's good? I'm just calling to make sure everything's cool on your end. You straight or what?"

"We're good. We just entered Ohio a minute ago, so sometime tonight the caravan will reach the D."

"Yeah, that's what's up then. Check it out, I got a few more moves to make, but when you arrive in the city hit me, all right?"

"I got you, nigga. I'm out."

Dre pushed the button to end their call. Rossi and his team were making good time on the highway, and Billy and Skeet were already in the friendly skies on their way to pay Torres. Everything was on point. Dre stared down at his watch. It was clear that the time had arrived to make his way to the meeting with Nut. He had a gut feeling that whatever Nut wanted to discuss wouldn't be to his liking. The fact that Nut hadn't been seen since he parted the club with Destiny had made Dre leery. Destiny was a declared enemy, and Nut seemed to have been siding with her. But those were thoughts Dre kept to himself.

*   *   *

Nut was caught up in his thoughts of grandeur as Ganz smoke engulfed the roomy GS 400 Lexus he sat in. Loud music resounded through the booming speakers. And although his life was already at a level that the average street nigga would kill to obtain, Nut's aspirations, thanks to the seed Destiny had planted in his mind, were soaring with the new position he would soon command.

Thanks to the strong weed, he no longer hesitated cutting all ties between himself and the Syndicate. The weight of the pistols that sat in holsters beneath his coat added an extra dose of power to the strength of will he had already built up in his mind. He gazed through the car window, seeing the sparse traffic through weed induced slits. Nut felt a sense of anticipation come over him. He took another toke from the blunt and peered at his Jacob & Company watch, wondering what could be keeping Dre. He became irritated that Dre was late, and he felt tired due to the strong weed. He reclined his seat and resigned himself to thoughts of controlling Detroit. With Destiny's connect behind him, Nut had no doubt the city would be at his mercy. Nut couldn't believe it took Destiny to make him aware of something he should have recognized long ago. However, the saying "better late than never" came to mind, making it clear that the decision he'd made was the right one.

"That's him over there. Sitting in the Lexus," Destiny announced, feeling a surge of excitement at his impending demise.

"So that's the deadly Nut, huh?" Omar questioned, chuckling at the view before him. "The nigga doesn't look so deadly to me."

Joining in on the laughter, Rico spoke into the walkie talkie. "Yo, I want the rest of you niggas to stay put. Me and Joe-Joe gonna handle this clown."

"Make it quick, and I don't want no mistakes. You hear me?" Omar spat in a no nonsense manner.

"Yeah, we got this nigga!" Rico exclaimed, before turning to Joe-Joe, who was busy placing an extended clip inside the Mac-90, hanging by a strap around his neck. "Let's do this shit, Joe-Joe," were the only words needed to set the murderous Joe-Joe in motion.

Destiny watched closely as the two assassins exited the truck and made their way across the street in the direction of the Lexus. Destiny shivered with excitement as she leaned forward in her seat to get a better view. In seconds, the first stage of her plan would become a reality. Once Nut ceased to exist, Dre's death would soon follow, and that more than anything was what Destiny wanted.

Peyton's attention was instantly drawn to the transmission he heard loud and clearly through the radio inside his car. "Our couriers have arrived. Repeat . . . the targets are exiting the plane. Everyone take up your position. It's time to rock."

Donning his DEA windbreaker and reaching for the MP-5 that sat fully loaded in the seat, Peyton fell in line behind the multitude of other agents that scurried in different directions to await the suspects. He received information from their Detroit office that they would more than likely be armed and dangerous. Peyton and the other agents who had flown in from Detroit and their Texas cohorts were prepared to use deadly force to apprehend them. He took up his position directly in front of the airport exit. Peyton swallowed the saliva that had pooled in his mouth, thinking that this was the moment he had awaited. He tightened his sweaty grip on the semi-automatic assault weapon. Though he was nervous, a part of him hoped the suspects would resist capture. He was looking for an excuse to exact a type of justice that exceeded the boundaries of the law.

"Let's grab those trunks and get the hell out of here," Skeet said, holding up his baggage claim slip to emphasize his point.

"Yeah, you must have read my mind, man. I'm ready to blow this joint too." Billy rummaged through the pockets of his Armani suit in search of his baggage claim slip. He matched Skeet's steps as he observed the many stares directed at them through his platinum Cartier frames. Though he was used to drawing attention wherever he went, for some reason the scrutiny they drew brought about a sense of paranoia.

"Damn!" Skeet grunted, hefting one of the large Louis Vuitton trunks on the revolving belt. He placed it upright on its wheels, released a tired breath and patiently waited until Billy retrieved the second trunk.

Billy shook his head at the overwhelming weight of the trunk. He sat down. "Let's go, pimp."

Rossi leaned forward in the seat looking upward, catching sight of the helicopter that seemed to have been in view ever since they left Torres' ranch. Though he wasn't prone to being delusional, Rossi couldn't shake the feeling that it was, in fact, the same helicopter. But he kept his thought to himself.

"Yo, what the hell you looking at?" Gus, the well-paid driver of the truck asked.

"What!" Rossi snapped.

"I asked you what the hell were you looking at? Shit, from the way you were staring, I figured you were either trying to spot a U.F.O. or become a professional bird watcher," Gus teased.

"Ha, ha, ha. That was real funny." Rossi flashed a phony smile. "Shut your fat, funky ass up and just drive the motherfucking truck, nigga." His abrupt remark quickly wiped the smile from Gus' face, bringing a round of laughter from two Syndicate soldiers who sat in the rear cabin with AR-15's draped across their laps.

"Yeah, drive the motherfucking truck, ho ass nigga!" one of the soldiers repeated loudly, attempting to catch his breath as another fit of laughter attacked him.

Rossi shook his head. He slightly leaned forward to check the sky once more. He couldn't shake the feeling that although the helicopter was no longer in sight, somewhere out there they were being watched.

"Can't wait to get back to the city," one of the soldiers said.

Rossi ignored him, still thinking of the possibility that they were being followed. He clutched the Calico-9 that sat on his lap. The enormity of the situation became clear for him. With the amount of narcotics they carried in each truck, there was no way that he or any of his cohorts would ever see the light of day again if they were caught. As the thought of their penalty festered in his mind, Rossi was determined that nothing short of death would ever stand between him and his freedom.

* * *

It was almost dusk as Agent Perez and a large contingent of agents surrounded the large hillside estate. He patiently awaited the cover of darkness, spying through the binoculars, searching for any visible movement inside the mansion. Though the city streets were abuzz with activity, due to the many simultaneous busts and seizures his army of DEA agents were orchestrating at that very moment, this was the target his personal time, energy, and vast resources had been directed at. He had become obsessed with Dre. There was even a hint of jealousy based on Dre being a teenager with the ability to regulate a multimillion-dollar operation that had been undetected by the agency until recently.

He broke his command to maintain radio silence at all costs, speaking in a firm, precise manner into the thin state of the art mouthpiece that ran from his ear to within an inch of his mouth. "All tactical team… this is Special Agent Perez. It is now seventeen-hundred forty-seven minutes. Set your watches by mine. At seventeen-fifty we will begin our insertion. Use the utmost caution. I repeat . . . use the utmost caution, because there is a great chance that we will encounter resistance." Perez's adrenaline instantly increased at the thought of what may or may not await them inside the house. Concluding his pep speech, he added, "I'll see you all on the other side."

He allowed his voice to trail off, and then his eyes were suddenly glued to his watch as each ticking second seemed to ring on in the air. The moment he had been waiting for was here, and as he rose from his crouched position and began to run toward the house in what to him seemed like slow motion, Perez could already savor the glory of victory.

# Chapter 23

"Shit!" Nut cursed, jumping up in his haste to wipe the burning ashes from his custom-made linen pants. He swept the ashes on his lap onto the floorboard of the Lexus, and then glared at the meticulously rolled blunt. His slacks were ruined, but he took another long draw on the weed. Exhaling a cloud of pungent smoke, he coughed. "Man, where the fuck you at?" he questioned Dre's late arrival.

Two male figures stepped from the curb, wearing long leather trench coats. Nut was so high and caught up in his thoughts of Dre and cutting ties with the Syndicate that he failed to take immediate notice of their suspicious demeanor. They whirled toward the driver's window and flipped back the flaps of their coats, revealing deadly assault rifles.

Nut was caught completely off guard, staring fearlessly into the faces of his assassins. Right at the moment when he was prepared to heighten his life to the greatest elevation he could fathom, he would be forced to pay the price for his murderous past. "Life's a bitch . . . then you die . . . that's why I get high . . . 'cause you never know when you're gonna go . . . " were the words he sang as his run came to a violent end.

Billy and Skeet exchanged light conversation as they made their way toward the airport exit. Billy was unable to control the fleeting glances he gave the crowd around him as they passed. Unlike Skeet, Billy felt an uneasy churning in the pit of his stomach. Then the tiny hairs on the nape of his neck suddenly stood at attention. He stopped and stared around the terminal in a slow sweeping motion.

Stopping a few steps ahead of Billy, Skeet asked, "What? What you see, dog?" He scanned the crowd in an attempt to figure out what had garnered his man's attention. Everything seemed normal.

"I don't . . . Uh, fuck it!" Billy stated, deciding that it was useless to involve Skeet in his paranoid delusions. He shook his head at the questioning look Skeet tossed him and continued on his desired path.

"Don't start buggin' out on me," Skeet said.

"Nah, it ain't like that."

Skeet paused to have one last look around. He exhaled, knowing something had gotten under Billy's skin to make him act so peculiar. It had to be, because he knew how Billy normally moved. With that thought in mind, he suddenly found himself more alert as he followed closely behind Billy.

They reached the door and headed out into the simmering heat. Billy noticed the suspicious stares from the numerous stone-faced men who were dispersed around the exit and in cars lining the sidewalk. The dark shades they wore along with the dark jackets with the DEA insignia etched into them left no doubt as to their identity. However, if their outfits hadn't distinguished them properly, the weapons they held did. They were holding everything from handguns to MP-5s and assault rifles.

Someone to his left yelled, "DEA. Get on the ground and keep your hands where I can see them!"

Billy instinctively removed his Glock from his waistband with lightning speed. He dropped to one knee and fired his weapon into the face of the sneering agent who stood to his left.

The agent dropped instantly by a DEA Suburban.

Skeet grabbed his gun a fraction of a second slower than Billy. His hand had been forced to go for his weapon had he wanted to or not. Once shots were fired, he knew there would be no stopping until death became him. As he fought to raise his weapon in time to defend himself, he had no real expectations that they would make it out of this showdown in one piece. Had he hoped for a miracle of that sort. But watching the agent's head explode from the force of Billy's bullets quickly dissolved that wish. He locked eyes with the lifeless gaze of the agent as he slowly slumped to the pavement with a loud thump. Skeet saw Billy turn his weapon on the mass of officers in front of him.

Billy squeezed off a shot into the crowd of officers who kneeled behind parked cars. Only the protection that their steel shields provided saved them from the hot lead. But the unwavering barrage of slugs that the agents returned left Billy and Skeet torn, disfigured, and utterly unrecognizable in pools of their own blood.

\* \* \*

Rossi, Gus, and the two soldiers in the truck with them were engrossed in conversation, making the best of an otherwise long and boring trip. They passed blunts as they laughed and joked in a joyous mood. They had no reason to feel any other emotion besides happiness, being that everyone in their organization was eating good. The enormous loads that were packed in each of the trucks were proof that their feast would grow even larger when they made it back home.

"Yo, two pulls and pass, nigga!"

"Man, we got more than enough Ganz for everybody," Rossi barked as he exhaled, staring over his shoulder at one of his loud-mouthed soldiers who sported a pair of chinky, bloodshot eyes.

"Man, chill with that shit. Damn, a nigga got this joint," the young soldier retorted, disregarding Rossi's command and taking another long draw off the blunt.

Rossi loved the fact that each of his young soldiers had the heart of lions. He ice grilled him to keep from smiling as he prepared to lay down a soft press game on the lil' nigga just to test his gangster. "Nigga, I ain't passing no fucking blunt to no lil' nigga with a big mouth. You heard me, mother—"

"Yo, Rossi . . . we got company!" Gus barked in a fearful voice, instantly causing Rossi to jerk his head back to the front of the truck and cut short any words he had planned to say.

"Oh shit!" Rossi said, stunned at the sight of the roadblock in the distance. He fumbled with the Calico-9 in his lap. "You niggas know what it is, so be prepared to set it," Rossi whispered. Turning to face Gus, Rossi saw nothing but fear in the old junkie's expression. "Listen closely, because I don't plan to repeat myself again.

Don't even think about stopping this truck! If you do, you die. Now do I make myself clear?"

Unable to speak for fear of not being able to form his words properly, Gus held Rossi with a wide-eyed stare and responded by shaking his head up and down in an erratic fashion. He began to shift gears, instantly causing the eighteen wheeler to leap forward.

The truck picked up speed. Rossi heard clips being loaded into weapons behind him as he in turn raised his own weapon in preparation for the battle that would soon ensue. Staring at the roadblock up ahead, they were only seconds away from meeting the deadliest challenge that had ever been laid before them. And even though Rossi was prepared to meet it head on, their chances for victory were slim. It was a harsh reality of the game that he always knew existed, but he hoped never to confront.

They approached the roadblock at top speed. Rossi braced himself for the impact that would come at any moment. He watched as law enforcement in FBI, DEA, and State Police outfits crouched behind their cars with weapons drawn. He whispered a short verse from a prayer he recalled hearing as a child. Rossi reared back and kicked several times with all his might, knocking the windshield out enough to fit his gun through it. He raised his assault weapon into firing position. Rossi had no fear as he pressed down on the trigger and released a torrent of fire. This immediately ignited the wrath of the fifty or more agents and State Police who opened fire, turning the suddenly out of control truck into a tumbling mass of steel and dead bodies as the truck flipped over.

\* \* \*

Dre pulled to the side of the street in order to allow the many police cars and a lone ambulance to pass. He gave the sirens and flashing lights time to make headway before continuing. He was accustomed to witnessing the scene that had just unfolded before him. But as he trailed the flashing lights off in the distance Dre found it odd that they seemed to be headed in the same direction he was going.

Dre reached for the phone to call and make sure everything was good on Nut's end. Just as his hand connected with the electronic device, the phone began to vibrate in his palm. "Hello," Dre stated, agitated by the sudden interference.

"Where you at, boo?" Stacy asked.

Dre exhaled as his girlfriend's voice instantly brought a calming change to his uneasy demeanor.

"I miss you, so you need to come home," she whined in a seductive tone, making him forget any other thoughts he had prior to her call.

"Is that so?" Dre questioned, grinning.

"Yup, I'm lonely, boo," she replied. "I was thinking that maybe if you hurried home I could give you a special treat before we go out this evening."

"Umm . . . now that is definitely a tempting reason to rush home," Dre stated, hoping the special treat she spoke of was a reenactment of last night's festivities.

"So hurry up, boo."

"Well, how about I—" He stopped short upon noticing the hostile glares reflecting on the faces of the men who pulled up beside him in a Monte Carlo.

"How about you what?" Stacy asked.

He returned the treacherous stares of the goon as he reached for the gun that rested in his waistband. Dre's mind was working in overtime. He tried to place the faces that held him in their unwavering gaze. He heard Stacy calling out to him, but he ignored her. The recognition he had searched for suddenly arrived. He remembered the new arrivals were affiliated with the Dexter Ave Dogs. And the weapons that slowly appeared over the door frame instantly set off alarm signals. He punched down on the accelerator in his haste to put some distance between himself and his enemies.

Shots from the speeding goons began sounding, whizzing past Dre's car. The men were regaining close proximity in the chase.

Dre ducked down as he whipped the Benz through traffic. He felt the bullets that crashed through the back window whiz past his head and exit through the windshield. Escaping death was one of the worse feelings he had ever experienced.

"Dre!" Stacy screamed, half-hysterical. "Dre. Talk to me, baby! What's going on?" she yelled with tears evident by her voice.

"Boo, please calm down!"

"I can't."

Though he tried to downplay the danger he faced, his nervous cracking voice defined the panic racing through his body as he pushed the Benz to top speeds.

"Please tell me what's happening," Stacy pleaded, crying loudly. "I hear gunshots. I hear your motor speeding. What's going on?" she asked as the sounds of the nonstop gunfire echoed.

Dre looked over his shoulder to gauge their distance. "They're on my ass and I can't seem to shake them, baby!"

"Who's on your ass? Baby, please make it home to me safely," Stacy frantically begged in a hoarse, cracked voice.

Dre tried with all his might to find the correct response to appease her. But the reality of the situation was it didn't look like he would be making it home. The bullet that ripped through his back at that moment caused him to lose control of the Benz. It was proof that his intuition may just have been on point. He slammed into a series of parked cars, smashing his head into the steering wheel as the Mercedes flipped on its side. Dre dropped the phone and immediately lost consciousness due to the impact of the crash. Not only was he unable to respond to Stacy's feverish questioning, he never heard the high-pitched screams or the loud shouted commands of the DEA agents as they stormed into his home, catching Stacy in an already vulnerable position.

Dre wasn't sure how long he had remained unconscious. His eyes slowly began to flutter open. The scene he observed upon regaining focus was far from what he recalled before blacking out. He sat in an abandoned building littered with glass and various other debris. His arms and hands and legs were tied to a chair. The pain that surged through his body and the fact that he was trapped felt recent. He had an eerie feeling that he had been there not long after the car crash. Angry voices and heavy footsteps approached him from behind.

Wincing in pain, Dre tried to wiggle free. The voices and footsteps kept getting closer. He wriggled his body, trying to free himself to no avail. Finding the task useless, Dre took a deep breath, closed his eyes and lay in wait of the inevitable. He heard familiar voices once the footsteps came to a halt as the figures walked from behind him to face him. He stared into the cold eyes that held him with a look of contempt. He knew who he was up against, and he knew his chance of surviving were almost none.

"Come on, let's do this nigga and get the fuck out of here!" Rico exclaimed in a matter of fact tone, pointing his assault rifle inches from Dre's face.

Rico stared from Dre's helpless form to Omar, who stood beside him. Rico glanced nervously around them, wondering what the hell they were all waiting on. He cut his eyes at Joe-Joe, who stood behind Dre in a world of his own as he too pointed his assault rifle at Dre's back with a sort of childish excitement.

"Hold up!" Omar commanded. "Go get Destiny."

"Fucking bitch!" Dre mumbled, shaking his head. Destiny had been the last person on his mind. But it was obvious that she had sent them. After raising him up, she was on a mission to tear him down. He wondered if there was truth in the rumors that she had also set his father up.

Joe-Joe walked in with Destiny, who was smiling as if she had hit the lottery for the second time in a week. Her heart was beating out of her chest as she lowered her mouth to Dre's ear and whispered, "Look at you now. You're not such a big man anymore . . . Are you?" Laughing, she added, "I just want you to know that I did this to you. Yeah, this shit is *my* work. And just so you know, before you take your last breath—*I* ruined your father the same way I'm about to do your punk ass."

"Fuck you, bitch!" Dre growled.

Omar watched Destiny carefully.

"Nope . . . you won't be fucking me ever again." Destiny giggled, waving her finger at him in a mocking fashion. "I'm sorry, boo, but you won't be fucking any-one anymore," she stated, turning to walk away without even taking another look in his direction. "Murder that ho ass nigga!" she tossed out the words over her shoulder.

"Come here, Destiny." Omar put his hand on her shoulder when she stepped over to him. He turned and screamed out, "Naiza!"

"Huh?" Destiny's eyes lit up. "What's she doing here?" Destiny asked as Naiza stepped through a door and walked toward Omar before sliding a mouthful of tongue inside his mouth.

"Trifling bitch!" Destiny blurted.

"No, you are," Omar said as he pulled out his Desert Eagle and jammed it in Destiny's mouth, then cuffed the back of her head with his other hand. "You fuck your best friend's man. You fuck my enemy, then fuck him over like you did his father." He turned to Dre, and then back to her. "Now it's time to join him." He fired a single .50-caliber slug that tore out the back of Destiny's head, dropping her lifeless body on Dre.

Dre was in shock. He could feel the warm blood and bits of brain on his face and neck along with the limp remainder of Destiny's body on his lap. Dre spat a piece of bloody tissue from his mouth and looked into the faces of his tormentors. He was finally on the other side of the gun, unlike the many times he had partici-pated in the destruction of people through bullets and barrels. Dre's thoughts began to drift back through time at the moment his assassins pressed their triggers.

*"I'm so proud of you for graduating in the midst of all you must deal with on a daily basis in this poverty stricken neighborhood, John Jr. Ford, Chrysler, or General Motors will be honored to give you a job.*

*However, if you decide to go to college instead, I'll find a way to scrounge up the money."*

*"Hello, I'm Destiny. And unless I'm mistaken, either my mind is playing tricks on me or you're John's son."*

*"I've got to go, but these are all my numbers. If you need anything, give me a call."*

*"Instead of the four-and-a-half ounces you asked for, I'm going to toss you nine of them things. Bring me $3,500 for the quarter key and we'll work from there."*

*"Come on, man. We don't have to get crazy over something as petty as a block. I'll retire. On my word, you can have the block, player."*

*"Please, don't do this. My woman and children are inside. I don't want to die in front of my daughters."*

*"Congratulations, player. After the move you pulled tonight, it's official. The block is yours now, so run it like you own it. "*

*"We want to thank you all for coming out to show us love tonight as we celebrate that nigga, Dre, from The Syndicate's birthday. "*

*"Hi, Dre, I'm Stacy."*

*"Detroit is where I rest. I'm from the Westside of the city."*

*"You actually supplied Dutch Jones?"*

*"Now that he's no longer with me, I need someone to take his place."*

*"Cells and caskets. There's never a shortage of prisons."*

All those thoughts and many more crossed Dre's mind at the moment he felt the hot slugs spiral through his face and upper torso, sending a deathly heat through him. He faded into the blackness that fought to envelope him. Dre's heart ached more for Stacy and the life they would never share than for himself. He wished that he had chosen another path, because life could have held so much more for him. Nevertheless, by choosing the path of riches, status, and notoriety like so many before him, Dre found out the hard way that there was a price to pay for the many sins he had committed. As he took his last breath, spewing a trail of blood from the corner of his lips, Nut's words from long ago suddenly held more truth than Dre had ever expected.

"We're playing a dirty game, cuz. Always remember that there is nothing fair in love and war, so let's get busy, nigga."

# *SPECIAL BONUS*

*For all of the readers of Wahida Clark's Thug Series. If you don't have access to ebook technology, on the next few pages, we didn't forget about you! Next up are those best-selling Letters that everyone has been raving about.*

*ENJOY!*

*The Letter*

# BY TRAE MACKLIN

Tasha,

I'm not good at apologies, mainly because I rarely get practice since I don't make a lot of mistakes. And that's not me on some conceited shit. Not making mistakes is a truth that helped me avoid death in the streets and make millions in the real world. In the life I live, mistakes can cost me my life and cause a nigga to go broke. So my words are well thought out and I think before I act. Usually.

I have sat and thought long and hard about you. About us. And I realized I strayed from the Trae I use to be. The Trae you fell in love with. The Trae that you committed yourself to. Instead I'm the Trae that fucked up. On the real I don't know how that Trae came into the picture. And I damn sure can't believe I'm keeping it 100 and admitting that I fucked up. Shit, I can't even believe I fucked up the way I did.

They say, "Love will make people do some crazy things." Crazy like me putting my hands on you, something I promised you I would never do. Crazy like me fuckin' that bitch Charli Li another thing I promised I would never do. The thing that hurts me the most was when you said my promises use to be something you *could put your life on and now those very same promises, they don't mean shit.*

*I know this might sound like a copout but being in love with you is the only way I can explain me blowing my cool and fuckin' up. That's not an excuse, it's an explanation. I'm just trying to make sense of all this.*

*You're probably wondering what the hell am I talking about? How did me loving you make me hurt you? Physically. You know how when people can't find something intelligent to express what they wanna say, they start cursing? It's all emotional and it's the same thing with not having an intelligent way to express your feelings through actions.*

*Sitting on that plane looking at you glow from carrying the next man's seed and then to add insult to injury, looking at those same lips that use to make my dick hard on sight, you had the nerve to ask about the next nigga. At that moment, I fucking lost it. If I didn't love you so much, it wouldn't have meant nothing to me. But I do. So I was angry. Hurt. Scared to death of the possibility of losing you. I didn't know what to say, what to do. On instinct, before I realized it, I'm choking flames out of you. Fortunately, I caught myself before I lost the only woman I ever loved to my own emotions.*

*Guess the bottom line of all this is we both fucked up. I didn't go to sleep and wake up with Charli Li, who you know I don't give a fuck about, in my bed. And we both know you didn't just slip and fall on Kyron's dick. That shit there was payback and I will have to live with the fact that my bullshit pushed you into the arms of another man, which I have to admit I'm still having a hell of time getting over.*

*When you left you took the best of me with you, REAL TALK!!! Shit, I went to Stephon's funeral just to* see you. Ain't that some shit? I'm at a service for some-body's death, and I'm there trying to get my wife and my life back. Guess that's proof I felt like I was dead with-out you. Ain't no chick never had me open like that. And I ain't talking about pussy. Everything about you is just right. Your smile, your eyes, your laugh, the way you whisper my name when I'm holding you. I was thinking back to when we first met and you use to braid my hair and play hard to get. I loved that shit. I played our song the other day and reminisced about my butterfly. I miss those days. I miss my wife. I miss us. I can't even front.

You have definitely done some shit that makes me mad, no doubt, but even when I'm vexed at you, I can't stop loving you. And I know you feel the same about me.

That's why after all the bullshit we always bounce back. That's why I'm here writing this letter, opening up to you like I would never do, and have never done to another woman. Ain't no flawless relationship, Tash. You need to come to grips with that. I'm trying to make sense of how I made some mistakes and how we can get pass this. In other words, I'm starting the dialogue between us. Talk to me.

Your Husband and Man fo' Life,
Trae Macklin

*The Response*

# BY TASHA MACKLIN

Tasha Macklin
*The Real Boss*

## *Tasha*

I was angry at Trae, so I refused to acknowledge his presence. He stood at the front door, on his way out. I walked right past him as if he wasn't even there.

"Why you got on my pajama shirt?" he asked me.

"Why do you care? You ain't here to wear it," I snapped and regretted the slip of my tongue. I kept walking, head held high until I got to my bedroom. My shoulders slumped and I sat on the edge of my bed, trying to fight back tears.

Trae had been playing these head games for the last two weeks and the shit was starting to get under my skin. We hadn't had sex in a while and my hormones were raging. This nigga would come home and spend time with the kids, and on those nights when he would stay, he slept in the guest room. In the morning, he'd fix breakfast and then leave. Some nights he would put the kids to bed and leave as if I was no longer in the picture. I'm like: What the fuck? Nigga, you made your point when you came and got my ass, so why you gotta drag the shit out?

For the last week or so he had been home every night. So seeing that, I was like: Okay, this game is finally over. I thought since he wanted to communicate through letters, let's do it. Getting a letter from Trae was new territory for me. So I figured since he wrote a letter, so could I. I thought it over for a couple of days and then I sat down, grabbed my pen and paper and I wrote.

I poured out my heart.

*Dear Trae,*

*I can't start this letter with apologies because truthfully I am not sorry for the shit that I did. Regretful? Maybe. No, that's a lie. I am sorry some days, sorry that I fucked with you. I read your letter and I felt everything you said, and I took it all into careful consideration. The fact that you sat down and wrote a letter gave you points in my book, but the pain you caused behind your actions that caused you to write it, fucked that up.*

*I never wanted to see us get to a point where seeing each other hurts. I know that you love me; there is no doubt in my mind of that fact, but you said it best yourself, you fucked up. It was you who fucked the next bitch. It was you who allowed the streets into our home, only to invade and crumble the very foundation that we fought hard to establish. I can't love you for both of us, Trae. I gave you everything you asked for. I gave in to you against my better judgment and gave you all of me. I gave you three beautiful children. I gave up my career to be your wife and raise our children. Then I gave up my dignity when I had to walk into a doctor's office and have them look me in the face and ask how many sexual partners I had because I had a fucking STD.*

*It was me who sat up nights when you were in those*

*streets, praying that you would make it home. It was me, who when pregnant, begged you to get out the game. And then when you had to make one more run, I had to bear the burden of losing our first child. Even when I didn't know if you were dead or alive, I never turned on you. I never left your side. In fact, I hauled my black ass to that jail when I found out you were okay and did the only thing a loyal bitch of my caliber could do: I stood by you through it all. And yes, I'm the same bitch that slept in a hospital chair for three months while pregnant again, nursing you, bathing you, and crying and praying for God to give you back to me. I refused to leave your side. Then to have you come back from death's door and years later pull the bullshit that you have been pulling. That shit is a slap in the face.*

*I'm tapped out, Trae. Not only have you fucked up, you put your hands on me. Love isn't supposed to hurt. Because of my love for you, I haven't loved me. I haven't been caring about myself enough to secure my feelings. Was fucking your boy's brother wrong? Hell yeah! I can't deny that. But knowing that I was giving you just a taste of what I went through was priceless. Was it payback? Shit . . . Payback ain't enough for what you put me through.*

*I wanted this letter to be a confirmation of my anger, but the more I write the more I realize that I still love you more than life itself. I can't throw away all of the good times that we had, all the drama we fought through to be together. I can't throw away the love that we share for each other. I can't forget the look in your eyes when you say the three words you love to hear and seem to know before I do, "Tasha, you're pregnant." Then the look on your face when you hold our baby in your arms for the very first time. And I damn sure can't forget that you are and have always been a provider and protector of our family. I too sat and thought back to how it all began with the chase, the catch, and the mind-blowing sex that kept a bitch cumming for hours. Yeah, I'm your butterfly, and yes, I whisper your name when you hold me close, because when I'm in your arms I lose my breath.*

*I don't want to hate you, Trae. What I wanted was for us to live a perfect life, but that shit obviously doesn't exist. We both fucked up and we fucked up bad, but going over the shit repeatedly does not change things. If we ever plan to get past this, there has to be some major changes.*

*I want to love you without pain again, Trae. I don't want to think the dick is all mine. I need to know it is. I need you to keep the streets away from our children and me. Keep them away from the home that we built together. And most of all, I need my Trae back, the Trae that doesn't lie to me. The Trae that doesn't hurt me. And definitely the Trae that would never put his hands on me. I know it wasn't easy on you when you found out I gave your pussy to another man, and it damn sure wasn't easy for me to know that the next bitch was getting my dick. But I think it's fair to call it even. If we can get past this, we have to bury this shit and start over fresh. No hate, no anger, no bringing the shit up when we feel down or get angry. We have to kill it.*

*First things first. Cali is a dead issue. This move fucked us up. We need to relocate. Second, we have to repair everything that is broken. Third, we have to love harder than we have ever loved before, having no secrets and holding no grudges. I love you, Trae. I want to be proud again to say I'm your wife. I want to be able to hold my head up high and not feel like the next bitch's joke. Lastly, I want my Trae back. The man that I first fell in love with. The man that had a bitch doing lap dances in the club. The Trae that had a bitch giving up pussy anytime and anyplace. The same Trae that holds my face and gives me tender kisses when I'm sleeping, and lays in bed with all of us around you and laughs at the crazy things our children say. I want my King back.*

*I don't want to live without you, but I know that we have a long road ahead of us before we can get back to life as we once knew it. If that letter was you opening the line of communication between us, I heard you loud and clear. And this is a sincere response. We need time to heal and whatever happens next has to happen on both of our terms.*

*Love Always,*
*Your Wife Tasha*

Three days went by and he hadn't even acknowledged that I wrote the damn thing.

But the kicker for me was, tonight I wanted some dick and this nigga was at the front door on his way out. I could just kill him, I thought to myself as I sat on the side of my bed and grabbed some tissue and blew my nose.

"What did you say smart?" Trae eased into the bedroom startling the shit out of me. I didn't even hear him come up the stairs. Now I grew even madder because he busted me crying. He stood in front of me. "What did you say smart?"

I rolled my eyes. "You heard what I said, Trae. You ain't here to wear the damn shirt."

Of course he had his signature smirk plastered on his face. The smirk that said, "Yeah, I won. I got the upper hand." The smirk that I wanted to smack clean off his face. He walked away, took off his jacket and threw it across the loveseat. He then leaned up against the dresser and stood there staring at me. "Fuck you, Trae!" I snatched up one of the pillows and threw it at him. I was mad, sniveling and blowing my nose. I felt vulnerable and more like a weak ass bitch.

"Take off my pajama shirt and come here, Tasha."

I ignored him. Tears were streaming non-stop down my cheeks, and I was still blowing my nose trying to get myself together.

"Baby, come here," he repeated.

This time I shook my head no. "Leave me alone, Trae. I'm not feeling you all up in my space right now." I was struggling, but slowly getting myself together. I stood and gathered my wet tissues. Fully composed, I looked back at my husband and said, "Make sure your ass is gone when I come out." I went into the bathroom, shut the door and then tossed the tissues into the trash. I placed a warm washcloth over my face until it cooled off. I slid the cloth onto my neck and looked at my red and swollen eyes in the mirror. Unhappy with my reflection, I turned the water off and hung up the cloth.

When I cracked the door open and peeked out, Trae was posted up in the same spot where I'd left him. I snatched the door all the way open and charged out. "Don't you have some place else to go?" I asked. When I got close enough, he pulled me close and hugged me.

"Trae, no. I see what you are doing." I tried to break free of his embrace. "You won. You got me back here. You got your family together and now you don't want me. And at the same time, you won't let nobody else have me. It took a minute, but I see right through your bullshit."

"That's not true."

"I'm not stupid. Get off of me and get the fuck out!" He held me tighter.

"Till death, Tasha. Till death do us part."

"No, Trae. I'm not going to let you do this to me."

"Do what?"

"Control me like this. Now let me go."

"Aiight, fine. You're in control," he said and let me go.

"Now leave," I told him as I pulled the covers back on the bed. I needed some quiet time without him all up in my space. I grabbed my Sudoku puzzle book and a pencil. Trae began to undress in front of me. Butt naked, he went into his jacket pocket, came out with a blunt and headed for the bathroom. I heard the shower come on and a few minutes later, the smell of purple haze floated up my nose.

## Trae

Tasha obviously got my point. She was mine, always would be, and I would never, as long as I was breathing watch her run off happily into the sunset with the next muhfucka. Took her long enough, but I believe she got it. Yeah, I was doing all that shit on purpose. I had to bring that lesson home somehow. I intended to drag the shit out a few more nights, but when she came walking past me with my pajama top on, ass hanging out, my dick started hollering, "My nigga, did you see that?"

I started talking back. "Yeah, I saw it."

"Well, what the fuck you waitin' on? Don't make me

starve again tonight. I can't take this bullshit much longer. So what you gonna do about it?" my dick asked me.

"The pussy ain't going nowhere. Be cool. You'll be all right for a few more days."

"Man, you got me fucked up. You ain't starving me another night. I need to be all up in that." And at that thought, my shit got rock hard. The next thing I know, I was climbing the stairs to my bedroom, following behind my dick.

I knocked off half of the blunt and took a nice, hot shower as I thought about how many ways I was gonna fuck Tasha. I knew my wife like I knew the back of my hand, and she'd been uptight as hell these past few days, needing to get dicked down. That's why she was doing all that damn crying. She was sexually frustrated.

I got out the shower, dried off, brushed my teeth and lotioned up. When I stepped out of the bathroom, she was sitting in the bed, puzzle book in her lap, tissue in hand, wiping away her tears. I pulled my side of the covers back, climbed into our bed and slid up next to her. I began unbuttoning my pajama top, the one that she had on, and she stopped me.

"No, Trae," she stated firmly.

"I want my pajama top," I told her as I went back to unbuttoning it.

"I'm not playing with you, Trae."

"I ain't playing, neither." I snatched it open, popping off the last of the buttons. They went flying across the bed. Tasha rolled her eyes. Her succulent looking breasts left me in a trance. Before I leaned in to her, I put a tit in my hand, brought it to my mouth and sucked on her pretty brown nipple.

"Trae, stop!" she said through sniffles.

I didn't stop until I had enough and was sure that her pussy was wet. I snatched the covers off her, ran my hand up her thigh until I had two fingers inside her. Yeah, she was ready. I leaned back in and flicked my tongue across her nipple as I fingered her pussy.

"Can I get that kiss you been saving for me?" She shook her head no and moved my hand from between her thighs. I pulled her down toward me by the neck. "I want my kiss." Roughly, I covered her mouth with mine, kissing her until her lips kissed me back.

Just as Tasha began thrusting her hips forward and whispering my name, we heard, "Mommy, I want some water." Caliph interrupted as he stood in the doorway.

"Okay baby." Tasha broke away and tried to get up, but I stopped her.

"Caliph, drink some water out of that bottle right there on Mommy's table and get back in the bed." I held onto Tasha's waist so she couldn't move. She still treated that boy as if he was a baby. I had to talk to her about that.

Caliph drank some water and set the bottle down. "Good night, Daddy. Good night, Mommy," he said as he made his exit.

"Close the door, Caliph." I still had work to put in.

I lay on my back, grabbed my dick and started rubbing him. He was so hard that when I turned him loose, he jerked back and forth all by himself. We both knew what that meant. "What you want to do with him? You want to tame him or what?" Tasha looked at him, trying to fight it, but just like my dick was talking to me, I knew her pussy was speaking to her.

She climbed over me, pussy in my face and her mouth at my dick. "Oh it's like that?" I asked her. I knew it was about to be on when I felt her lips wrap around my tool. Then, the next thing I knew my shit was down her throat. I couldn't let her outdo me, so I spread her pussy lips and ate her at the same rhythm as she was sucking my dick. Electricity shot down to my toes. It was obvious that my head game was winning; she released my dick and was moaning, groaning and grinding against my mouth. I could tell she was about to cum, so I slapped her on the ass and stopped.

As she changed her position, I grabbed another pillow and put it under my head. It was time to watch my baby ride. She locked gazes with me as she straddled my dick and slid all the way down on him. She whispered, "Trae, I hate you right now, but this dick feels so good." Tasha placed her soft hands on my chest and started ridin'. I watched my baby get her fuck on, sliding up and down, side to side until she finally screeched, "Oh my God! My spot. My spot!" I gripped her ass and plunged into her pussy as deep as I could. "Oh that's my . . . right there, baby. My spot. Oh my God, that feels so good."

I got a kick out of seeing her face twisted all up and could feel her pussy contracting. Once her head fell back, I knew she was gone and she started cumming. My shit throbbed and was now on maximum swole. She fell forward on top of me, and I whispered in her ear, "I still want my kiss." Tasha was still breathing hard and trying to recover from that orgasm. Still deep inside her, I turned her onto her back and placed her legs over my shoulders.

"Baby wait," she purred.

"Wait for what? I'm the nigga you love to hate, remember?" I was on my knees digging deep. She couldn't move; she couldn't get away. All Tasha could do was roll her head from side to side and moan. I had complete control of the pussy.

"Trae, baby, please. Ohmygod! Baby, my spot. My fuckin' spot!" she screeched, and at the same time she started cumming again. It was on. In this position, there was no hittin' and missin'. All I could do was hit it.

"This is what you needed, right?" I asked her as I kept punishing her spot.

"Okay, baby. I had enough." She shuddered all over.

"But I didn't come yet," I teased her. "You don't want big daddy to cum? That ain't fair. I know you said you hate me, but damn." I was so deep into the pussy, that when I did decide to cum she was getting pregnant. Her body trembled as I got my grind on nice and slow. I lived for these moments.

"How does this feel?" I asked her. She was so gone, she couldn't even answer. I guess my baby had had enough. "I need you to come one more time for Daddy." I rocked her body in sync with mine. Her pussy was feeling so good, I knew I wouldn't be able to hold back much longer. The pussy at this point . . . was bliss. "C'mon baby, move with me. You can take this big dick a little bit longer." Finally, my baby rolled her hips for me. We were as one. Fucking at the same pace. Slowly. Those slow orgasms seemed to be a little more intense than when you were fucking wild and hard. The slow ones came up on you from deep within. Finally, we started cumming at the same time.

## *Tasha*

I hadn't realized that I needed some dick that damn bad. I went from having a crying fit and on the verge of telling him to go fuck himself, to, I really love sucking your big black dick and I love you more than life itself. Love is crazy I tell you. Looks like I'll never understand the shit.

Here we lay at the foot of the bed and I couldn't even remember how we got here. I believed I came at least three times. Lying on my side with my eyes closed, Trae gently kissed my shoulder and told me how much he loved me . . . And my pussy. I knew he was sincere.

That was the last thing I remembered as I woke up to my phone ringing.

## *Angel*

"I need a damn vacation," I mumbled when I heard a series of knocks on my office door.

"What!" I yelled out, annoyed because I had just decided to take a break for at least an hour. Things had been a circus around our office for the last few days.

My door flew open. "Good morning, Mrs. Santos. You are not going to believe this." I could hear the excitement in my assistant's Deidra's voice.

"Believe what, Deidra?"

"You have got to see this," she said, coming around my desk and placing her Nook in front of me. Why she was reading on her Nook smack dab in the middle of the workday, I had no clue.

"What are you doing?" I tried to move back.

"I can't tell you. I have to show you. First, look at this." She tapped my keyboard and began typing. Twitter appeared on my screen and then I saw a page that read: Trae Macklin. I sat there waiting to see what this shit was all about. She scrolled down the page showing me bits and pieces of conversations about Trae publishing THE LETTER. It appeared that he had been chatting with random females about his and Tasha's relationship. I had a chance to read a few tweets, and then she held up her Nook revealing a book cover. The title was THE LETTER by Trae Macklin, and there he was posing on the fucking cover with his damn chest out. I was like: What the fuck is this?

As I read this 'apology letter,' I tried to hold my composure in front of my secretary, but inside I was losing it. "Okay, thank you," I said in a tone that let her know she was dismissed. She smirked and took her little Nook from me and slowly began exiting my office. She was one of them bitches who had a thing for Trae.

"I'm on break so hold all of my calls," I told her.

The second that door shut, my fingers were on speed dial. "This bitch better answer."

### *Tasha*

I looked over at the clock, then at my ringing phone. I started not to answer because I could feel that it was getting ready to be some bullshit. Against my better judgment, I took the call.

"Why you always call me so early?" I asked, still half asleep.

"Bitch please, it's noon over here and I need to talk to you," Angel yelled.

"What's up, Angel?" I asked, already knowing that this was going to be a daunting conversation.

"Why did that little secretary of mine just walk into my office and show me your husband's bullshit Twitter page?"

I took a deep breath. I was not ready to have this

conversation, so I hoped to push it off until I had a chance to wake up and prepare for the onslaught of questions coming my way. "Can we talk about this later?"

"Heeeell no, Tasha," she responded, not backing down.

"It's not that serious, Angel."

"He's on Twitter and on Nook. God knows where else. What is going on? He's telling all of y'all's business."

"Trae wrote me an apology letter. I read it and then threw it in the garbage. He found it and got pissed off, and then posted it for his little fan club on the Internet."

"So that's how we doing it now? Posting shit on the Internet?" Angel asked with an intense sarcasm.

"For real, I don't know what Trae is into nowadays."

"Bitch, that is your husband. You should know everything that he is into. Posting your shit online. . . ."

Angel obviously was feeling some type of way over all of this. Wait until she found out I was getting ready to post my shit as well. She'd probably have a heart attack.

## *Angel*

I sat on the other end of that line trying to read her emotions but couldn't. Tasha was always good at hiding shit.

"So what are you and Trae doing over there? Because I saw your little post on the end. And don't tell me that you are even thinking about doing the same bullshit!"

Tasha took a deep breath then answered, "We are trying to get things back on track."

"Angel, I never would have thought that we would end up this fucked up."

I could hear the pain and despair in her voice. But I would have to feel sorry for her later because I had a few things I needed to get off my chest.

"So, are you going to post all of your business, too?"

"No, Angel. I'm not."

"Good. Because I can't say it enough. Y'all moved way out to fairytale land and lost y'all gotdamn minds. And while I'm on the subject, that snake ass cousin of yours, no disrespect to the dead, but he saw that shit coming. Him and Trina had major roles to play in all of this bullshit. Trae's ass went and jumped into some foreign pussy and then you turn right around and fuck family."

"Look, don't judge me." Tasha was getting all riled up. "He started the shit and I finished it. He knew what type of bitch I was when he married me. I told him up front, 'Fuck up and I'ma have some serious payback for that ass.' And I meant that shit. I don't know why y'all can't seem to understand that."

"I don't have a problem with payback. He fucked up, no doubt. But out of all the dicks in the world, you had to slide on Kyron's. Tasha, you are not that naïve. You had to know that it would cause a major riff between Trae and Kaylin."

"Honestly, at the time I didn't give a fuck. I was doin' me. Shit, I'm grown. I can fuck who ever I want."

"Doin' you? Don't hand me that bullshit. Ain't no doin' you when we are a family. And now your shit is in jeopardy because you were so-called doin' you." A couple seconds of quiet passed. "Tasha, you are my girl and I love you to death, but Kaylin is my husband.

His whole brotherhood with Trae has been compromised."

"If your husband is going to let what happened between me and Trae get between them then they need to reevaluate their so-called brotherhood," Tasha stated.

Silence fell over the line. I couldn't believe what she had just said. "So you really don't know what Trae did to Kyron?" Fuck me! I wasn't supposed to say that. Loose lips sink ships. This was exactly why Kaylin didn't want me talking to Tasha.

He knew I would be the one to spill the beans.

## *Tasha*

I sat straight up in the bed, put my feet on the floor and braced myself for what Angel was about to reveal.

"What happened, Angel?" I asked.

"Oh, don't ask me shit. Ask Mr. Internet."

"Don't play with me." I stood up and walked to the window to see if Trae's truck was outside, but it was gone.

"Hold on, I have another call." Angel obviously thought she was going to dodge my question.

"Angel, don't you fuckin' answer that call. What happened?"

"I gotta go."

"Angel, wait! You bitch!"

She hung up.

*Shit Just Got Real*

# BY TASHA MACKLIN

## Tasha

I couldn't believe Angel hung up on me after not telling me what Trae did to Kyron. I called her ass back and of course, she didn't answer. *Why was I so out of the loop? And what did Trae do to him?* Shit, he was laid up in a hospital bed the last I heard.

I dialed Trina. Now that I thought about it, it had been weeks since I'd spoken to her. When she didn't pick up, I sent her a text and then I called Trae.

"Hey babe, what's up?"

"You tell me. You do remember our conversation, don't you, Trae? We had an agreement. No more secrets, no more lies." His silence let me know that he could sense where I was going with this. "I heard some shit about what you did to Kyron, but I want to hear it from you. What did you do to him, Trae?"

"We'll talk when I see you."

*"We'll talk when I see you?"* What is that supposed to mean? Just tell me what you did to him. How hard is that?"

"Why the fuck do you care, Tasha?" he barked. I then knew that I had to choose my words carefully. "Tell me. Why the fuck do you care?"

"Forget it, Trae." I took a deep breath, regretting where this conversation was headed.

"Forget it my ass! You called me asking about the next nigga. And when I tell you we'll talk about it later, you start pressing me. What the fuck is that about!"

"Forget it, Trae." I hung up on him. Frustrated, I folded my arms, sat back in the chair and began running Angel's words through my mind. Fearing the worst, I picked up the phone and called Trina again.

"Hello."

My sister sounded as if she didn't mean to answer the phone. "I just tried to call you," I told her. "What's up with you? Where have you been? I haven't heard from you."

"Trying to stay my ass outta trouble. What's up with you?" she answered, all dry and shit.

"Trying to find out what's going on. What's happening?"

"Shit," she said all nonchalant.

"When is the last time you spoke to Kendrick?" I didn't have time to beat around the bush.

"Last night. Why?"

"So what's up with Kyron?"

"What do you mean 'what's up with Kyron'?"

"Trina, don't play dumb. Trae did something to Kyron and I know you know all about it."

"I don't know shit, Tasha. If I did, you know I would have told you."

I thought about what she said, though I wasn't totally convinced she was telling the truth. "If I find out you lying it's going to be on and poppin'."

"Do you think Kendrick would tell me something if they did do something to him? C'mon now, Tasha."

*Okay. Now I know this bitch is lying. She probably don't believe the words coming out of her own damn mouth. Something isn't right. I just can't put my finger on it . . .*

"Yeah, all right Trina. Let me get off this phone. I'll talk to you later." I hung up and jumped out of bed. Then I threw on some jeans and a T-shirt, brushed my teeth and washed my face. I went downstairs and thought about how convenient it was to have Aunt Marva around. The kids were finishing up breakfast. I kissed my sons and Aisha on the cheek.

"Marva, I gotta go check on my sister. Can you keep an eye on them until I get back?"

"As long as you're back by two. Me and Cheryl are going by Daisy's."

"No problem. I will be sure to be back by then."

"Ma, can I go?" Shaheem asked me.

"You are not even dressed, Sha. Mommy gotta go and check on Auntie Trina. I'll be right back."

During my drive to Trina's, I kept thinking about Trae asking me 'why do you care'. Shit. *Why was I so concerned*? I knew damned well why. I couldn't front. I did catch some feelings for Kyron. It was mostly lust, but the feelings were there. I hated to admit it, but it was fun while it lasted and it felt damned good to give Trae a dose of his own medicine. Of course, I didn't love Kyron, and Trae had my heart. I knew Kyron and I could never be. Trae would never allow that to happen, and on the real, neither would I. More important, I will always be in love with Trae Macklin.

I arrived in front of Trina's place in thirty minutes flat, shut my ride off and headed up her stairs. I knocked on the door and waited. As I stood there, my mind flashed back to that day when Trae stood out here pacing like a raging caged animal waiting to pounce. Quickly, I tossed that scene out of my head. I never want to go through that shit again. Again, I banged on the door and then pressed my ear up against it. I knew the bitch was home because her car was parked out front. I pulled out my key and used it.

"Kendrick, is that you? That was quick. You came back?" Trina came from the back wearing a wife beater, shorts and sweat socks. I saw a dark purple bruise on her arm and when I looked closer a bruise was healing on her jaw.

"What the fuck happened to you?" I squinted as a frown came over my face and I eased into investigation mode.

"He dumped me, Tasha." Tears started rolling down her face. She folded her arms over her chest and looked down, avoiding eye contact. "Kendrick dumped me. Can you believe that bullshit? The nigga dumped me!"

So that's why I hadn't heard from her ass. I followed her into the kitchen. She filled up a teapot with water.

"You want some tea?"

"Tea?" I asked her.

"I got cramps, bitch. Yes, tea. You want some tea or not?"

"No, I don't want no gotdamn tea. What I want to know is what happened to your fucking face?" I walked over and grabbed her chin, turning her toward me.

"What happened, Trina? How did you get the bruises? You let the nigga beat on you?"

"Hell no! Me and his bitch got into it." She pulled away from my grip.

"He got a girl?" I grabbed one of the kitchen chairs

and sat down. She didn't answer my question. Instead, she decided to get right to what I wanted to hear.

"After Trae stabbed Kyron in the throat, all types of skeletons started falling out the closet. They thought he was going to die, girl. After that happened, the nigga flipped the script. That's when the nigga started treating me like I was the enemy. I was like shit, I wasn't the enemy when Kyron was fucking my sister and I was fucking you!" She grabbed a cup and a tea bag.

"Stabbed him in the throat? Damn, you brushed past that shit like you were asking me if I wanted paper or plastic. How long ago did he stab him, Trina?"

"It's been almost a month."

"A month? Why are you just telling me this?"

"I don't know." She shrugged. "You got enough shit to worry about. Plus you told me to stay out of your fucking business, remember?"

*No the fuck she didn't*, I thought, looking at her sideways.

"And why do you care anyway? I thought he was just a revenge fuck? Let me find out you done caught feelings for this nigga," she said with a half a smile as she began pouring hot water into her cup. I wanted to toss that shit in her face.

"You know what, Trina? Fuck you. You told me what I wanted to know. Let me get up outta here." I stood up.

"What? I hit a nerve?" the bitch had the audacity to ask me.

"No, you didn't. I'm good." I threw the same fake ass smile back at her.

"Then why you got to leave when I mentioned that you caught feelings?" She sat down and crossed her legs.

"I gotta get up outta here, Trina. But I'ma tell you

this, there is one thing for sure and two things for certain: Karma is a bitch." I walked out, leaving my miserable sister all by herself. I didn't know her involvement in the shit, but something was up.

As I drove back home, my thoughts were on Trae, and the reality of his actions felt like a mack truck smashing me into brick wall . . . *He almost killed the nigga. How was he able to get that close to Kyron to stab him in the throat? And how did I not know about this? What if he would have killed him? Now what? Are they going to keep going tit for tat? This shit has to stop somewhere.*

"How are you, Mrs. Macklin?" I heard the greeting come from my opposite side as I pulled into my driveway.

"I'm okay, John," I said to the mailman. Instead of putting the mail in the box, he handed it to me.

"Have a good one," he sang, and then started whistling.

"You too." I parked the truck in front of the garage and went into the house. I set the mail on the dining room table.

"Marva, I'm back," I yelled as I tossed my keys onto the table. On my way to the kitchen, something told me to look through the stack of letters. I picked the stack back up. *Junk. Junk. Bill. Junk. Bill. Junk.* I tossed each one on the coffee table. Then I came to a red envelope addressed to me. It had nothing for the return address, but the postmark was from New York. I started to tear that shit up, but as I flipped it over, that unmistakable fragrance struck my nose. At that moment, I knew where this shit came from. *Speak of the devil.* My heart pounded double time at the thought of what could be inside. I dropped it on the table and stared at it. Folding my hands together, I brought them to my mouth as I contemplated whether I should burn the shit or open it. Just as I had decided to burn it, curiosity got the best me, causing me to snatch up the envelope and find a corner somewhere.

"Marva, I'll be upstairs!" I hollered, and then I heard little people running my way. "What I tell y'all about running through the house?" My three sons stopped dead in their tracks.

"Send them out back. I'll be out there," Marva yelled out.

"I'll take them outside, Auntie Tasha," Aisha said.

I stood there and watched my wanna-be-grown niece line the boys up and give them instructions as she pointed her little finger at them. Then she marched them out of the dining room. I headed upstairs to my bedroom and shut the door. I went over to my desk, sat down and slowly opened the letter. If felt as if time stood still. I began to read . . .

*Tasha, Tasha, Tasha . . .*
*There's a part of me that wants to knock you the fuck out, then stomp the shit out of you while you're on the ground. But another part of me wants to give you a hot sponge bath, pat your body dry with the best towel money can buy, then plant kisses all over your body before I make love to you all night long. This Love-Hate thing may sound crazy but I'm not insane. I didn't just smoke some dust before I penned this letter, and I ain't poppin' pills like some white boy from a trailer park in Milwaukee.*

*I'm pointing fingers and you're the target. You led me to think you was divorcing that muthafuckin' clown Trae. You fucked me, allowed my seed to start developing in your womb, made me think I was the shit times ten, then after I done went against my own brother for you, at war with your punk ass husband over you, and what you do? Go running back to this lame nigga Trae and tell me I was just a revenge fuck. Then to top your bullshit off, you get on some right to choose Planned Parenthood shit and abort my child. Our Child. Fuck abort, you killed our child. On some G shit, you ain't no better than me and every other thug that caught bodies on the street. And as vexed as I am, as unbelievable as your actions are, a part of me still got love for you.*

*The funny part is, this whole shit revolves around you, but it ain't about you. It's about Me. This shit may sound insane, but I ain't crazy. See, you are one of them high-maintenance Hos and the problem with high-maintenance Hos like you is y'all think your pussy is made of platinum and your clit is a 10-carat princess cut diamond. I don't know about Trae and all these other tender dick clowns with they nose up your ass like it's a bouquet of roses, but every move I made with you was calculated for my benefit.*

*You're probably saying to yourself right now, "You wasn't talking all that shit when you had your face between my legs or when I was riding your dick!" The typical response from a Ho who don't understand men. You riding my dick is about Me. Me bustin' a nut, Me laying back while you work, Me proving that your high-maintenance ass ain't no different than these broke Hos in the projects fucking for Chinese food and a Tyler Perry flick. Me, Tasha. It was always about Me. Bottom line.*

*Although it may not seem like it, the same shit goes for me eatin' the shit out your pussy. The better I eat your pussy the better you gonna ride my dick. Nine times out of ten you Hos go running back to your friends bragging, then your friends come creeping behind your back into my bedroom. So even when it looks like I'm going all out to please you, I'm doing some minor shit to benefit Me in a major way. Half you Hos never had an orgasm anyway, so all it takes is for me to give you one for you to return the favor and unconsciously convince your friends to fuck me by bragging to them. Angel, Kyra, Jaz.*

*You think none of them ain't entertain the thought of creeping into my bed like crackheads wasting they time chasing that first hit? Go figure.*

*You probably thinking I'm full of shit because I'm the same dude that copped you a brand new Jag. If you thinking like that, you must've really went for that bullshit about me not being able to have you running around the city flagging down taxis. Then you went bragging to Trina about the car being in your name. Only if you knew it was in your name because it was a stolen car that was tagged. And as far as you riding around town, yeah I wanted you in something hot. The better you look, the richer I get.*

*See, motherfuckas in the hood is nosey, always got some shit to say and they always countin' somebody else's money. And everybody run with the winning team. Reebok ain't come to some underground rapper for a sneaker deal, and Bill Gates ain't give no dude with a 99-cent ebook a million dollars to promote it. Reebok went to Jay-Z for them S.dots and Bill Gates pieced off Jay-Z with a mil to promote Decoded. Money attracts money. If people think you got money,* *they think you know how to make it. So they'll put their money in your hands. You know how many people gave me bricks on consignment because of you? How many people offered me buildings to set up spots because they see you in that Jag? Every time your silly ass zipped up and down the street in that $90,000 car that only cost me five stacks, you caused some up-and-coming hustler to get at me so they can find out how to get behind the wheel of a car that do 0-60 in less than five seconds. I got two goons in Brooklyn that will kill for me and a top lieutenant off the strength of your pretty ass whipping that Jag. How could I not love you? But you were just as happy as a Ho on payday to be in a car you think is increasing your wealth while all you were doing was raising my stock. Good lookin'. I appreciate that. Even though the spotlight was on you . . . it was always about Me, Tasha. Never forget that.*

*When I say I love you, I'm really saying I love Me. That may sound crazy, but I'm not insane. There really is no you; Tasha just don't exist. Your Jag, I bought it. I picked the model, the color, all for a specific reason that really had nothing to do with you. But your stupid ass started to define yourself by that car. Same thing with the money I would give you to tear down the mall with. And you had your weight up already, your own money. But I wanted you to splurge with mine. So the car you drove, the clothes you wore, even the perfume on your skin, all of that was an extension of Me.*

*Why do you think I was so caring and nursed you back to health after you twisted your ankle running from Trae? It seemed like I cared about you, but I cared about you being able to hit the gas on that Jag, hop out and walk around switching that big ass, keeping men thirsty and people talking, wondering about how much money I got. All because I could toss it around on you. Why do you think men call women Hos? It ain't got nothing to do with you fucking, at least for me anyway. Everybody like fucking. It's about you hittin' the pavement and strollin' your ass around town, so you can make me look good and attract potential investors for me. You're nothing more than a walking billboard.*

*Remember, Tasha . . . I may sound crazy, but I'm not insane. So when I say I hate you and love you—don't take it personal. It really has nothing to do with you. It's all about Me.*

*Dueces*
*Kyron, that boss ass nigga*

I ran through the pages in minutes and by the time I got to the last page I was fuming.

"No this muthafucka didn't." I sat there stunned. I started not to even dignify that bullshit ass letter with a response, but fuck that! He obviously felt he needed to get some shit off his chest, well so did I. I opened the drawer, grabbed my favorite notepad and a pen and started writing this bitch ass nigga back.

Just as I finished and was about to read it over to make sure I didn't leave anything out, Aisha came barging into my room yelling, "Auntie Tasha! Kareem bust his head. He's bleeding. Aunt Marva said come here. You might have to take him to get stitches." She was sweating and all out of breath.

"What?" I jumped up and hauled ass downstairs to check on my son.

## Trae

Right before I got some bullshit ass phone call from Tasha, I was actually on my way to talk to her. Not *talk* to her, more like tell her some things that I had been keeping to myself. I was going to tell her what went down with that stalking, crazy bitch Sabirah and what I did to Kyron, especially since the shit was most likely caught on camera. If the detectives or really care or if Mama Santos or someone decided to press the issue, I'm fucked. Benny, my attorney, said my biggest concern was my prints. If my prints popped up, that would change the whole fucking game. The worst of this shit stemmed from Sabirah, and if I get picked up, Tasha needed to be prepared. Then to really rain on my parade, I get a bullshit ass phone call from Charli. This ho calls me out of the blue talking about she needs to see me. So I definitely needed to get to Tasha and tell her this shit before I made my next move; then here she comes calling me, drillin' me on some 'what I did to the next nigga' bullshit. I pulled the phone back and looked at it, thinking she obviously was smoking something.

When I got to the house I walked up in there ready to go to war.

"There you are. Where have you been, boy? And why don't you live here anymore?" My aunt met me at the door with her nosey ass. I paused and looked at her like she was crazy, but she kept on going. "Anyway, Tasha left to take Kareem to the hospital. He fell on that pile of bricks that you have back there and he's going to need stitches. Take that frown off your face. The boy is not dying. He will be fine," she said it all casual as she began picking up toys off the floor.

"Fine my ass. Who was supposed to be watching them?"

"Boy, they are kids. Kids play. They run, they get hurt. So watch your mouth. We can't watch them 24-7. Shit happens," my aunt snapped.

"Who's here now?" I looked around her.

"Tasha took Kareem and Aisha with her to the hospital. Caliph and Shaheem are having lunch. Are you hungry?"

"Naw, I'm good."

"Good, because I gotta get out of here. Daisy and Cheryl are waiting on me. Glad you came home."

"Do I have time to jump in the shower right quick?"

Aunt Marva looked at her watch. "Boy, you better be glad I love you. Hurry up!"

We were just on the court shooting some hoops and I was sweaty as hell. I hit the stairs and at the same time started taking off my T-shirt, looking forward to a nice hot shower. Better yet, I wanted to jump in the pool and do a few laps.

When I got to my room I walked straight to the closet, tossed my tee into the hamper and grabbed my trunks. As soon as I walked out of the closet, I saw that Tasha had been at her desk. Her little flowery notepad was flipped open and her fancy pen lay on top of it. *Awww shit.* We hadn't been spending time together, so I was hoping she didn't write me no Dear John letter. I went to the desk and my eyes went to the sentence, "and don't write me no more, bitch!"

*What the fuck? Don't tell me Charli is up to her bullshit again, sending letters and shit.* I flipped to the front page and saw *Kyron, Kyron, Kyron.* I was hoping that my eyes were playing tricks on me. I focused and those three words were still there. I thought I was about to lose it. *Why the fuck is she writing this lame? And in my house. No wonder she wanted to know what I did to this faggot. This bitch done lost her damn mind. She still fuckin' with this nigga?* I couldn't even see straight, let alone sit down. I ripped the pages out of the notebook and forced myself to read this shit.

*Kyron, Kyron, Kyron . . .*

*First of all, Nigga, you bitch made. Here it is you over there recovering from a life threatening injury and the first bitch you holla at is me? You talking all that shit about Jags and money and connections, who the fuck you tryna convince that you the shit, me or your-self? Talking about you love me and you hate me. What kinda fag shit is that? You* wish *you hated me. You don't know who you fucking with, so you better check my re-sume. I will bet anything that your dick is hard right now as you read and anticipate my next line.*

*My nigga, why can't you just accept it? You were just something to do for me . . . simply a revenge fuck. I gave you some payback pussy on my terms and you got pussy whipped and fell in love. That's why you laying over there crying and shit. And you have the audacity to call me a Ho? Fuck outta here with that bullshit. You don't even know how you mustered up the energy to call me a Ho. No nigga, I ain't your Ho; you're my bitch. Sheeeit . . . gonna call me a walking billboard? If I am that, you best believe it reads, "Kyron's a fuckin' sucka!"*

*I recall you saying three important things: 1. You went out 2. You made my money 3. You kept me fly, then gave me the dick if and when I decided I wanted it. But then I fucked you so good you thought I was going to take you to the top of the world and had you beg-*

ging: *Marry me, Tasha! Be mine, Tasha!* I had your punk ass pulling out rings and shit. So, that sounds like you the Ho. Nigga, I pimped your ass real good, had you trained well, and even after you got that ass whipped you still brought momma her money. Yeah, I rode your dick . . . good enough to make you lick where another nigga slides his dick. How does Trae's cum taste? Is it as good to you as it is to me? And then you brag about a bitch serving her purpose. No nigga, you served your purpose. I wasn't even fucking you and you were coming up off stacks and scheming on ways to steal me from Trae. And you are boasting about a Jag? You a low budget ass nigga if you think a Jag gets you a come up. Them fake ass, so-called, loyal niggas you got on your team are laughing in your face because they got a bitch for a boss, or should I say a broke ass co-worker? Bitch ass sitting here whining about a car, page after page. Nigga please! I bought Trae a fuckin' Maybach. And you obviously forgot that I told you I have a Spyker C8 Aileron Spyder sitting in the garage that I don't even drive! That Jag was like a punch buggy compared to my shit. That's why Trae busted the shit up. You think your money is long? Get the fuck outta here; your money is as long as your dick . . . and that ain't long enough.

Since we keeping score, let me Ho check your ass real quick. You called me a Ho, but I'm the same bitch that had you turn your back on your family. It was Me, Tasha, the same bitch that had you eating pussy, and it ain't about you making me cum, nigga, I'm married to Trae Macklin. My pussy is well trained. And yes, I'm the same bitch that turned you into a marked fucking man. So watch your back, bitch ass nigga. You do the math. Calculate that shit. Tasha, a ten... Kyron, a zero.

*You asked yourself, are you insane? Hell no! You in love and I can't fault a nigga for that. You just like every other nigga that gets the pleasure of Tasha. You sprung the fuck out. The proof is in that long ass letter going on and on and on about what you lost and what you wish you still had. Gonna write me a punk ass letter. I can't get over this shit. What? You ain't got shit else to do? By the way, where your bitch at? You had a so-called bad bitch that held you down the whole time you was doing your bid, but as soon as you fell into this boss pussy you forgot all about that bitch. I had your ass moaning and groaning my name. Tasha. While thinking Mari who?*

*Oh, and I didn't kill your seed. The little muthafucka committed suicide when it realized it wasn't the child of a real boss. So fuck you and die muthafucka!*

*The Boss Bitch,*
*Tasha Macklin Forever*
*P.S. Don't contact me no more. Bitch!*

I finished that shit, not knowing what to think. I stood with the shit in my hand as my blood began to surge through my body like hot lava. *She caught feelings for this nigga?*

"What are you doing reading my shit, Trae?" I didn't even hear Tasha come in the room.

It was on . . .

Available wherever books and e-books are sold

## Exposed by Naomi Chase

On the brink of a major promotion, Tamia Luke is within reach of the glitzy life she's always dreamed of—until her client, Dominic Archer, blackmails her into becoming his mistress, threatening to reveal her scandalous past. Tamia has no choice but to submit to his demands. But the tables turn when her hostility towards Dominic is replaced with insatiable lust. No man—including her boyfriend—has ever satisfied her the way he does. And as her infatuation grows, the closer she comes to losing everything—including her life . . .

## Most Wanted by Kiki Swinson and Nikki Turner

Gigi Costner needs four million dollars she doesn't have and time she hasn't got. Her ex-con ex-lover swears to make her pay for the multimillion-dollar stash of diamonds she stole as she ditched him for a new life as a suburban wife. With time running out, will Gigi's new plan get her in front of the drama or drag her back into hood madness . . .

## Heist by Kiki Swinson and De'nesha Diamond

Accustomed to a life of luxury, Shannon Marshall is devastated to lose everything after her husband, Todd, is sent to prison for gun running. So when Todd plans the ultimate stickup from behind bars, Shannon's ready to put her neck on the line. But she'll have to pull off the hustle of a lifetime and play one dangerous gangster who always gets what he wants . . .

Turn the page for an excerpt from these exciting stories . . .

# From *Exposed*

"Your nine o'clock appointment is waiting in the conference room. I offered him coffee, but he declined."

"Thanks, Marjorie." Tamia rushed past the receptionist, barely sparing the woman a glance. She was ten minutes late to a meeting with a new client. Not exactly the best first impression to make. Thank God her boss was out of town this week, or she'd be in a shitload of trouble. Hell, if the client decided to go with another agency after today's consultation, Tamia could pretty much kiss her promotion good-bye.

Reaching her sleek glass cubicle, she stowed her Coach handbag in the bottom drawer of her desk and grabbed her OneNote tablet. Out of habit, she inspected her appearance in the hand mirror she kept hidden under a tray on her desk. Her MAC makeup was flawless, perfectly accentuating her dark, slanted eyes and full, juicy lips. Her lustrous black hair was cut in a stylishly layered, Rihanna-inspired bob that drew compliments wherever she went. Her silk button-down blouse molded large C-cup breasts, while her black pencil skirt showed off a round, healthy ass and long, toned legs.

As she hurried from the nest of cubicles that housed the agency's brand creative team, one of the copywriters popped his head up.

"Hey, Tamia, I need the final mock-up—"

"Not now," she said, cutting him off. "I'm meeting with a client. We'll talk later."

She headed quickly down the corridor, passing walls that were covered with framed awards, plaques, and press clippings the firm had garnered over the years, establishing it as one of Houston's top advertising agencies. Tamia had worked there for seven years, diligently climbing her way up the ranks. As an account executive, she'd spearheaded several successful ad campaigns and now boasted an impressive client list.

She loved her job. More important, she was damn good at it. So she had as good a shot as anyone else to land the coveted promotion to assistant brand manager of advertising.

Reaching the end of the corridor, Tamia strode briskly into the large conference room. A tall, broad-shouldered man stood at the huge picture window that overlooked the glistening downtown skyline. Dominic Archer, a Crucian-born businessman who'd made his fortune selling prepackaged Caribbean food products.

"Good morning, Mr. Archer. I apologize for keeping you wait—"

As he turned from the window, Tamia promptly lost her train of thought. The man was at least six-four and copper brown, with sleepy dark eyes and a manicured goatee that framed full, sexy lips. Beneath his expensively tailored Gucci suit, his body looked well-toned and muscular. Solid as a rock.

*Oh dayum,* Tamia thought. *This brotha is foine!*

Recovering her professionalism, she stepped forward with an outstretched hand. "Tamia Luke," she introduced herself.

He clasped her hand, his eyes roaming her face. "Dominic Archer." His deep voice held a hint of a lazy island lilt. The scent of his expensive cologne wafted up her nostrils, subtle yet intoxicating.

Tamia smiled at him. "It's a pleasure to meet you, Mr. Archer. Are you sure you don't want any coffee, tea, or juice?"

He smiled, revealing a set of straight, white teeth. "No, thank you. I'm fine."

*Yes, you are.* Clearing her throat, Tamia motioned to the long glass conference table. "Please have a seat."

Once they were both settled at the table, she got right down to business. "I understand that you want a memorable advertising campaign to launch your first Caribbean-style restaurant."

"That's right." As Dominic leaned back in his chair and casually crossed his legs, Tamia's gaze was drawn to his Dolce & Gabbana black calfskin leather loafers. The man had style, which boded well for their collaborative partnership.

"I want something that's gonna grab people's attention," he explained to her. "Something that'll lure customers who've never even *thought* about trying Caribbean food. And I want something that'll drive as much traffic as possible to my restaurant."

Tamia smiled at him. "Then you've definitely come to the right agency. We have a proven track record of satisfying our clients' needs."

"So I've heard." Dominic's eyes gleamed. "I've been a fan of your work for years."

"Really? I'm so glad to hear that." Tamia was thoroughly stoked. "Now, before my team gets started on developing the creative concept for your ad campaign, I need to familiarize myself with your restaurant so that I can decide on an effective target market. So let's talk about—"

"You're even more beautiful than I'd imagined," Dominic interrupted softly.

Her cheeks warmed from the unexpected compliment. "Thank you."

"No, for real. I mean it." He held her gaze. "I always wondered what you looked like behind that black mask."

It took a delayed moment for his words to register. When they did, Tamia's blood ran cold and she stared at Dominic, stunned. "W-what did you just say?" she whispered.

A slow, knowing grin spread across his face. "Does anyone still call you Mystique?"

The room swayed. Tamia swallowed hard as a clammy sweat broke out over her skin. "When . . . how . . ." Her throat tightened, choking off the rest of her question.

Dominic grinned harder. "Like I said, I've been a fan of your work for years."

Tamia got unsteadily to her feet, crossed the room, and closed the door. She couldn't risk any of her coworkers overhearing the conversation she was about to have.

As she made her way back to the table, Dominic's eyes traveled over her body as if he were picturing her naked. When he licked his lips, Tamia felt dirty in a way she hadn't felt in years.

She stood behind her high-backed chair in an attempt to shield her body from his view. "What do you want?" She forced out the words past dry lips.

Dominic reluctantly lifted his eyes from her cleavage to meet her accusing gaze. "Why did you stop acting? You were a natural, Mystique."

"My name is Tamia."

He smiled, slowly shaking his head. "To me, you'll always be Mystique."

Tamia's manicured fingernails dug into the soft leather of the chair. "Again I ask. *What do you want?*"

His smile widened. "I want you to come out of retirement. Become Mystique again."

"That's not gonna happen."

"You misunderstand me." Dominic leaned forward in his seat. "I don't want you to perform for strangers. This time around, I want you all to myself."

Incredulous, Tamia stared at him. "You're out of your damn mind!"

He chuckled quietly. "If I am, Mystique, it's your fault."

"Don't call me—"

"I own every last one of your movies. I can't tell you how many times I've watched them, wishing *I* was the lucky man you were fucking so enthusiastically. It never seemed like you were just acting. Like I said, you were a natural."

Tamia felt sick to her stomach. "Look," she said, darting a furtive glance toward the door, "I don't know who the hell put you up to this, but you wasted your time coming here. I stopped doing those movies a long time ago, and I have no intention of coming out of retirement for you or anyone else. Now you need to leave before I call security."

Dominic laughed softly, unfazed by the threat. "You won't call security."

"Think I won't?" Livid, Tamia spun away from him, rounded the conference table, and marched toward the phone at the opposite end.

"Do your colleagues know about your past life as a porn star?"

That stopped her dead in her tracks.

She stared across the table at Dominic. The wicked gleam in his eyes chilled her to the bone.

"Do they know about your alter ego Mystique, the submissive with a sublime pussy?" he taunted. "Do they know how much you enjoyed being spanked and fucked in the ass? Do they know how much you loved sucking your master's big, black—"

"Stop," Tamia whispered, feeling faint. "Just *stop*."

But he ignored her. "What about your boss? When I contacted the agency and specifically asked to work with you, he couldn't stop singing your praises. But does he know how *truly* talented you are? Would he risk the company's outstanding reputation by promoting an employee with a . . . checkered past?"

Tamia gaped at him in horror. "Are you *blackmailing* me?"

Dominic smiled narrowly. "Blackmail is such an ugly word, you know? I prefer to think of this as a business transaction, one that can be mutually beneficial."

"How?" Tamia hissed. "*You're* the only one who'd get something out of this damn deal."

"That's not true," he countered mildly. "In exchange for your cooperation, you'd get my sworn promise to keep your dirty little secret."

Tamia glared at him. "And if I don't 'cooperate'?"

"You will," he said with certainty.

Panic gripped her chest. "You can't make me do anything!"

"No?" he challenged, raising a thick brow. "Tell me, Mystique. Does the lieutenant governor's son know that you used to be a porn star?"

At the reference to Brandon, the blood drained from Tamia's head.

Dominic smiled, slow and satisfied. "I didn't think so."

"Why the hell are you doing this to me?" she cried.

"I already told you. I'm one of your biggest fans. I couldn't pass up the opportunity to meet you in person, to see if reality lives up to the fantasy." He looked her up and down slowly, visually peeling away each article of clothing. "So far I haven't been disappointed."

Nausea churned in Tamia's stomach. "It's time for you to leave."

He raised a brow. "But we haven't discussed my ad campaign yet."

*Is he serious?* Tamia wondered incredulously. "Under the circumstances, I'm sure you can understand why I'd have a problem working with you."

"You're up for a promotion," he smugly reminded her. "Can you really afford to turn away clients?"

Tamia didn't reply, but she knew he was right. Landing another major account would bolster her chances of receiving the promotion and give her an edge over her competition.

*But at what cost?*

"Why don't you give it some more thought?" Dominic suggested mildly. "I'd hate to have to tell your boss that you forced me to take my business to another ad agency."

Tamia glared at him, her jaw tightly clenched. The bastard knew how to play dirty. "You need to go."

He smiled, then unhurriedly rose to his feet, smoothing a hand over his silk tie.

As he rounded the table and came toward her, Tamia didn't know whether to bolt or grab the first sharp object she could get her hands on. She had time for neither before Dominic reached her. She folded her arms across her chest, a protective gesture that had the unintended effect of drawing even more attention to her cleavage.

Dominic stared at her bulging breasts, then licked his lips and gave her one of those lascivious smiles that made her feel violated. Powerless.

She closed her eyes and averted her face as he leaned close, his warm breath fanning her cheek. "You have twenty-four hours to consider my offer," he whispered in her ear. "Don't keep me waiting, or I promise you'll regret it."

Tamia swallowed hard, shaking from the inside out.

When she opened her eyes again he was gone, leaving behind a white business card on the table and a subtle trace of his cologne.

# From *Most Wanted*

"Hey, baby?" I sang into my cell phone as soon as I heard Sidney's sexy voice come through the line. I could actually picture my husband smiling on the other end of the phone. He always smiled when it came to me.

"Guess where I am? No, silly, I'm not at home butt naked waiting for you." I laughed at his joke. "Seriously, I'm two minutes from the lot. Thought I would surprise you with lunch and a quick midday kitty call," I said seductively.

Sidney sounded excited to hear my voice. He just loved when I did little impromptu things like this. It wasn't always easy finding time to be spontaneous with him being such a busy businessman. He was much older than me, and I guess his previous relationships weren't as much fun. Sometimes I had to pull him out of his shell. It was nothing for me to try to keep him happy, so long as he kept making money.

"Don't worry about what I'm wearing . . . you'll see when I get there," I cooed. He was saying something when my phone line beeped with another call interrupting our sexy talk. I pulled the phone away from my ear and saw that it was my mother. I blew out an exasperated breath. She always knew how to interfere at the wrong times. Sidney was saying something dirty, acting like the dirty old man that he was, but I had to cut him short.

"Look, baby, that's my mother on the other line. Let me holla at her and see what she wants. I'll see you in a few. Be ready for me," I told Sidney. He sounded excited as shit as we hung up.

I clicked over and put on my mental suit of armor. I loved my mother, but she could be a nag and annoying as hell too. It didn't make things easy that she basically lived off of me . . . well, my husband really. The days of living off of me were long gone. I had come into some money, but I'd burned through it just as fast as I had gotten it. My mother had been right there burning up my little windfall with me. I had done some nice things for her because she raised me as a single mother in the rough streets of DC when most mothers were leaving their kids to go smoke crack and shit. Still, my money was gone, and she and I were basically dependents right now. Sidney took care of me, and in return I took care of my mother.

"Yes, ma. What's up?" I answered the line, my voice dull and lifeless. Nothing like how I'd just spoken to Sidney. I wanted her to know I was busy and didn't have a lot of time to yak it up on the phone with her.

"Gigi?!" my mother belted out, damn near busting my eardrum. I pulled the phone away from my ear for a few seconds and frowned. She was bugging! I could hear her yelling my name again. "Gigi!"

"Slow down, lady . . . is everything all right? Why are you yelling?" I asked, concerned. I hadn't heard her all loud like this since she thought she'd hit the lottery a couple of months back. Long story. "You okay?" I asked again.

"Yeah! Yeah . . . everything is just fine. I got some news, baby!" she shrieked excitedly. *You got a damn job and no longer need to live off of us,* was what I was thinking, but I didn't dare say that. Once I realized her high-pitched voice wasn't caused by someone kicking her ass, I calmed down for a few seconds. I let out a long breath waiting to hear some crazy story of hers.

"Okay?" I said expectantly. "What is the news?"

"You will never guess who I spoke to today!" my mother yelped. Before I could even ask who, she volunteered the information. "Warren! I spoke to Warren! Your Warren, baby! He said he is coming home in less than a month and he wants to see us . . . well, really, he wants to see you the most," she said excitedly.

I felt like someone had just punched me in the side of my head. An immediate pain crashed into my skull like I'd been hit. "Warren?" I mumbled, my eyebrows immediately dipping on my forehead. I wished my ears had deceived me. A cold feeling shot through my veins and I almost dropped the phone and crashed the car. My heart immediately began thumping wildly, and cramps invaded my stomach like an army going in for the kill.

"Yes! Warren! He is getting out early on some kind of deal or good behavior . . . something like that! Isn't that good, Gigi?!" my mother continued.

I was speechless. I couldn't even think. Flashes of Warren's face started playing out in front of me. The last time I saw him haunted me now.

"You there, Gigi?" my mother inquired, her voice changing as she must've realized her news wasn't so good. I swallowed hard before I could get the words to come out of my mouth. I cleared my throat because the lump sitting in the back of it made it hard for me to talk. I could feel anger rising from my feet, climbing up to my head.

"How the hell did Warren get your new number?!" I asked through clenched teeth. My voice had no problems now. My nostrils flared and I gripped the steering wheel so hard veins erupted to the surface of the skin on the back of my hand.

"When I moved you from the fucking hood in Southeast DC, I told you to leave that shit behind altogether!" I chastised. "What is wrong with you?! You just couldn't leave well enough alone!" I barked some more. I was full on sweating now. My head was spinning a mile a minute. She had no fucking idea what she had done. "Whose side are you on?!" I screamed.

My mother was quiet at first. I'm sure she was looking at the phone like it was an alien from outer space. I guess she didn't know how to process my anger. She also didn't know the details of my history with Warren after our arrests, which probably confused her even more. It really wasn't her fault. My mother had always liked Warren for me. I mean, he had scooped me up out of the hood and given me a life my mother knew she could never give me. He didn't spare a dime when it came to her either. Sometimes my mother had seemed more enamored with Warren than me.

It was understandable given her history with men. As a kid, I had watched my mother go from one no-good bastard to another. My father had left as soon as I was born . . . typical hood story. My mother had always tried to find that perfect man, so most of my life her bedroom was like a revolving door. There would be one dude this month and another dude the next month. She would always come to me and say, "Gianna, I think this one is going to be your step daddy for sure this time. Baby, we gonna have a good life if it's the last thing I do." Pretty sad when I think back on how desperate my mother had been to find real love. I had watched niggas beat my mother, take her money, steal our TVs, and leave her so depressed she wouldn't get out of bed for weeks.

I was determined to be better than that when I grew up. I wanted to finally give my mother that good life, but school and hard work wasn't in my DNA.

When I met Warren, he became my security blanket. He bought me food, clothes, and eventually, shelter. My mother was love struck herself. I would even catch her blushing sometimes when Warren would come to the house and joke around with her. I don't know why her staying in touch with Warren came as such a shock to me now. I always knew she'd probably pick him over me in a close call situation anyway. Plus, I had never told her what I'd done to him after he and I got knocked riding dirty. After Warren went to federal prison, I played the whole distraught girlfriend role in front of my mother, never letting on to the truth of the situation. She had seemed torn even then.

The news my mother had just dropped on me had me reeling. I started calculating shit in my head. I had been given a false sense of security thinking Warren was going to do much longer in prison. I didn't think he would be getting out so soon. . . . It had only been four years and according to the information I got, Warren had been charged with all types of gun charges, RICO shit, and the whole nine yards. I was under the impression from the feds that Warren would have the book thrown at his ass when he got sentenced.

Someone had fucking lied to me. This was definitely not part of the plan I had hatched back then.

Even still, I thought for sure I had made provisions where Warren would never find me. I had changed my name slightly—no longer going by Gianna, I was now simply Gigi. I had moved out of DC, finally settling in country-ass Virginia, and started living the quiet, kept life as the wife of a fucking old rich dude, who technically could be my father. It would take my mother to fuck that all up!

"Ma . . . how did Warren get your phone number?" I asked again, finally able to calm myself down. My jaw rocked feverishly waiting for her answer. I was praying it wasn't her. I was hoping deep inside Warren had just paid a private investigator or some other Lifetime movie type shit.

"Gigi, when we moved from DC, I stayed in touch with Warren. I thought you would get over being mad at him one day and get back with him. I didn't know you were going to marry so fast. Warren was the only man who had ever done anything good for us and I felt obligated to him. He didn't have any family, so I wrote him letters and sent him packages. Not like you . . . you just got a new man and moved on," she replied.

All of my hopes of my mother NOT being the culprit who blew my cover were dashed. I wanted to scream at the top of my lungs. What a dumb bitch! How fucking stupid can you be?! I couldn't say those words, but I sure as hell was thinking them. Panic hit me like a wrecking ball going into a building at top speed. Warren was the last person on earth I wanted to see or hear from right fucking now. I had to breathe slowly through my mouth to calm down enough to keep talking to my mother. I also had to pay attention to the road.

"What have you told him about me?!" I inquired

loudly. My voice quivered just thinking about ever seeing Warren again. This was definitely not what I had
planned. Again, I silently hoped that my mother had
never discussed me with Warren.

"Everything. He knows you're married. He said he
is happy for you. He knows you are doing well living
here in Virginia Beach with your new husband. I didn't
see the problem. The man is locked up and he was still
asking about you. I think he always loved you, Gianna.
All I can say is sorry, but Warren seemed very happy
for you," my mother said apologetically. Something
like a cord just snapped inside of me. I was literally
coming apart at the seams listening to her.

"You are stupid! You had no right telling him my
business! He is my ex and you don't know what the fuck
I went through with him because I never told you! Just
because you would do any fucking thing just to say you
had a man doesn't mean I grew up to be like you!" I
boomed, the cruel words hurling from my mouth like
hard rocks. I breathed out a long, hard windstorm of
breath.

"Did you also tell him who I am married to? Anything about where I live? Or maybe you gave him my
fucking social security number while you were at it?" I
asked, trying to sound as calm as I could. It wasn't
working; the bass in my voice was deep and intimidat-
ing.

"Well, excuse me! I thought you would want him to
know how well you were doing now seeing that he almost caused you to go to prison right along with him.
He didn't even sound like he was interested in getting
back with you at all. His questions were all general . . .
seemed to just want to know you were all right. I'm
sorry if you feel like I did something wrong, but the

last time I checked I don't have anything to hide," my mother retorted.

I immediately felt guilty for calling her stupid. I had to try and pull myself together. It wasn't her fault.

She was right. She had no idea what had happened, and maybe she just wanted Warren to know that despite the jeopardy he'd put me in four years earlier, I was doing just fine. There were a few minutes of awkward, eerie silence on the phone line. My mother wasn't the quiet type, so I knew the silence meant she was truly at a loss for words.

"I gotta go," I said. I didn't give her a chance to say a word. I just hung up the phone. A loud horn blaring behind me almost caused me to drive off the road. I swerved my car a little bit to keep from hitting others.

"What the fuck?!" I screamed, looking into my rearview mirror. I swerved onto the shoulder of the road. The string of cars behind me passed by, drivers cursing at me and laying on their horns. I was shaken up. I clutched my chest. I had been so distracted by what she was telling me that I was driving slow as hell, holding up traffic. The news from my mother had fucked me up so badly I couldn't even drive. I put my car in Park and sat there for a few minutes.

"Warren is coming home early and knows where I am," I said out loud as if I had to convince myself that what I'd heard was true. My insides churned and I felt like I had to throw up. My legs rocked in and out feverishly. I could see the snarl on Warren's face as clear as day in my mind's eye. I knew him so well. I knew how he was when it came to shit like loyalty too. I had made a promise to him that I hadn't kept. I had also seen Warren's wrath firsthand. There was no way he would just let go of what I had done to him. I could hear him speaking to me now. "No matter what, just never cross me. I can live with everything else. Just never betray me." Warren had said those words to me on several occasions. The same words over and over, he never changed it up. Each time he had said them, in return I promised him that I'd always be loyal, never cross him. I had sworn. I had pledged my allegiance to him. But then I'd turned around and committed the worst Judas act of treason against him.

"Fuck!" I screamed, slamming my fists on my steering wheel until they hurt. "Fuck! Gigi! What the fuck have you done?! What the fuck are you going to do now?!" I yelled out loud. Where Warren and I came from, what I had done was a cardinal sin. In any hood I knew of, snitching and stealing were both acts as heinous as raping a child or killing your own parents. That is how seriously street niggas took it. Most of the niggas I knew, Warren included, lived by the death before disloyalty creed. I was terrified just thinking about the consequences. Maybe he'd shoot me execution style right in front of my mother. Maybe Warren would torture me with battery acid and jumper cables before finally putting me out of my misery. I could only imagine. I closed my eyes and all I could do was think back to how things had gone so wrong. How we'd gone from being so happy—the hood's Prince William and Kate— to being the hunter and the hunted. I kept thinking. Thinking. Something I had tried to avoid doing for four years now. I couldn't help it. My mind went back.

# From *Heist*

CRASH! BANG! "What the fuck?!" I was out of bed and on my feet with one big jump when I heard the sounds of crashing glass and wood smashing. I immediately started searching the side of my bed for my ratchet. I felt down around on the floor in the place I usually kept it.

Nothing.

"Fuck," I cursed as the sounds grew louder and louder. Shannon had moved my shit. I told her not to ever move my shit without telling me. She was always so worried about guns being around Lil Todd.

"What the fuck!" I exclaimed as I heard feet thundering in my direction. My heart pounded through my wife-beater like the shit was going to jump loose of my chest bones. My mind was not foggy with sleep anymore; I was wide awake and on alert.

I didn't know if it was jealous motherfuckers from the hood or those hating-ass five-o bastards who had a vendetta against me, banging up my fucking minimansion doors. The shit sounded like a fucking earthquake was happening right there in my crib. At first I didn't hear them say "POLICE!" but as soon as I was facing down the end of an MP5, I knew what the fuck was up.

"Get on the floor! Get the fuck on the floor!"

Those commands were very familiar. I put my hands up, folded them behind my head, and assumed the position. I was pushed down to the floor roughly, and about five of those bastards dropped knees in my back and legs. My arms were yanked behind my back, and I was cuffed and made to lie facedown on my own fucking floor. Those fucking pigs were swarming my crib like flies around a pile of freshly dropped shit. It seemed like there were a million of them. All of them against just me.

"Punk bitches," I grumbled under my breath. I recognized one of them—a big-headed white boy who thought he was the shit. A snake motherfucker named Labeckie. He was the sergeant of the Norfolk Police Department's narcotics and gun unit, and he hated my ass.

"Take out that wall! Tear this fucking place up until we find some shit!" I heard that bastard yell as he looked down at me and smiled.

I closed my eyes when I heard them axing down walls and cabinets. Didn't they fucking know they could've just opened that shit up? My mind was racing, and I immediately hoped that Shannon didn't walk in on this shit with Lil Todd.

I lay there, facedown, knowing right away that somebody in my camp had snitched. I knew my gun-running shit and five-o radar were airtight. There was no fucking way they could have known about my operation unless somebody told them. It had been three years since I had done my last bid on a drug charge, and when I got home, I had gone into a different line of work. Before I got knocked on the trumped-up drug charges, I was one of the biggest kingpins in the Norfolk area. I had all of Tidewater on lock, and I was bringing in at least fifty thousand a week. Almost all of the trap boys in the area were employed by me. I ran a tight ship, and the narcos found it hard to get my ass. The cops who arrested me the last time weren't gonna rest until they got my ass. I had beat so many charges because of my high-paid attorney, and those fucking pigs were mad as hell, so when they finally got me on some ol' caught slipping shit, they was happy as hell.

When I came home, I promised my wife I was leaving the drug game behind me—the money, the bitches, and the fucking five-o too. I knew she was tired of riding with me through all this bullshit, so I told her I was going legit, and that is exactly what I did . . . at first. I opened my own short-distance trucking company. That shit was all good, but it wasn't enough money for me. Shannon was used to living a certain lifestyle, and I was going to provide it. I got into the gun-running shit by coincidence, and it was all up from there. I was bringing in cake, and my wife and kid were fucking happy. I was sure I was careful, and I surrounded myself with only a few cats who I thought were real. It seems one of those motherfuckers wasn't a real cat but a fucking snake-ass rat.

These bastard-ass cops had me facedown on the floor for mad long. The circulation in my hands felt like it was completely cut off. All I could hear was them destroying my beautiful home and rummaging through my shit. I bit into my cheek until I drew blood when I heard one of them whistle and say, "Hmm, the missus must be a pretty bitch—look at these pretty-ass panties." Then the bastard took a long sniff and said, "Ahhhh, pretty pussy smell. Think I could fuck his wife while he does his life sentence?" and then he started laughing. I squirmed around with the handcuffs biting into my skin. He was so lucky I was shackled like an animal or else I would've fucked his ass up. Shannon was my world, and I didn't want a nigga, especially a bitch-ass pig, even looking in her direction.

"Yo, these cuffs is tight!" I called out while they continued going through my shit.

"I don't give a fuck! You lucky we don't hog-tie you like the animal you are," the pig guarding me barked in my ear. His punk ass knew if I could get out of the fucking handcuffs, his wig would be twisted back.

It seemed like they were searching for days when one of them yelled, "Jackpot! I knew we would find something!" I just shut my eyes and thought about Shannon and our little man. I was a three striker, and my ass was going down. I had always made it a practice not to bring my shit where I live, but Jock—one of my boys—had met up with me the night before with a military-grade AK47 left over from his sales meeting. Apparently the cats he met up with had gotten cold feet on that shit and didn't buy it, leaving Jock to drive around with the shit on his way back to Norfolk. Jock was shook and didn't know where to take the shit, so being the man I am, I met up with Jock and took that load off of him. My intention had been to get that shit sold today. Either I was a few hours short or I was set the fuck up.

"Yo, I get a phone call, right?" I asked as two cops hauled me up off the floor.

"Don't ask for shit!" one of them barked.